FIRETEAM ZULU

a Terran Shift novel

JAMIE ALAN BELANGER

Cover concept & design: Jamie Alan Belanger

Cover art contains a Public Domain image from NASA, free Photoshop brushes by Denny Tang and revn89, and a free Barrett M107 model from Turbo Squid. None of these people endorsed my work or probably even know about it. But I wanted to mention and thank them.

Published in 2012 by Lost Luggage Studios, LLC
through Amazon CreateSpace.

ISBN: 978-1-936489-09-1

Printed in the United States of America.

I can't possibly publish anything without thanking my brother Paul for tirelessly reading and re-reading the beta versions of my books. Without his contributions, this would be a much less cohesive work fraught with strange inconsistencies. Thanks bro.

-- Jamie Alan Belanger

8 FLORA

F ire in the hole!" shouted Tex as he sailed through the air over the shipping crates piled in the receiving dock of asteroid colony A8-2239. Sarge shook his head but dutifully capped his hands over his ears. The shock wave of the explosion shook the station's walls and threatened to shatter the thin nanoglass windows, which bowed outward to accommodate the shock. The windows strained at their limits, then shivered back into place.

Tex popped his head up over the edge of the crate to inspect his work. "Yee-haw!" he shouted. He fired two rounds from one of his pistols, the cracks of the gunfire acting as a sharp contrast to the strange sucking sound of the plasma weapons the pirates had. He looked a little ridiculous holding a couple of six-shooters; bringing plastic projectiles to a plasma fight. Sort of like trying to defend yourself from a school bully with a Kleenex. But that was Tex, it was part of his signature style. He saw himself as a cowboy born a few hundred years too late. "That's how you do it, Sarge!" he exclaimed, then fired another shot.

An answering shot rang out from down the hall, the sharp high-pitched crack of a pulse rifle. A thin beam of light cut through Tex's cheek and sprayed blood on the wall behind them. He collapsed to the floor and held one hand to his cheek.

Sarge glared at him. "That's how *you* do it. Don't get sloppy now."

"Yes sir," Tex responded while searching his pocket for a med pack. He pulled one out and slapped it to his cheek, wincing as the patch adhered to his skin and medicine entered his bloodstream. Wasn't the first time he'd taken damage in a firefight.

Sarge, on the other hand, had a lot more experience in fights. One thing that he'd learned well over the years he spent in the military was that a smart commander called for backup when he needed it. He pressed a small button in his cheek with his tongue. "Tank," he said.

"Sir?" came the response in his ear implant. In the background he could hear the sharp report of Tank's pulse cannon.

"We're pinned down, could use a hand." As if to accentuate his statement, a fresh volley of blue plasma pelted the shipping crates and the wall behind them. "Looks like these bastards got themselves a plasma rifle," he said.

The government had outlawed plasma weapons almost two centuries ago, but criminals still got hold of them somehow. The weapons weren't really any more dangerous to use than standard pulse rifles, if the wielder was properly trained. In fact, pulse rifles used the same ammunition, but fired it in much smaller, more focused amounts. The problem was that the people who liked the dangerous plasma weapons were never the ones who were trained to use them. The weapons needed little precision to work, and usually caused more collateral damage than necessary to get the job of killing people done.

Another blob of plasma sailed over his head and smacked into the wall behind them. It sizzled as it melted the steel. A few more well-placed shots would punch a hole through the wall and expose the mining colony on 8 Flora to the vacuum of space.

"Tank?" Sarge asked again.

"Sort of busy myself," Tank said, "but I think Ghost is already en route."

"Copy that. Carry on." He pressed the button with his tongue again to sever the connection.

"Tank coming?" Tex asked.

"No," Sarge replied, "Ghost is. Get to the cafeteria area and see if Tank needs some help. This is under control."

"Sir," Tex replied, starting to add something else but thought better of it. He nodded and moved down the hallway behind them.

Sarge shifted his position and pointed the muzzle of his pulse rifle around the crate. He flipped a switch on the gun and the vision in his left eye cut out, replaced by the live stream sent from his rifle. He peeked around the corner with it, studying the pirates at the end of the hall. Most of them were standing out in the open like the amateurs they were, but it looked like three had the good sense to fire on his position from cover. He watched as they fired, impressed that they had the coordination to stagger their reloading so they could keep a constant stream of suppression fire going. Military training? Or just a lot of hours logged in video games?

He heard something hit close and pulled back. The pungent stench of burnt electronics hit his nose. Sarge glanced down and saw a plasma burn straight through his left hand. He held it up and looked through the hole. Inside his hand, the titanium bones sizzled from the plasma. He clenched his fist to make sure the fingers still functioned, and they did. Minor damage. Much more lucky than last time...

*　*　*

Sarge was younger then, and in charge during combat for the first time. He'd made a similar mistake, poking out from cover for too long. His orders were to take and hold a bunker on Mars. Some separatists had managed to infiltrate a military base and had killed some soldiers. The bunker was their stronghold. His commander's hope was that taking the bunker back by force would end the conflict sooner.

Sarge hated the idea of sending these young kids assigned to him into battle. He was young too, but some of these kids weren't even shaving yet. One of them looked like he was twelve, even though the lieutenant had insisted he was eighteen. Sarge issued the orders and their eyes welled up, shoulders sinking toward the ground. Halfway into their graves and they hadn't even moved from behind cover. One of them had made a snide comment about Sarge going first.

"I'm going first," he had responded, doing his best to appear like he hadn't heard the comment. The confidence in his voice surprised them all, himself included. "Stay close."

He leapt from cover and was immediately thrown back to the dirt with biting pain down the left side of his body. He managed to work himself to a kneeling position and looked at his arm, detached, flopping on the ground. He fired a few rounds toward the bunker and pressed the muzzle to the remaining stump. He grit his teeth and turned his nose from the sizzling flesh.

"Are... are you okay, sir?" one of the privates under his command had asked.

"Always," he replied. "Always."

Then he charged, screaming as he ran to the bunker, firing all the way. He hadn't taken more than a few steps before he heard screaming behind him, and the air filled with plasma bursts from both sides.

Sarge couldn't remember much more than that.

He'd blacked out, but when he came to several hours later, he was in the bunker. His soldiers noticed he had awakened and crowded around him, telling him what he'd done. What *they'd* done. The bunker was secure, and reports were coming in that the remainder of the separatists had seen the battle and thrown down their arms. Their squad of eight marines had stormed a bunker defended by thirty men, and won. Thirty dead separatists, and the attacking marines had lost only one of their own. Sarge lost his arm. The rest had only minor burns.

Sarge figured he'd be discharged at that point. But within a week he was on the operating table, getting a whole new arm. A better one, full of all sorts of enhancements. One of the privates under his command had joked that he was now part cyborg. Sarge challenged the kid to an arm wrestling contest, but the kid wisely declined. Sarge chuckled in response, but inside he was the saddest he'd ever been. He'd had enough of fighting, but now he was combat-ready again. Every time he got wounded, the military fixed him up and sent him out again.

"You ready to go back into the fray?" one of the doctors asked. He smiled too much. Too cheerful. Too eager to send the newly fixed soldier back into danger. Maybe that was part of his contract -- sending soldiers back to the front as quickly as possible ensured his job security. He watched Sarge wiggling the digits on his new hand, glancing between that and his computer display screen.

Sarge studied his new hand intently. Titanium bones wrapped in artificial flesh, linked to his nervous system with a new fleet of nanobots. He was ready for combat again. Ready to be sent out again. Another injury fixed, another chance to die for his nation.

Am I ready? he thought.

"Always," he responded.

*   *   *

Tex followed the tactical map of the mining colony in his HUD until he could hear the sound of Tank's pulse cannon. He sprinted down the last hallway and entered the cafeteria, where he found the mountainous man standing behind an overturned table, muscles bulging and dripping sweat, firing short bursts from his massive pulse cannon into the kitchen. He looked a little like an automatic turret, rotating with perfect precision to provide maximum suppression fire. Anyone who didn't know the tactic would have thought at least four marines were firing. Every few blasts, someone in the kitchen poked an arm above the counter and returned fire with a pistol, sending plasma in some random direction. Tex gave a short whistle and pulled his six-shooter pistols. Tank grunted in response and continued his barrage. The muzzle of his cannon was glowing a soft red from the heat. Tex guessed it must have been running low on ammo as well.

Tex crept along the wall until he could see into the kitchen. He could see what looked like three of the pirates, huddled amongst a pile of pots and pans. One had dropped his weapon and was hugging his knees to his chest, rocking back and forth. Another poked a pistol above the counter to return fire. Tex aimed and fired, striking the man in the back of the head. The third pirate reacted by aiming his plasma pistol at Tex, but he was too slow. Tex fired off two rounds, one from each pistol. The remaining pirate slowly reached for his pistol.

"Don't do it," Tex warned. The man did not heed the warning, and Tex shot him before he could aim the pistol.

"I'll cover this room," Tank said. "You check out the storage rooms beyond the kitchen."

"Great, a bug hunt," Tex said. He returned one of his pistols to its holster and stood with his back against the wall. He reached for a grenade on his belt, pulled the pin out with his teeth, and spat it out. "Eyes and ears," he said, tossing the grenade into the first storage room. The flashbang grenade detonated with a loud pop, showering the room with light and blasting it with sound. Tex ran into the room and checked, but didn't see any movement. "Well, that was a waste. Looks clear."

"Better to waste a grenade than to get shot," Tank said.

"True," Tex replied, emerging from the storage room. "Looks like the next storage room is a little-" he stopped and listened. He made a sweeping motion with his hand, then held up two fingers. Tank shook his head and held up three in response. Tex waved his hand past the entry and someone inside fired in response.

"Bang it," Tank said.

Tex reached for his belt, but his grenade hooks were empty. "I'm out."

"Here," Tank replied, tossing a grenade to Tex. "Last one."

Tex looked down at the grenade and was about to pull the pin. He stopped short and regarded it. "You want me to *frag* them?" There was some muttering from inside the room.

"Probably have to kill them anyway," Tank said, "might as well have fun doing it."

"True," Tex said, pulling the pin.

"What do you say?" Tank asked.

"Huh?" Tex said, pausing to look back at his companion. He spat the pin out. He had a firm grip on the grenade, so the timer hadn't started yet, but he was eager to get rid of it nonetheless.

"What do you *say*?"

"Um... thanks?"

"No, no," Tank said. "I mean-" he paused as the pirates inside the storage room fired. "I mean, when you throw a flashbang, you warn your team to protect themselves. You say 'eyes and ears.' What do you say when you throw a frag?"

Tex frowned. "I don't know. How about, 'Nuts and butts!'"

With that, he tossed the grenade into the room. The blast came two seconds later, shaking the kitchen and rattling pans. Tank turned, surveying the other entrances to the cafeteria as Tex rushed into the storage room. Tex emerged shortly after and said, "All clear."

* * *

Sarge used his gun to peer around the corner at the pirates who continued to fire on his position. They had moved forward a few meters to another set of crates, still firing and reloading in some of the best symmetry he'd seen in a long while.

Then there was a flash, nothing more than a shadow, noticeable only because he was looking for it. A slender girl glided in from a side hallway behind one of the pirates and sliced his neck wide open with a small blade. Before any of his friends could even register something had happened, she was gone.

Another flash of steel on the other side of the hallway ended another life, and again she was gone. One of the pirates paused shooting to look at his comrades. Sarge took aim at him, waited for the superimposed reticle to turn red, and fired two rounds into his chest. Aiming was slower this way, but being able to kill from cover was priceless. That was one advantage he still had over these pirates.

On the video feed in his eye, he watched his other advantage make another quick slice, followed by a shower of blood splattering on the wall. The remaining pirates turned to fire at her, wildly peppering the walls with plasma bursts. Sarge popped up from cover, took aim the old-fashioned way, and dropped three of them before the remaining pirate turned to flee. He got as far as the hallway entrance before Ghost stopped him.

"Good work," Sarge called down the hallway while checking the charge on his pulse rifle. Half ammo. Not bad for a day's work.

"Thank you, sir," came the reply. Ghost stepped from the shadows and stooped to wipe the blood from her blades on a pirate's shirt. She sheathed the blades and strolled down the hallway toward Sarge. She stopped before him and closed her eyes. When she opened them again, she nodded. "Three more, sir. Tex and Tank won't need much longer to finish this."

"No more on the ship?"

"Already taken care of, sir."

"Outstanding. Did you see anything worth salvaging on their ship?" He dreaded asking the question. Anything they found on a pirate's ship would have been stolen from someone they didn't have a chance to help. But times were tough, and they could use all the supplies and extra pay they could muster.

"I already confiscated some cash I found in the Captain's quarters. Weasel's reviewing their cargo manifest but thinks it's mostly junk."

"Sir," Tank's voice came in clear over the com in his ear, "area secure."

"Good work. Clean up what you can and I'll meet you back on the ship."

Sarge flipped the safety on his rifle and handed it to Ghost. He walked down the hallway, footsteps sending echoes out around him. Hallways that would be full of life, full of people working the mines on the asteroid if not interrupted by the pirates. The police and military were nowhere to be found. Colonists had extended themselves so far that the available forces for protecting people were stretched too thin. It wasn't much of a problem until the pirates showed up. Bunch of neo-punks looking for quick profits in the budding space age. The colonists had no one else to turn to -- Fireteam Zulu was their last line of defense. Four ex-soldiers out on their own, acting as a ragtag vigilante force trying to save the whole damn solar system. Too bad they couldn't be in more than one place at a time. Too bad nobody else seemed to want to join in on the defense.

Sarge stopped before a door with a small sign that declared it the "Recreation Room". He knocked on the door three times, paused, then twice more. The door opened, revealing a room packed with colonists, cowering and sobbing in the warm stale air. Their leader stepped out into the hallway, peered around Sarge, barely listening to what he was saying. But Sarge was used to this. He'd given this speech to a hundred different people in a hundred different places after a hundred different jobs. It was always the same speech:

You're safe. The pirates are dead. We can't be bothered to clean up because there's so much fucking work for us to do. Thanks for the cash, goodbye and good luck.

Not verbatim, of course. After a few dozen such speeches, he'd learned to avoid the f-word, and had even added some of those flowery words that politicians and colony leaders seemed to like. But the content of his speeches never wavered. He was terse, he was firm, and then he was gone.

What he didn't tell them was that it was highly probable the pirates' friends would return, and by then Fireteam Zulu would be millions of kilometers away. There was no sense in alarming them. If they were nearby, they'd be back. If not, well, then this place would become another statistic on the United Earth Federation's weekly report. He had read many of those statistics in the past. Hell, he'd put a few of them in there. When orders came from above, you didn't question them, that's what they drilled into you. Be a good little soldier. Those aren't really colonists; appearances are deceiving. Do what you're told. Refuse and you become the target. Well, now he was in charge. He gave the orders. And killing colonists, regardless of what label was slapped on them this week, was not an order he would give to a subordinate.

Sarge finished his speech and cleared his throat to signify that he was done. The colony's leader broke from his trance and extended his hand. There was hope in his eyes, hope written on all the faces of the people in the room. Sarge's face reflected none of it.

"So," the leader said, looking a little lost. "You're off to save someone else now?"

Sarge stared at the man, then slowly nodded. "Always," he said, then he turned and walked down the long hallway back to his ship.

AUTOMATIC SNIPER

I t was a typical cool night on Mars. The red dust sparkled from the first
rays of the rising sun, minute silicate fragments reflecting the reddish
hues of the sky. Faint scent of locally run farms carried in the wind,
animals and crops, all grown naturally in the absence of bugs and predators.
Mars terraforming was taking nicely. The planet was a prime candidate --
very close to Earth in some ways, and yet so very alien in others.

Dust storms were still a problem, but the United Earth Federation scientists claimed they were close to suppressing them completely. They had
solved the same problem in the Gobi Desert on Earth more than a hundred
and forty years prior, and they knew exactly what to do, step by step. Mars
had the same problems, just on a much larger scale. All they needed was a
few more years. In that time, they could finish building the oceans and planting the grasses in the Southern hemisphere, and the dust storms would sub-
side once and for all. In some ways, the people of Mars looked forward to
that day. It meant more predictable rainfall and easier working conditions.
But a lot of other people dreaded the coming day, for they knew what else
the end of terraforming would bring: a tourist trade. Millions of people flood-

ing to the planet for holidays, polluting their pristine world with diseases and garbage. How many years would it be before Mars was just another disaster area, like Earth?

A massive railgun scanned the horizon, slowly rotating to the left on its tripod, silently gliding along a well-oiled path. Its left eye transmitted an infrared image to the monitor behind it, the right transmitted green-tinted night vision, its display shown beside the left's on the monitor. The machine reached its limit, paused, and started rotating to the right.

The operator seated behind the monitor squinted at the images a moment before returning his attention to the electronic puzzle game in his lap. Sergeant Richard Collins fixed a blank stare on the game's screen. The puzzle game, undaunted, continued waiting for his move. His heart just wasn't in it tonight. Or this morning. He'd been given the worst shift of them all: dawn patrol. Just him and an automatic sniper, monitoring the northern flank of United Earth Marine Outpost MP-2184, a small military establishment on the surface of Mars. Their assignment was classified, their personnel strictly limited. Something to do with making sure the farmers and scientists in the area did what they were told, and protecting them from pirates if necessary. Pirates rarely made planetfall, so that part of the mission was the least likely to occur. Collins was never quite clear what the actual mission was, but that went with the territory. It was far above his pay grade, and he knew better than to ask. All that mattered to him was that this mission and base were classified, so that meant a Remote Outpost Bonus. His tour of duty was almost up, and this tour counted double. That meant retirement, and a sergeant's pension was enough to live on, if he spent it carefully.

He tapped the game's screen to select a piece and moved it to the other side of the board. The game displayed a message that it was thinking, running calculations so it could respond with the best possible move. Collins was getting used to this thing's AI and knew it would no doubt make a perfect move and win. Again. He watched with dismay as it moved a piece he didn't even think could move that way and declared itself the winner. These games were all calibrated to provide a challenge to players augmented with all sorts of nanotech implants for processing data. Normal people like Collins were at a distinct disadvantage.

Norms, he thought with a snort.

Just another derogatory term from years long past that some people still used. He didn't care for Norm politics, he just didn't want the military to jack him up with their usual cocktail of biological and nanotech implants. There were a lot of people who didn't trust the implants, in civilian life at least. The military judged trustworthiness of technology by different standards. Collins had to take a lot of shit from his fellow marines and the officers who commanded them, but it was a small price to pay to know that he was, in fact, normal. At least, normal in the sense that humans used to be.

The automatic sniper stopped rotating, focusing its attention on a lone figure walking toward the outpost. "Alert," it said through its speech synthesizer. It zoomed in, optics in both lenses framing the figure's face for a snapshot. The on-board computer created a composite from the two shots and altered the tint to approximate daytime vision. It beeped and displayed the image on the monitor, then sent it off for processing. The response was instant. This person was a local farmer, and most definitely not authorized to be here.

Collins read the information. Human male, about two meters tall and two hundred and fifty meters away, moving slowly, staggering. Wasn't the first time some drunk farmer stumbled their way into a restricted area. Probably wouldn't be the last. "Warning shot," he said.

"Affirmative," the automatic sniper responded. It lined up a shot and fired, the electric path of the railgun's shot lighting the night sky while sending a single depleted uranium round into the dirt at the man's feet. A cone of dirt shot into the air up to the man's waist, then slowly rained back down. The man stopped and watched the dirt for a moment, then peered into the darkness around him. "Subject not fleeing," the automatic sniper said. "Use of deadly force is acceptable. Awaiting operator authorization."

Collins sighed and watched as the figure glanced around, then resumed walking toward his station. Some people were just plain stupid and there was no alternative. Luckily for him, he had authorization to use deadly force, so the paperwork would be brief. Not that it made him feel any better about making the decision. "Kill him," he said.

"Affirmative."

The automatic sniper charged another round and sent it out, this one penetrating the man in the center of his chest. He sank to his knees and placed his hands on the soft dirt, head sagging. Collins watched the video feeds from the automatic sniper and waited. The man rose to his feet and continued his journey toward the outpost. The automatic sniper registered this activity and fired another round, this one penetrating the man in the abdomen. The man took one step back and then continued forward.

The automatic sniper switched itself into full automatic mode and let loose, firing rounds at its maximum rate of over ninety rounds per minute. Round after round struck the man, but still he stumbled on. He paused and pitched forward, then two rounds caught him in the shoulder, ripping his arm off and pulling him back upright. Again he resumed his staggering. Collins dropped the electronic game machine and reached for his pulse rifle.

The computer terminal beside him beeped and a tired face came into view on it. "Collins! What in the hell's going on over there, soldier? You got the night lit up so much I can't sleep." The Colonel looked even more annoyed than usual. It was bad enough that he was woken up several hours too early, but add in that he had to call Collins the old-fashioned way and you had one pissed off officer.

"Sorry Colonel," Collins responded over the din, "got someone approaching and he ain't dyin'. I'll patch you in." He pressed his finger to the monitor and dragged the live feed to the Colonel's screen. The machine notified him that the live uplink was established. The Colonel's eyes widened as he watched the railgun rounds penetrating the farmer, who continued staggering toward the base. Two steps forward, one step back. Sometimes falling, sometimes lurching forward, sometimes being pushed back several steps. But always moving forward.

Then the automatic sniper stopped firing. The sudden silence was as jarring to both men as the full-auto railgun had been. Collins looked and saw the figure laying in the dirt less than fifty meters from his station. He glanced at the readout from the automatic sniper, blinking warnings that it was in danger of overheating and almost out of ammunition.

"Well," said the Colonel, "looks like he's done for."

"What kind of man takes over two hundred railgun rounds to kill?"

The Colonel fell silent for several moments before responding. "Reload the gun, soldier. I'm sending your replacement. When he arrives, I want you to bring that corpse to the morgue for analysis and then report to me."

"Yes, sir."

The screen turned black. Collins replaced his rifle, checked the automatic sniper's imaging and warning readouts, then reached for the nearest ammunition box. His shift would be over early, but he had a sinking feeling that his day was just beginning.

HUNTER

I n the dim light of the ship's bridge, a single man stood before a telescreen, studying the facial expression of the woman he was conversing
with. Something wasn't being said, that much he was sure of. But what
it was couldn't be discerned. At least not from this distance, not without considerable effort on his part. He knew from experience that the effort required
would exhaust him. The last thing he wanted to do was to show any sign of
weakness to this woman. She was a shark, and would sink her teeth into any
such display without hesitation. Corporate types always tried to hide things
from him. At least when the orders came from the military, he knew he was
being told what he *needed* to know. Civilians would omit details they thought
dangerous, or unimportant. But he'd been tracking people for so long that
he'd become accustomed to gathering all the information he could before
even setting out. Every detail was important. Knowing was paramount.

He studied the woman's perfect haircut, light brown locks pulled back
into a twist, not a single strand out of place. Well-ironed navy blue suit, sharp
tie fitted just right. Her skin was taut, like a teenager's, but he knew she had
to be pushing seventy, at least. He could see it in her eyes. Even through the

augmentations she had, there was a depth of soul that only came with wisdom. She was a hard woman to read, well-versed in the deceptions needed to rise to the position she held.

The woman flinched under his stare and averted her gaze. "So?" she asked, trying to mask her apprehension by glancing around her office casually. "Can you do it or not?"

"That depends on what you aren't telling me," he said. She made an elaborate sigh. He waved his hand to dismiss the gesture. "Never mind. Do you want captured, or dead?"

"I want them alive. It's very important that they face trial, for vigilantism. A very public trial."

He snorted. "You'll never find a jury to convict them."

"It won't be a civilian court-"

"Then why not issue orders to me through military channels?"

"Make no mistake, Mr. Owens, this *is* a military operation. I am speaking to you with full military authority-" she waved her hand and a badge appeared in the corner of his screen, gilded and rotating. After three revolutions, his screen beeped and printed an authentication confirmation. "The only reason I'm approaching you this way is because I believe good work should be rewarded. Fifty million credits for the capture of Fireteam Zulu, tax free, wired to an account of your choice."

"Understood," he said. "But I want you to understand something as well. I am Woden. Call me by my real name again, and no authority will protect you from me."

"Is that a threat?" she asked, looking more amused than alarmed. She leaned into the screen with a playful smirk as she studied his image. She had the look of a young girl peering into a cage to see a cute little animal scurry about.

Woden furrowed his brow and stared at her. Beads of sweat formed on her forehead and slid their way down her cheeks. She grasped her throat and gagged. He smiled and turned away, releasing his grasp on her. He had known for a long time that he could command nanobots in other people's bloodstreams remotely. But affecting them over a Solar Net connection was something new he had been playing around with. He was quite satisfied with the results. Part of his body ached, but he could hide the discomfort. He wouldn't have been able to kill her this way, but she didn't know that. He'd made his point. "No authority, Mrs. Anderton, do you understand me?"

She panted as she stared at the screen, horror in her eyes. "Yes... Woden."

He regarded her cowed response with distaste. "I'll contact you when I have something to report." He waved his hand and cut the transmission.

The conversation had been longer than he wanted. Being a hunter had made him paranoid -- always worried that someone was hunting *him* and listening for transmissions over the Solar Net. Encryption could only protect you so much, and anyone who knew him would know to look for heavily encrypted traffic. Sure, the probability of someone decrypting the message was slim, but you didn't have to decrypt the message to know that *someone* was sending *something* of importance. Search for an enormous, well-encrypted transmission, someone sending a large amount of data. Follow the trail, and...

Woden shook his head and sat in his pilot's chair. His ship was following a pre-programmed trajectory, traveling toward the asteroid belt from high Mars orbit. The course had been set hours ago, back when he first received the message from Gabrielle Anderton. Before returning her call, he did his research, as he always did. His ship was already on its way to a rendezvous.

He looked to a window he had left open on his computer screen, showing a distress message sent hours ago. A mining colony on 8 Flora that was under attack from pirates. Fireteam Zulu would be there, he was sure of it. All his research indicated they were predictable do-gooders.

Two other documents were open beside it.

The first was the planned trajectory for a ship with no cargo manifest or name. But he knew its name. He knew who was on it and what it carried and where it was going.

The other document was all the information he had already gathered on another ship in the local area. Pirates. Some small-time punks looking for a big score. And he had just the kind of target they were looking for.

TETHERED

Weasel shifted in his chair, as much as the cable plugged into the base of his skull would allow, listening to the loose bolt creak in that strangely comforting way. Of course, if that bolt ever gave way or fell out, he'd be in a world of pain. The cable plugged into his skull could be wrenched free, or the pole supporting the chair could be thrust into a most uncomfortable spot. He kept telling Sarge the chair needed to be fixed, but they never had enough time in port. Pirates, always the pirates. That's all Sarge seemed to care about these days.

A jolt of electricity surged through his body, starting in his brain implant and continuing down to his toes. His muscles spasmed in response for twenty solid seconds, then relaxed. Daily exercise. It wasn't enough. He could feel his muscles atrophying, which they should be, considering he'd been confined to this chair for almost nine months straight now. His Turina Jack was connected directly to the ship's computer and he was in full control of it, could feel every part of the ship. He had access to all of the communications equipment, every monitor, every process and every apparatus on the ship. Connecting this way was rare these days; the newer ships were being built with more traditional bridges, like they used back when people were first starting to colonize the solar system. There was still some stigma surrounding T-Jacks, but Weasel didn't mind. He rather enjoyed plugging into the ship. He had supreme control, ultimate maneuverability. He just couldn't move physically as long as they were away from a port. If he fell asleep or died liked this, the whole ship would shut down. A rock, a tomb, floating in space, no life support, no thrusters. Giving up his own mobility was a small price to pay; he had grown used to being alone anyway. In a strange way, he was never alone this way. He always had Zulu Prime. He always had a connection to the Solar Net.

Zulu Prime was a small ship, originally intended to deliver a single squad of eight marines to a drop zone. The military developed the Broadsword-class ship more than a hundred years ago, and the fact that most of them were still flying was a constant reminder of how well constructed the ships were. The biggest advance in the construction of the ships was with the power supply -- the ship's entire exterior was a solar panel, coated in thick transparent metal. Just floating through space provided a constant stream of energy from the sun. Excess energy was stored in a battery array in the aft engine compartment.

The marines on the ship were split into two rooms with four bunks each. The sergeant in command of the squad had his own private room, across the hall from a common bathroom. When he'd acquired the ship, Sarge had converted one of the common bunk rooms into a rec room, complete with provision storage and a small telescreen for some entertainment. Fireteam Zulu hadn't used that room in months. There wasn't any time for relaxing. Fight pirates, eat something, sleep a bit, then repeat. The more humanity expanded into the solar system, the more active the pirates became.

The Broadsword ships were never intended to be a home for the marines it ferried, but Sarge and the rest of the Zulu team did treat it as such. In fact, the only person the military had intended to remain on the ship for extended periods of time was the operator. They had constructed the brain interface to the ship based on the assumption that one operator would stay tethered to the ship for months at a time. Drop off a squad and then return to grab another group. Deploy, depart, keep flying. The ships worked best when they were almost never shut down.

Weasel's eyes stared at the plain gray steel ceiling of the ship, a boring view that he tolerated only because it provided good contrast for the text prompts the computer in his head superimposed over his vision. He scanned the text message he'd just received -- another distress call, another ship besieged by pirates. He sighed as he scrolled through the bright green text. Almost the same text as the last few. Like a form letter, some kind of office suite template. Pirates were unusually active for this time of year. Zulu Prime had emerged from the asteroid colony's landing bay not even an hour earlier, and here was another job.

Weasel tapped the button inside his cheek and said, "Hey Sarge."

There was a muffled curse somewhere in the ship, then Sarge's voice, "Yeah?"

"We got another job."

"Fuck a duck, already?"

"Busy year."

"Where's this one at?" Sarge grumbled.

Weasel double-checked the message. The header contained coordinates, not a colony reference. He pasted the coordinates into his chart system and it responded with a blinking dot in a sea of black. He rotated the image to find a reference point, stopping when he saw Mars. "Looks like high Mars orbit. Five, maybe six hours out."

"Shit. Poor bastards will probably be dead by then." A pause, and another grumble that for Sarge usually indicated reluctant assent. "Alright, head for it. We'll get some shuteye in the meantime. Wake us in four hours."

The com line clicked off. Weasel entered the navigation coordinates and started the program that would compute an optimal trajectory. He then turned his attention to an alarm program and entered a request that would wake his friends in four hours.

Friends, he caught himself thinking. More like employers, at least in the way they treated him. Four ex-soldiers adrift in space with him acting as eyes, ears, and brain for the lot of them. He turned his gaze downward and the chair shifted to accommodate his ocular movements until he could see out the viewport. The asteroid belt stretched as far as he could see, and from his vantage point he could pick out a good half dozen colonies on the larger chunks of rock. His colony was somewhere out there. Or, rather, was. He was born on the asteroid 1 Ceres twenty-eight years ago. His parents were in the original group of miners sent to harvest the iron and carbonates. He was amongst the few who managed to make it to the escape pod before the pirates poured into the base. Just docking at 8 Flora was enough to bring a tear to his eye.

Weasel had grown up in the slums of South Africa, orphaned and forced to learn the laws of the street the hard way. He had a good routine going and a tentative relationship with a local fence who bought anything he could steal. One day his fence introduced him to the world of hacking, and that's when the real money started to pour in. When he'd earned enough, he hopped a transport to the new promised land of the twenty-second century, Mars. One day en route, a ship docked to trade supplies. That ship turned out to be an earlier Zulu Prime, mobile home of the already famous Fireteam Zulu, a battered ship that barely looked fit to fly. Weasel picked the wrong pocket that day, but a witty retort and a hearty laugh later and all was forgiven. Sarge took him in, taught him to fly the ship and he'd been with them ever since. A few years later they acquired the ship they were currently flying, which Weasel much preferred since it let him use his T-Jack and hacking skills much more than the older hand-flown ship did. That old junker didn't even have a functioning computer, let alone a Solar Net uplink.

An alert window scrolled into his view to notify him that the computer had finished plotting the course he programmed. Zulu Prime's engines whirred to life and the ship accelerated through the void.

*   *   *

"Four hours? You serious, Sarge?" Tank asked after Sarge had finished relaying Weasel's message. He peeled the combat armor off his massive chest while staring intently at Sarge.

"Always."

Tank shook his head and sagged his shoulders, mostly for effect. When

Sarge said *always* in that certain way he spoke, you knew he meant it. There was no arguing with that tone. "You know I'm always up for action, Sarge," he said while stretching his arms, "but we need down time too, sir."

Sarge didn't miss a beat. "Then you should bed down instead of debating it with me, soldier. Now hear this, CFB. There are people on that ship who'll get permanent down time if we don't help them. Take the four hours, get some shuteye, and be ready for action. Is that understood?"

Tank snapped to attention and saluted. "Yes sir," he said, then pivoted and approached his berth.

Tex and Ghost had enough sense to keep quiet after that conversation. They had most likely chosen to let Tank speak for them, as they knew the two soldiers had served together at some point. If anyone had rapport with Sarge and a chance to sway his orders, it was Tank. But Sarge never changed an order. He made a decision, and stuck to it.

Sarge surveyed the team. He could see the exhaustion in Tex's face. Ghost's was solid as stone. Even her hair moved with her face, clinging to the same spots as if glued there.

There was certainly no shortage of work. But Tank was right about one thing: they did need some down time. Without it, someone was bound to do something stupid.

Speaking of stupid, he thought while watching Ghost tending to the laser burn on Tex's cheek. She worked with steady hands, slowly moving the medical unit over the scar in precise lines. Tex winced as the machine repaired the skin, sending the stench of charred flesh into the air around them. He'd forgotten the first rule of any operation: caution. He'd paid the price, but did he learn the lesson? Sarge hoped so. Good soldiers were hard to come by.

REGRETS

C ollins finished reloading the automatic sniper by pushing the ammo box in with his boot. Once again, a disadvantage. Most soldiers had enough strength to handle pushing the boxes in with bare hands. He had to struggle and kick it a few times to get it in. Even now, the box was in, but the machine expected more force to lock it in place. He pulled his leg back again and kicked the box as hard as he could. The machine beeped to let him know it detected a completed reload operation. The screens blanked and filled with diagnostic readouts. Collins sat and was studying the data when he heard footsteps behind him.

He stood and turned to face his replacement -- a private that everyone called "Jane" because nobody could pronounce her real name. She had a mixture of European and Middle-Eastern ancestry and a surname that pushed twenty characters in length. Her black hair was cut to the regulation ten-millimeter length. Her eyes sparkled in the twilight, light violet color speckled with pink. Collins never asked, but he assumed they were dyed nanotech eyes. Standard-issue augments with a feminine twist. She was beautiful, but in a plain sort of way, where most men wouldn't give her a second thought.

But Collins liked her and found any excuse he could to spend time talking with her.

"Morning, Jane," he said.

"Richie," she replied, then her demeanor turned professional and she stood at attention. "I mean, *sir*."

"Relax, I'm off duty."

She smirked. "True, sir, but I'm not. I'm here to replace you."

"You still look tired. They woke you up for this?"

"I was already awake, sir." Jane cleared her throat with a polite cough. "Someone decided to play reveille with a railgun."

Collins laughed. "Sorry 'bout that."

"It's okay, I was supposed to be up for duty in an hour anyway. Don't think the rest of the platoon will be as understanding, though." She sat on the chair behind the monitors and double-checked the readout. She stifled a yawn.

"They really that mad?"

"Some of them were just getting to sleep. There was talk about lynching."

"Oh, the fun never stops in the 1209th, does it?"

Jane smirked, then a look of concern crept onto her face. "Can I ask you something?" she asked.

"Sure."

"I mean, as a guy, as a soldier, not as an officer."

"Go ahead."

"You ever have..."- she paused and glanced over her shoulder -"regrets?"

Collins frowned. "About what?"

"All this. The military, the daily grind, the marching and saluting and training. It's just... it's just not exactly what I thought I was signing up for. I don't know," she said, looking down. She noticed her hands shaking and placed them on her hips. "I feel like I should be doing something more than double-checking supplies and babysitting machinery."

"Of all the places to babysit machinery, this is one of the best."

"How so?"

"Thanks to our good pal, Rob," Collins said with a smirk. When he saw the confused look on her face, he added, "R-O-B, the Remote Outpost Bonus. Eight years of fun here counts as sixteen. Add in the first four-year term I served and that equals twenty years. Regulations state that if you serve any twenty-year term that includes time at a remote outpost, you get to retire early with a nice pension."

"That's easier to say when you're so close to the end. Not as easy when you've only been here *one* year. Sometimes I just want to go back home."

"And miss out on all this fun?"

She smiled at him in that way that made his skin tingle. "Oh yes, this place is all sorts of fun. Speaking of fun, I believe you have some cleaning to do." She pointed toward the farmer.

"Oh yes, I have a date with some drunken idiot farmer. Thanks for reminding me."

"A date?" Jane asked.

"Yeah," Collins replied. "Worst first date *ever*."

Jane laughed. "See you later, then."

Collins turned and walked around to the front of the automatic sniper, which focused on him for a moment before it returned to scanning the horizon. He pulled on gloves and focused his view on the farmer's corpse. He paused and turned his head halfway to facing Jane. He wasn't quite sure how to say what he'd been feeling for the past few weeks, or if he even should say anything. There were nights that the two of them would stay up hours past their curfew, laying in their bunks, talking in whispers about all manner of topics. He wasn't exactly sure what it meant, but that sort of thing had led to relationships before. Jane was a soldier, as was he, but he didn't stay up nights talking with the others in the barracks. The only thing he knew for sure was that she was on his squad, and he shouldn't be thinking the things he was. It was a breach of protocol, if nothing else. Even if she wasn't on his squad, rank would get in the way.

"Yes," he said, finally making a decision to say something. "Sometimes I do have regrets. Places I'd rather be. Things I'd rather do." He gulped and cleared his throat, felt his hands start to sweat inside his gloves. He focused his gaze on the farmer again. "Things I'd rather say," he added, wondering if she understood his meaning or even felt the same something. He didn't turn to see if she had any reaction to his words. He wasn't sure he could deal with any response at this point. He took a deep breath and started walking to the corpse.

THE BARGAIN

The airlock door cracked open with a hiss and slowly slid to the side. Behind the door was the adjoining ship's airlock, dimly lit by small red lights set along tracks in the ceiling.

A single man stood within, staring straight ahead until the door finished its journey, hands clasped behind his back. He stepped into the brightly lit cargo hold, dressed in a simple black jumpsuit, skin-tight, with a single zipper stretching along the front. Wild blond hair, unkempt looking, like he'd been living in a forest his whole life. His cold gray eyes scanned the interior of the cargo hold, passing over every curve of the ship's interior, pausing at the barely visible seams where walls met. Every time his eyes passed over one of the crew, they continued without recognition, as if the crew weren't there at all.

Victor Wells was uneasy about this entire meeting. The only reason he'd accepted the offer to meet in person was that his men had been complaining for days about wanting some action. He'd promised them action, and money, and more. He had provided for them in the past, but their memories were shorter than their credit lines. Things had been tight lately. They needed a score, and this man promised a bargain like none they'd ever had before. An easy mark; low-hanging fruit ripe for the picking. Victor scratched his protruded belly. He'd been eating as well as usual, but his supply of liquor had dried up days ago. Sobriety was not a state he cared to continue in. He had to admit that he was interested in a lucrative score as much as his men. The four men he'd brought with him to meet this stranger watched with intense stares, nervous hands perched on their pistols. They were some of the most loyal men in his crew, but that wasn't saying much. Their loyalty was in direct proportion to how much and how often he paid them.

"So," Victor said, trying to hide the tremor in his voice by raising the volume, "what is this about?"

"A bargain," the stranger replied. He seemed interested in the ceiling, at the moment.

"A bargain, yes, you said that earlier. It better be a good one to justify meeting in person."

"Oh, I assure you it is. There's-"

"Wait," Victor interrupted with a wave of his hand. "I don't deal with strangers. First you tell me your name."

The stranger's eyes ceased their roaming and settled on the Captain. "I am Woden."

"That's an odd name. Where did-"

"Do you want to discuss name origins, Captain Wells, or do you want to become very, filthy rich?"

Victor glanced down and shuffled his feet. The men behind him perked up. One of them prodded him in the back. "Yes. Yes, of course, right," he said. "What is this bargain then?"

"There's a ship, somewhere between here and Mars. It's a government ship, unmarked, traveling without an escort," Woden said. He paused when he saw Victor's reaction and waved his hand dismissively. "No worries, it's not a military ship. Strictly research. There will be no guns, no soldiers, no guards. Easy pickings. Most of the research they do is classified, so the contents won't even be acknowledged should they go missing. Even better, the ship is instructed not to send any distress signals should they come under attack." Woden handed the Captain a small bundle of papers. "Here is all the data you need to find the ship, and an authorization code that will allow you to dock with it."

Victor took the papers and gave them a cursory glance. The ship's schematics showed it to be a decent size. The authorization code looked like any other code of its type, but the surrounding connection instructions were gibberish to him. He pursed his lips and nodded as if he knew what it all meant. "Interesting. But why tell us about it? If it's such easy pickings, why not just get it yourself?"

"The men on board are instructed to send no distress signals. They are, however, instructed to destroy the ship, and the cargo, should they find themselves under attack."

"So you need more hands to take control of the ship before they can self-destruct?"

"Exactly."

"And how much of this cargo will you require as your share? Twenty percent? Thirty?"

Woden shrugged. "I don't care about the cargo. I don't care about the ship. You can have it all."

There was a murmur behind the Captain. He turned his head briefly to shush them. "What *do* you care about, Woden?"

"I want to send a distress signal once we get on the ship. Open band on the 'Net. Then I'll stay on board, and wait."

Victor laughed. "There's only one ship that would give a shit."

"Precisely."

"You mean to tell me that you *want* them to come?"

"Yes."

"I see..." Victor said, glancing at one of his men. "So... you want us to board this ship and rob it, and while we're busy doing that, you want Fireteam Zulu to show up? If you're planning to double-cross someone, you usually don't tell them."

"This is not a double-cross, Captain. It's a trap."

"Call it what you will. I don't appreciate being trapped and screwed over, with or without advance warning. Oh, we'll go after this ship, rest assured, but there will be no distress signal. Just a loot and leave. As for you..." he motioned and one of the men behind him drew his pistol and fired.

Woden tilted his head to the side. The air in front of him shimmered. The projectile slowed, halting near his face. Woden examined it with mild curiosity. Small piece of black plastic, hardened to withstand the detonation that sent it from the pistol. It was one of the newer bullets of its type, designed to work like older lead projectiles, but with a plastic coating that would shatter on impact with something harder, like a ship's hull. Safe for everyone except the person you fired it at. Woden plucked the bullet from the air and tossed it to the man who had fired it.

"You misunderstand me, Captain," Woden said. "This is not a trap for *you*. This is a trap for Fireteam Zulu."

BALLS

Four hours, Tank thought. *It would have to be enough. I've gotten by on less.* He paused before his berth and glanced back to watch Ghost tending to Tex's wound. There was something going on between them, or there had been. He was sure of that. And it bothered him. Personal attachments complicated things. He needed to know that his teammates had their minds focused on the mission. It wasn't that he wanted her for himself. She was pretty, and had a certain feminine grace that he found attractive, and he certainly respected her combat ability. Something inside him knew they weren't compatible. He had accepted that a long time ago. They were both killers. But she killed with the steady hands of a surgeon, while he would much rather use something more direct, like a tank.

He turned his attention back to his berth and smiled. *Like a tank,* he said to himself while laying down on the soft padding of his bed. He closed his eyes and thought back to the day his platoon had given him his handle. *Like a tank. What a fun little war that was...*

*   *   *

The whole platoon of marines was pinned down, which was something

they were extremely unhappy about. The Lieutenant was barking orders, trying in vain to motivate the young soldiers to leap over the embankment and
charge the enemy. Every one of them might have considered that course of
action had the Lieutenant had the balls to do it himself. But he was fresh out
of the academy. He knew the art of war, he was highly trained, he was well-
versed in all the rules and regulations the military had drilled into him, and
he was completely useless in actual combat.

Charles Tenneson was only a private first class then, but already he had
the good sense not to run at a hundred pissed off farmers armed with pulse rifles. They were just a bunch of farmers, sure, but even in the hands of an am-
ateur, a pulse rifle was a fearsome weapon. Anyone could aim at a target as
wide as a platoon of marines charging over a ridge and luck into at least a
few kills. So he chose to not charge in, and was instead laying in the dirt beside his friend, a new recruit by the name of Hewitt.

Poor kid, Tenneson thought as he watched Hewitt flinch with every
round that sounded close. It was the kid's second day as a marine, and here
he was in combat. At least he had Tenneson to rely on.

The conflict started only a week prior, and was already close to being re-
solved. The military leaders for United Earth had declared war immediately
after the farmers in Mars colony MP-2169 had decided to strike. Their com-
plaints filled fifteen printed pages and mostly amounted to low wages for
long hours. The people wanted fair wages for the food they were growing.
The government wanted cheap food in return for the money spent to get the
people there in the first place. The response was swift: quell the rebellion before it starts. Nobody counted on the farmers being armed.

And oh how they were armed.

They had pulse rifles, boxes upon boxes of ammunition, and even a laser
cannon. Thankfully, they hadn't yet figured out how to use that, but there was
no guarantee they wouldn't figure it out eventually. They had all this gear because some nameless private made a minor calculation error when air-drop-
ping supplies to the local marine base. Now those same marines were pinned
down, out-numbered, and out-gunned. By farmers.

The Lieutenant was still trying to motivate them to charge the farmers, barking orders in three different languages. Everyone understood the standard Terran language, but he kept lapsing into a local Martian dialect and his native language. Hewitt seemed to understand the latter, but it didn't change his desire to stay put.

If their Sergeant were here, he would have grabbed his pulse rifle and been the first on the open plain. The whole platoon gladly would have followed him, even if it meant certain death. Their Sergeant had his whole arm blown off in the last battle, but that didn't stop him. He picked his rifle up with his other hand, fired a few shots, and used the heated muzzle to cauterize his own wound. He claimed he couldn't remember much about that battle, but the marines with him knew what he'd done.

Are you okay, sir? Tenneson had asked while shielding his nose from the stench of burnt flesh.

Always, came the reply. *Always.*

Then he'd charged, and Tenneson followed. All of the marines followed, driven forward not by any desire to achieve an objective, but by sheer inspiration in their commanding officer. They followed him into hell -- a military bunker with thirty armed men. Their single squad made it to the bunker, and their Sergeant dove in head-first through the front gun slit, without hesitation, firing all the way. He hit the dirt, rolled to the side, and rose. Tenneson knew he couldn't fit through that slit, so he hit the dirt outside the bunker and fired in, covering the Sergeant as best he could. The Sergeant took a few rounds in the leg, but still he managed to limp to the door. He dropped his pulse rifle and opened the door. The rest of the squad poured into the bunker and finished the battle.

Their Sergeant was a brave man who never flinched when confronted. He followed his orders, then, and achieved an impossible objective at great risk to his own life. He didn't hesitate. He didn't complain. He accepted his orders with a slight nod of his head, barely even blinking. When asked if he was ready, he gave his standard response: "Always."

In short, their Sergeant had balls.

Balls that were currently in the stockade, thanks to the Lieutenant. Sarge was sent away to get a new arm, and then was sent back to the front to kill more farmers. He refused. Sarge had balls, Sarge liked combat, but Sarge didn't want to kill farmers. He'd killed enough already, he said, not knowing for sure who they were or what they'd done.

Some part of Tenneson agreed with that sentiment, but the rest of him followed orders. Except this one. He wasn't throwing his life away for the Lieutenant. Running out into the open was suicide. There had to be a better way.

"Get out there you pussies!" the Lieutenant shouted over the steady thumping of rounds hitting the dirt around their makeshift foxhole.

Somewhere to his left, Tenneson heard one of the privates mutter, "You first, asshole..."

That set off the Lieutenant, sending him on another tirade. His face tinted crimson as he tried to balance embarrassment with orders while also trying to find the private who had insulted him.

"Dammit LT, what're we s'posed to do?" a rookie next to him asked, sending the Lieutenant into another red-faced tirade. The firefight drowned out most of his screaming, making him look like a child being taught the meaning of 'no'.

"What's an LT?" Hewitt whispered.

"Lieutenant. Lazy Trooper. Take your pick." Tenneson turned his head to the right, away from a fresh volley of verbal carnage that was about to engulf the platoon.

And that's when he saw her, beautiful in her rusted armor plating, guns poised yet silent. Sleek lines, some battle scarring on the side but something about that made her even lovelier. She was no doubt the most welcomed sight he'd seen all day. He dropped his gun and, crouching, ran to her. He pressed his body to hers, rubbing his hands over her sides lovingly. Someone behind him shouted a warning as rounds starting hitting around him, pelting the dirt and pinging off her armor. He knew there was only one safe place, and that was inside her. He clambered up the rungs, opened the old rusty tank's hatch, and climbed inside.

The tank had obviously been abandoned here years ago, probably some-thing sent as a precautionary measure yet never used. It was a relic from days long past, and was probably rusty on Earth before they shipped it here. Martian sand had covered and hidden the vehicle. Only recent wild shots from the farmers had managed to expose it, and even then there was so much rust on the armor plating that it was difficult to tell where the armor ended and the sand began. But one patch of plating had avoided the rust, hidden and protected beneath the sand, and it glinted in the sunlight.

Despite the layers of rust on the outside, the inside was pristine, scent of new leather and gunpowder filling the air around him. A slight layer of dust coated everything. Tenneson analyzed the interior as quickly as he could. He guessed there was room for five soldiers, maybe six. He found the main power switch and pushed it. Something clicked and the controls all around the interior lit. He glanced at the main turret, with the racks of ammunition beside it. He didn't know how to load it, and the controls for firing were not labeled in any language he knew. But that didn't matter much.

All he needed was balls. Like Sarge.

Tenneson sat in the driver's chair and reviewed the startup checklist taped to the wall beside him. He flipped through a few pages until he got to the one in English. He followed it dutifully, but the tank protested when he got to the part about stirring the fuel tanks. There was a note about the biodiesel fuel having problems in low temperatures, but the reserve battery had already fired up and the tank had some electrical power. Tenneson flipped a switch to run power to heating coils wrapped around the fuel tank, waited the twenty seconds as instructed by the checklist, and tried again. The tank sputtered and roared to life.

The controls were easy enough to figure out. Push here to go forward. Pull to go back. He didn't anticipate needing to go back. All he needed was forward and stop. He pushed the controls and the tank lurched forward, rusty tracks tearing at the Martian soil, digging its way toward the farmers. Constant pinging from the farmers' pulse rifles ricocheting off the tank's armor. Tenneson had never been in a tank before, but he was fairly sure that small arms fire wouldn't penetrate the armor plating. Individual pulse rifle rounds were too focused to be a problem, and the farmers weren't trained well enough to concentrate their fire. He hoped they didn't have any anti-tank rockets or plasma weapons in that marine care package.

As the tank rumbled forward, shaking the ground around them, the farmers panicked. Some dropped their weapons and ran. Others froze in place, watching the machine lurch toward them. The unfortunate ones who ran into the open field were shot to death by his platoon. The others hid in their houses. Still the tank continued on, over the embankment outside the small village, and over the farmers who had stayed behind. Tenneson pulled another lever, sending the tank into the largest building he could see through his little viewing port. After the building finished crashing around him, he stopped the tank and opened the hatch.

Outside the tank, the air was filled with the sounds of screaming, the shrieks of the dying, and the stench of old biodiesel. The marines had charged in his wake and were spilling into the village, the Lieutenant calmly strolling behind them, careful to not actually be engaged in any combat. He stepped carefully over a giant farmer stain on the soil and followed the bloody tank tracks to the collapsed building. Tenneson climbed out of the tank and planted his feet in the soft soil. He turned to watch his comrades overrun the rest of the village.

"Splendid job," the Lieutenant said to him when he'd gotten closer. He tried to look like he was examining the tank and the building as he read Tenneson's name tag. "Good work, Tenneson. You got balls, son."

"Thank you, sir."

Some cheers erupted from the marines, signifying an end to the combat. The few farmers who lived through the battle were rounded up and forced to sit on the ground and wait while the marines called for a transport to take them away. The village was mostly intact, except for the building Tenneson had driven the tank through.

The Lieutenant covered his ears and spoke in happy tones to his commanding officer, claiming that the farms could be up and running again in a matter of hours. All they needed were some more complacent farmers; men and women who were more inclined to work.

Hewitt had taken a hit in his shoulder, but it hadn't soured his mood. In fact, he showed it off like a medal he had earned, his own personal badge of courage. This from the kid who had spent most of the day cowering with the others. Hewitt had Tenneson's rifle slung over his shoulder; he returned it and they walked back to the transport together.

Later that night, back in the base, the other marines congratulated Tenneson on his solution to the problem. That night, he earned the handle 'Tank', given to him by his fellow marines.

For having balls.

For reminding them of Sarge.

For driving over farmers with a tank.

Norm

From his office, the Colonel could see most of the Quad -- a large central area formed by the null space between the armory, the barracks, the garage, and the mess hall. It was big enough for two platoons to assemble, or, in an emergency, for a ship to land. There was a gap between the barracks and the mess that allowed him to barely make out the turret that Collins was appointed to. Collins was standing there, talking with his replacement. The Colonel took a sip from his coffee and waited. He found it was generally a good idea to let soldiers chat, but most had the good sense to work while they did it. Collins was a different type of soldier, not like the rest at all. The only problem with him being a Norm was that the other soldiers knew it, and would often tease him about it.

Hide it as long as you can, the Colonel had told him on his first day. *Don't let them know or they will never forget it.*

He took another sip from his coffee as Collins started the arduous walk to the farmer's corpse.

Collins hadn't hidden it at all. Like many of the original Norms, he was proud of his normality. That pride came with a price, for once bio-tech became standard treatment for a wide variety of afflictions, Norms became out-casts. The only respite they'd had in more than two hundred years was pro-vided by the sun. The Great Solar Storm of 2096. Humanity had thought they knew how to predict the sun's cycles. Scientists were sure they could give ample warning, but the sun proved otherwise. The first electromagnetic shock wave was actually a double wave. We shut down satellites and other electronics, hiding from the onslaught, then turned everything back online just in time to lose all of it to the second wave. Our early warning systems were knocked out. Billions of people died instantly when the pulse killed the nanobots that governed their entire bodies. Many millions of others were left paralyzed or disabled. War broke out, the greatest military mobilization we had seen yet, and it probably would have been worse had we not lost so many people already.

Nations were busy building offense and defense when the third electro-magnetic pulse hit the planet, taking out most of the military machinery. The Norms, outcast from regular society, became the majority. When the dust set-tled there were few people left who could fight them. If they had had some measure of foresight, they would have seized all positions of power when they had the chance. But many of them decided to revert to simple lives of farming, raising livestock, almost like a complete reversion to medieval life-styles. The Norms who did seize what power they could were quickly re-placed when the world stabilized.

Now humanity had come full-circle. Norms were the minority again. Most people were tinkering with bio-tech and nanotech again. Anything they could get pumped into them to make their lives better. People experimented with everything from cosmetic augments to age extension. Common dis-eases, including ones that were fatal in earlier times, could be cured with a single injection of nanobots that were programmed to fix you and could even learn to combat mutations. Another injection would let you change your eye or hair color on a whim. It was a slippery slope for some people -- most start-ed with augments that made it possible for them to continue living, then moved into augments to provide convenience.

The military was the biggest endorser of augmentations. They were always searching for ways to make better, faster, smarter soldiers. They had augments for communications, augments for combat, and augments for tactical coordination. Maps were installed into soldier's heads, visible on ocular implants. Encrypted radio receivers for receiving orders and displaying waypoints on the soldier's maps. Soldiers had a wireless link to their pulse rifles, so they could aim and fire around corners, or from cover, without exposing more than one hand. The list of augments grew every year, and every soldier would get upgraded at the start of each new service term.

All of these augmentations were used with little thought given to the problems a person would experience should history repeat itself.

But the Norms had succeeded in one very important respect. While in power, a visionary in the upper echelons of government had laid down laws within the core doctrine of the United Earth Federation to prevent hate crimes. Included within were clauses that made it illegal for anyone, even the military, to force any member of the Norm Party to receive augmentations of any sort. Some had taken advantage of this clause to enter the military without sacrificing their normality.

People like Collins, the Colonel thought. *People like me.*

There was still a price to be paid. Other soldiers viewed Norms with disdain, for they were crippled in comparison to their augmented counterparts. Some refused to be put on squads with Norms. Every possible advantage needed to be exploited in combat, and Norms were more of a liability than others. That made some things tricky. Some very talented Norms could hide their lack of augmentation with superior skills. The Colonel had done that. He was such a good marksman in his day that people assumed he had ocular implants, but the reality was that he had just trained harder.

Things were going well for him, until Beijing.

He was in charge of an entire regiment, a much more fitting job for a colonel. His job wasn't that tough: maintain the border. Then they captured a Chinese general and were to hold him until he could be collected. He posted a fireteam on guard duty composed entirely of Norms. Nobody wanted to fight with them, so he worked on getting them to work together, to show what Norms could do in combat. Most of the soldiers viewed this as a good move, because none of them wanted to go into combat with a Norm. Nobody knew the Colonel was also a Norm, or it would have been viewed as some sort of favoritism.

Everything was going well, until she came.

Nobody saw her, nobody could stop her. She swooped in like a phantom and killed the Chinese general before anyone even realized she had been there. Even to this day, all he knew about her was one frame from the security camera footage, one hazy glimpse of her from behind. One mistake on her part, but the only thing revealed was her gender, and even that much was just an educated guess. The footage was confiscated and hidden, then mysteriously misplaced.

The resulting investigation blamed the entire incident on the Norm fireteam. The military considered leaving it at that, but the Colonel had insisted on defending his subordinates. His attempts at protecting his soldiers resulted in the exposure of his own Norm status. His superiors didn't hesitate to hang the albatross around his neck. Technically speaking, he hadn't done anything wrong, so they couldn't court-martial him. But they had a platoon on Mars that was currently under the command of a very talented captain who deserved a chance to rise to something more suitable. It was as good a place as any to let a Norm ride out the rest of his career.

The Colonel frowned as he saw Collins almost at the medical office, dragging the corpse by hand behind him. He'd given every break he could to the boy, but this was going to be a hard one to cover up. He sighed and took another sip of coffee.

"Sir?" his adjutant said as he entered the office. "There's a priority one call from Fleet."

"I'll take that in here."

He turned to face the video screen, wondering why Fleet would want to talk to him.

ANATOMY OF A TRAP

W oden pointed out the viewport. "There," he said, indicating a ship that was growing in the window.

The pirate captain regarded the ship with growing interest. "Doesn't look military." He shifted in his chair and glanced around the bridge of his ship.

Captain Victor Wells' men conducted themselves with the same lack of discipline they usually had. Only one of them was worth a damn, the rest he'd replace in a heartbeat. The good one, a wiry Latino kid who said his name was Trey ("with an 'e'," he'd emphasized many times), worked hard at his controls, running every scanning program he'd managed to steal from the Solar Net over the past three months. He was the only crew member who would do anything without being prompted, bribed, or coerced. That made him irreplaceable in Victor's eyes. But Trey had one annoying flaw.

"It is military," Woden replied. "UEF research vessel TA-8291, code name Orion."

"Looks 'bout the right size to have a reasonable cargo hold."

Woden nodded. "Trust me, Captain, there's quite a haul in there."

"And we're to leave you there, alone? How're you gettin' back to yer ship?"

"After I deal with Fireteam Zulu, I'll use their ship. Just loot the cargo hold and go, Captain. I will handle the rest of the plan."

Trey raised his hand. "Um, mister Captain, sir?"

Victor rolled his eyes. The flaw. It made him feel like he was a teacher in an elementary school classroom. Still, Trey's discipline was remarkable compared to the rest of the crew, and Victor did his best to put up with these constant requests for permission to speak. "Yes, Trey?"

"Cap'n, I'm in. UEF Orion, like he says. Forged dockin' procedures authorized. Good ta' go. Five mins."

The Captain exhaled. "Alright," he said, "let's do it." He reached to his console and pushed a button. "Listen up," he said, his voice echoing around the ship, "we dock in five. Get to the airlock and get ready."

The Captain led Woden from the bridge, down the well lit corridor to the airlock, where his men were already assembled. Seventeen men, bastards all. Murderers, rapists, scum of the galaxy. They were a ragtag group he'd picked up over the past thirteen months. He didn't trust a single one of these men, but as long as he provided them with money they at least wouldn't turn on him. He hoped. He still felt nervous around the men, and tried to hide his shaking by folding his arms behind his back, which he had strategically placed close enough to a wall so that he could at least see mutiny coming.

Woden stood still while the men prepared. Passive, his face clear of emotion. He ignored the foul language and anticipatory stories they were swapping. They were amateurs, punks. One of them scowled at him, and still he showed no response. Not a single man there scared him. Even if all eighteen rushed him at once, he knew he'd barely break a sweat dealing with them.

Four more minutes went by, and the assembled men slowly sank into silence. Then the sound of metal scraping metal echoed through the room, shaking the floor. It ended with a thud, and a red light above the airlock door turned green. Four eager men up front threw open the hatch and rushed into the other ship's cargo hold. Woden waited for the rest of the men to filter into the UEF Orion before following the Captain in.

Captain Victor Wells looked around the cargo hold as his men exchanged eager comments. "That's a lot of cargo," he said, giving the hold another look. Crates were stacked from floor to ceiling all along the perimeter of the room. In the center were several rows of palettes, bearing smaller crates. Most of it was military cargo, stamped with the UEF logo and a list of contents. Food concentrates. Medical supplies. Terraforming equipment. Small arms. Machinery. Enough supplies for a year at a small starter colony. "I think we'd need at least four trips to loot all this."

"Easy, Captain," Woden said. "You only have time for one load. But first things first-"

"One load?" one of the men said. His dismay echoed amongst the other pirates.

"Where are you going to store the cargo?" Woden asked. "You can't fit it all in one trip. Do you have some secret hideout nearby with enough storage for all this?"

"Actually, we *do* have a place," Victor Wells said. "My brother-in-law has a place on Deimos. It's not too far. We could do a round trip in about an hour."

Woden bit his lip. He surveyed the cargo a moment, then waved at the crates in the middle of the room. "These medical supplies in the center are the most valuable. Start with them. Although, I'd recommend against taking those in the *very* center. The crates with the white markings on the sides. Too... fragile."

"And Fireteam Zulu?" the Captain asked.

"Last I saw, they are about four hours away, in the asteroid belt. I'll send the distress signal when you come back from the second trip. That should give you enough time to get it all. Except, of course, for *those* crates. Trust me, Captain, you don't want to deal with those. And don't bother with the crew quarters. These are scientists. They don't get paid in cash."

"Alright by me," the Captain said. He ordered his men to start loading the crates in the center, and repeated the warning about the crates Woden indicated they should leave. Some of the men grumbled, but they grabbed crates nonetheless and started moving them back to their ship.

Woden motioned two of the men over. "Take this," he said, handing them a small black box. "I need you to install this-"

"Main electrical box," one of them said. "I've installed these before. No prob." He took the box and raised it above his head. "Hey guys? Trey, I'm installing an inhibitor. Get the portable lights."

"Trey?" Woden said. "I recommend that you cut power to your own ship as well."

"To our ship as well?" Captain Victor Wells asked. "What about oxygen? We'll be breathing heavier while doing all this work."

"Life support is an emergency system. The inhibitor will not affect that."

"But if we needed the engines... if we had to get away-"

"The intention, Captain, is to make it *look* like both ships are derelict. If someone floats by, you want to be ignored."

Trey started to raise his hand, but Captain Wells wasn't looking at him, so he cleared his throat and said, "Cap'n? I know a way ta' cut power ta' make it look like that, but we'd have full engine usage in less than a minute."

Captain Victor Wells glanced at Woden, who nodded. "Good, Trey. Do it," he said.

"Good," Woden said as Trey set down a box and disappeared into the pirate ship. "And now if you'll excuse me, I have a distress signal to compose."

With that, Woden strolled from the cargo hold, down a hallway that led to the ship's bridge. He couldn't help but smirk. Every part of his trap was coming together. It was all a matter of timing.

He knew the crates he'd indicated were not the most valuable ones in the cargo hold. But they were the heaviest, and would take the longest to load. Several of them were also rather bulky, making them even more difficult to take. Some of the pirates would ignore him and attempt to loot the crew quarters. That extra bit of havoc would help, and in many ways was necessary to his plan. The crew of the ship would cower some place defensible, like the galley. And then the power would be cut.

Fireteam Zulu would answer his distress signal. He was sure of that. But if there were no pirates here to fight, they might not even board the ship. He had to be sure they boarded. Cutting the power was one way to ensure that.

This ragtag group of pirates would pose no threat to Fireteam Zulu. Even with eighteen-to-four odds, they wouldn't last more than a few minutes. But they'd be just enough distraction to give him the opening he needed.

The hardest part was the timing. Fireteam Zulu would need about four hours to get to them. Keeping even this group of pirates busy that long was an impossible feat. He hadn't counted on them having a base nearby to ferry stolen cargo to. In a way, that worked out better than he had planned. This gave them the hope that they would be able to take it all. That greed meant there was a good chance they'd take their time with the first load, packing as much into their ship as possible while congratulating each other on their newly acquired wealth. Still, he hadn't expected them to have a hideout near-by. At the time he constructed his trap, he was counting on the pirates not be-ing on board the Orion for very long. The timing was very critical. The trap worked better if Fireteam Zulu arrived in time to fight the pirates. That's why he had sent the distress signal hours ago, before he had even contacted Victor Wells. And Fireteam Zulu was almost here.

New Texas

Tex looked at his reflection in the mirror, turning side to side to compare the difference between cheeks. Ghost had done a good job repairing the laser burn. He had to zoom in on the reflection to pick out the details. Other than that it was not noticeable.

He removed his shirt and hopped onto his bunk. Tank was on the lower bunk, already snoring. Tex envied people that could fall asleep that quickly. His brother was like that, hit the pillow and sound asleep. The only time Tex could ever do that was in New Texas, with the warm summer breeze flowing through the windows. The aromas of his mother's cooking permeating the entire house. Fill your stomach with two generous slices of whatever pie she'd just baked, then sit in that old comfortable chair in his father's den. Instant sleep.

He closed his eyes and focused on those thoughts, wishing for sleep to overtake him.

But the more he wished for sleep, the more awake he felt.

He had grown up in New Texas, many years after the area was declared safe for people to live in again. Nobody really knew why it was called New

Texas. Not much had changed. The borders were the same as they had been after Mexico had reclaimed the land. The cities kept the same names. The people were largely the same -- some of Mexican descent, some of Texan, some mixed. People still tipped their hats in greeting while subconsciously resting hands on their pistols. The cattle still roamed the plains, even more oblivious to the passage of time than the people. Boys still grew up with dreams of being cowboys.

Barry Swenson was one of those boys. He spent most of his youth digging through every online archive on the Net, searching for all the Western movies he could find. Most of the modern movies made with synthetic actors were boring, cookie-cutter plots with perfect people speaking perfect lines with perfect timing. There was nothing magical about the new movies. No emotion, few variations in movements or vocal inflections. Computer generated landscapes that looked the same in almost every movie -- a jumbled bunch of recycled polygons and speech synthesizers, fitted together according to set algorithms. Barry tried to track down older movies, before the changes in the media industries, but they were few and far between.

Until he found the server. An old Usenet server, sitting in the local dump, buried under piles of machinery and forgotten. He rescued the server and had to recruit three friends to help him figure out how to connect the thing. It required some hacker know-how, so he told Tyler about it. But Tyler couldn't do anything until it was plugged in, so they had to get Sebastien involved. Sebastien knew about electronics and his dad had an old soldering iron that still worked. Took him almost a week to figure out what was wrong. He said it was the power supply, not that that meant much to Barry.

Turned out that fixing the power supply was only the start of the project. The machine rumbled to life. Fans on the back spewed chunks of dust out of the case. But they had no place to plug in their VR goggles. No ports for data gloves. They tossed around ideas at lunch the next day and heard muffled laughter from the next table. The laugher was a Korean kid, said his name was Kim. "If that server's as old as you say it is," he said, "you need a monitor. And a keyboard too."

"Of course!" Tyler replied. "But where the hell are we supposed to get those?"

"I think my dad has some spares," Kim said, voice trailing as he regarded their reactions.

"What d'you want in return?" Barry asked.

"Just want to see the server. And the data. If you guys found what I think you found, well, working on something that old would be a lot of fun."

"Deal."

They went to Kim's place after school, got a keyboard and an old LED monitor. Neither one fit, so Kim had to dig a little deeper into his dad's shed. Down near the bottom of one junk pile in the corner, he found an ancient cathode ray tube monitor. The connector fit, but there wasn't enough left of the monitor to actually use. Sebastien had to spend an entire afternoon soldering an adapter for the LED monitor. It worked, mostly, but the screen refresh was wrong. Sebastien spent another few days tweaking the connection to get the flickering to stop. While he was busy with that, Kim found a second keyboard, one with a connection that fit the server.

Once they had the server connected, Tyler got into it but there was just too much data. "Terabytes of unorganized crap," those were his exact words. Not a lot of data in the grand scheme of things, but the way it was organized didn't make any sense. They dug through some old manuals they found in Kim's dad's shed. Tyler swore at those manuals more than he had in history class. Sebastien stood by, watching them flip through the last of the manuals. He told them they'd have to go to the edge of town. He knew someone who just might be able to help.

After school the next day, they went to the edge of town, to Old Man Cletus. Sebastien said he'd gone there for old parts before, and knew the way. Their parents had told them not to go. That was one area of town they were strictly forbidden to visit. But they had to know what was on the server. There was a chance, a slim chance, of something that was worth watching.

Cletus laughed when they finished explaining what they needed help with, a big hearty belly laugh. "Theh's na way ta get tha' data off," he had said, "ya won' even get tha' thin' wiyah'd ta a mod'n display unit."

But they showed him the server, and the interface that Sebastien and

Tyler had built. His tone changed immediately. In an instant, Cletus had taken on the air of an excited teenager. Just another one of the boys, helping with an after-school project.

"Tha probl'm," he told them, "is tha' ya needa news readah. Ya canna jus' use tha data like mod'n fials. Back then we had ta have speh-shul prohgrimms ta piece thin's t'getha. See? Look heah, this is a fial. One fial. Not twenny fials."

Tyler got excited. "Yeah, I see it now. One file, but it's split into twenty parts."

"Zactly," Old Man Cletus said. "People would encode fials, split 'em inta pahts, and upload tha pahts."

"Why?" Tyler asked.

"We did'na have tha bandwith back then! People had ta connec' over tel'phone, oha cable lines. Slow as molasses in winta, boy. Tha only thin' wohss than spendin' half a day downloadin' fials was findin' out they wasn't complete. So they split tha fials. Ya downloaded tha pahts, pieced 'em togetha, and if one paht was fucked up ya just downloaded that one paht agin. Oha ya could get these fials- see theah? P-A-R-1. P-A-R-2. Checksums, payrih-tee fials. Ya'd run a proh-grimm ta rebuild the missin' pahts from those. Beauty o' a scheme, fo' tha time."

Then he showed them how to use the news reader to piece the parts of the files together. Once they knew that, they cloned the server's data drive and each rescued the files that interested them. Even Cletus took a copy of the drive's data. He mumbled something to justify his action, but by then he had already drained half a jug of dark liquor and the boys could no longer understand him, except that it was something called *Moooonshaaaahn* and they were welcome to try it. Only Tyler was curious enough to try, and his reaction was enough to keep the others away.

Barry spent most of the next few years tracking down and decoding old Westerns, the ones that were worth watching. The ones with Gary Cooper, Clint Eastwood, and John Wayne. He went to his local library node on the Net and tracked down a list of all the old movies and didn't stop looking for files until he had completed his list. He watched every movie several times, memorizing lines, studying reactions, learning from the masters of the genre.

When he was older, he and Tyler enlisted in the army. But that wasn't all it was cracked up to be. Barry was handed a pulse rifle and battle armor. It wasn't what he wanted. He wanted a six-shooter and a dusty stetson. Maybe a cigar butt to grit in his teeth as he told people to get some coffins ready. He begrudgingly took the military augmentations but as soon as his four years were done, he left.

Once reunited with his movie collection, he started to seek out other enthusiasts. He found a group in Hong Kong that had a small collection of Italian Westerns, redubbed in English and subtitled in Mandarin. They agreed to trade their collection for his. They were so impressed with the size of his collection compared to theirs that they sent him money as part of the exchange. Barry spent most of the money to purchase his six-shooters and a vintage stetson. Little wear and tear around the brim, but nothing that compromised the usability of it. He practiced daily until he ran out of ammunition for his gun and was forced to learn how to make his own.

Barry went to talk with Old Man Cletus one day, finding him with a young woman he awkwardly introduced as his friend Shelly. Barry found her attractive, and wanted to do his best to impress her, so he placed one hand on his six-shooter's butt, tipped his stetson, and introduced himself as Tex. Shelly was obviously trying not to laugh, hiding her amusement behind a head nod and a smile. Cletus snorted and shooed him out, saying that he had some business to attend to.

That was the last time he saw Cletus alive.

He got a video from Tyler the next day. Tyler had seen the news report on Cletus' death and offered some explanation. Apparently, Old Man Cletus had discovered some files on the news server that the government wanted suppressed. He had posted the files in every public forum he could find, trying to call as much attention to them as he could. Word on the forums was that they had sent one of their assassins to take him out, and were actively searching for other people connected with the discovery of the Usenet server.

Tex, startled, grabbed his six-shooters and his stetson, and tucked his disk drive with all his movies into his bag. He had nothing else worth keeping. He hopped on the next transport off Earth, a ship destined to dock with the bustling metropolis on Luna. There was no telling who knew of his connection to the server. He figured it should be easy enough to disappear in the moon colony, and everyone said work was plentiful there. Halfway to the moon, his ship was boarded by pirates. He did what he could to fight them, but they were too many, and he was low on ammo. He was forced to lock himself on the bridge with the rest of the survivors.

Fireteam Zulu boarded the transport and chased off the pirates. The firefight was long and bloody. Most of the pirates perished, and one member of the legendary Fireteam had as well. The leader knocked politely, entered the bridge, and introduced himself as Sarge. He rattled off a short speech and then asked for help in carrying his fallen comrade back to his ship. Tex volunteered without hesitation; it seemed like the noble thing to do at the time.

"What's with the hat?" Sarge had asked as he lifted his fallen comrade's arms.

"Texas thing," replied Tex, picking up the man's legs. "Ever watch old Western movies?"

Sarge snorted. "Don't have time for movies. Got work to do, and now I'm down a man."

"Fighting pirates? I'm looking for work-"

"With what? I don't need some kid with a toy gun and a dream."

"I was in the army," Tex said, "stationed in New Texas. Served four years."

"Augments?"

"Standard mix."

"You just got a bit more interesting, kid. How are you with fighting completely unfair battles for little to no pay?"

Tex shifted the corpse to get a better grip. "Sounds like the Magnificent Seven," he said with enthusiasm.

Sarge paused and frowned at him. "There's four of us. Three-" he turned his head to the side and added, "understood Weasel, we're on our way." Sarge turned back to look at Tex. "We got another job but there's only three in our fireteam. We need a fourth, if you're interested."

Unfair battles. Incredible odds. Winning would be glorious. Even losing would be glorious. Seven against an army. Four against dozens. Tex couldn't think of anything he'd rather do.

Blood Trails

Collins grunted as he hoisted the corpse onto the examination table. It wasn't that the corpse was particularly heavy, actually it was quite a bit lighter than it should have been because of all the holes in it. But it was those same holes that made it troublesome to transport. In retrospect, he should have pushed the corpse onto a tarp before attempting to move it. He was sure the Colonel would chew his ass out for leaving the sticky blood trail from the field to the medical office. And he was also sure that it would be him who would be ordered to clean it all up. Even while dragging the corpse, he knew he'd done it wrong. The whole situation reeked of twenty-twenty hindsight.

"What's this?" asked Doctor Dmitri Vladlodikov, a kindly man of Ukrainian descent who was well liked by most of the soldiers at the outpost. He peered at Collins over the rims of his glasses as he pulled his clipboard a little closer to his chest.

"It's a corpse, Doctor D."

"I can see that," Dmitri sighed. "I suppose I should have asked *who* is this."

"Some farmer," Collins said. "Approached from the north about half an hour ago. Took over two hundred railgun rounds before he dropped."

"So I have *you* to thank for the early rise."

"'Fraid so. Well, him too. Colonel wanted me to turn him over to you."

"Where's his other arm?"

"I have to go back for it. Got shot off somewhere around two hundred meters out."

Dmitri looked at the corpse from head to toe before nodding. "Tell the Colonel I will report when I have something to report. And I highly recommend you step into the decontamination shower in the corner before leaving."

"Got it," Collins said. He stuck one hand under the other arm and pulled, removing his glove. He stepped into the shower stall and closed the door. The shower registered his arrival and beeped twice. It warned him to close his eyes and hold his breath, which he did after putting his glove back on. Nozzles set in the wall sprayed him with a strong jet of gasses laced with a white powder. The floor rotated, turning him in a complete circle before stopping. Another beep emanated and the shower informed him to remain still. A grate in the floor slid open and the shower sucked the extraneous gas from the chamber. The door clicked open. Collins stepped out and looked himself over. His gloves and uniform were clean. All the blood had been removed.

Collins left the medical office and headed straight for the Colonel's building. The Colonel was standing in his office, framed in the window like a perfect picture of unhappiness, sipping coffee and watching as Collins approached. He turned his head and said something. As Collins got closer to the building, the door opened, held by the Colonel's adjutant. Collins didn't even bother with pleasantries. He marched directly into the Colonel's office and stood at attention. "Sergeant Collins reporting as ordered, sir."

The Colonel continued to sip his coffee while watching the reflection of Collins. After another sip he turned. "I've studied the data from your automatic sniper unit. You killed a local farmer. But, given the circumstances, I believe you acted appropriately."

"Thank you, sir."

"I was going to commend you for doing your duty. But then you went and screwed that pooch when you dragged that bloody mess across my base. I don't have to ask you where you got the corpse from or where you brought it to. I got Fleet calling and asking what the problem is. Fleet. *Fleet!* They can see that blood stain from *orbit*, Collins! How the *hell* am I supposed to tell the General that a soldier did his duty when he makes a two-hundred-meter-long blood stain all through my damn base?"

"S... sir..." Collins stammered.

"Not to mention the shit we're going to get from the General and the farmer colonies when word gets out that not only did we kill a farmer, but we blew over two hundred rounds doing it! *Never* in all my years of service have I *ever* seen a single corpse make such a bloody fucking mess. I'm not doing the paperwork on this one, Collins. No, oh no, I'm going to make *you* do it."

"Sir, yes, sir!"

"But before you do that, you're going to get a shovel, and a mop, buckets, whatever the hell you need to clean up that fucking mess you made. I don't want to see a single drop of blood in the quad. It may be dirt, but it's *my* dirt, and by God it's going to be clean, marine dirt. And I'm assuming you made a similar mess *inside* the medical offices"- he paused long enough for Collins to gulp -"then by tomorrow, I want those floors clean. Shining, like a mirror, you understand me, marine?"

"Sir, yes, sir!"

"And after all that is done, you're going to clean some *more*. Effective immediately, I'm replacing your normal duty with janitorial services. I don't *ever* want to see you make a mess like that again, got it? You make a mess like that again, it damn well better be your own fucking corpse that does it."

"Sir, yes, sir!"

"Dismissed."

Collins saluted and left the building, stumbling on his first step outside and almost falling. He took a deep breath to calm his nerves. He thought briefly of returning to his bunk to sate his fatigue, but he was a marine and knew better. He'd already been yelled at once today, and the sun hadn't even finished rising yet. He proceeded directly to the janitorial closet, a small room built as part of the medical offices building but accessed from the out- side. He pressed his thumb against the security lock and waited for it to scan his print before opening the door.

Inside, he surveyed the cleaning supplies. The room was small, and was so packed with supplies that there wasn't much room to walk. Anything you had that needed cleaning could be done with something in this room -- mi- crobes for biological messes and nanobots for repairing buildings and weapons. They even had a couple jars of microbes for cleaning guns so the marines didn't have to do it manually. But the Colonel didn't tell him to clean up the mess he had made. The Colonel had said to get a shovel, and a mop, and buckets. That meant he had to clean it the old-fashioned way. There was a distinct difference between cleaning something efficiently and cleaning something as a punishment. Collins decided he'd best start with the outside of the base, and grabbed a good-sized bucket and a shovel.

The sand around where the farmer had collapsed was stained from his blood, dark spots barely visible in the red sand. Collins followed a sporadic trail from there to the severed arm, careful to wrap it in a small towel before putting it in the bucket. He shoveled the blood spots from there back to the original mess, where he spent more than an hour shoveling what tainted sand he could see into the bucket. As the sun continued to rise, the spots got a lit- tle easier to see, forcing him to return to the same areas repeatedly. When he was sure he'd gotten most of the big mess the farmer had made, he started working his way back toward the base. The mess *he* had made.

By the time he was done with the blood trail outside of the base's perime- ter, he had made twelve return trips to dump the tainted sand in a pile near the janitorial closet. He brought the arm to Doctor Dmitri, wincing as he saw the mess inside the building that he would have to clean later. Some nearby marines snickered, but none of them said anything to him. Heckling a fellow marine who is performing disciplinary duties is tantamount to volunteering assistance. Even Jane knew better than to offer more than a sympathetic glance.

Several hours went by before Collins got close enough to the medical office that the shovel was no longer useful. He returned to the janitorial closet, dumped some antibiological microbes into the bucket and sprinkled some more on top of his pile of tainted sand. He entered the medical office with a mop and a fresh bucket. He started swabbing the bloodstains on the floor, slowly making his way to Doctor D's office. When he got closer, he could hear voices inside.

"Weeks?" the Colonel's voice asked, sounding even more agitated than before.

"At least," Dmitri replied. "Possibly as much as a month."

"You want to tell me how it's medically possible for someone who's been dead for weeks to walk seven kilometers and then take two hundred and seventeen railgun rounds before stopping?"

"It's not. It shouldn't be."

"These weren't practice rounds, Doc. Full-on depleted uranium, government issued, delivered by a railgun. This guy had no armor. That first round to his chest would have vaporized his-"

"I'm well aware of the effects of your weaponry, Colonel." It was Dmitri's turn to sound agitated. "In fact, the rounds did what they were supposed to. Notice his liver? His heart? Lungs?"

There was a pause before the Colonel responded. "I don't see any of those here."

"Precisely. Your railgun vaporized every one of his internal organs."

"Well can you at least tell me who he is?"

"Not yet."

"What do you mean by that?"

Dmitri grumbled something Collins couldn't hear.

"You can't be serious," the Colonel replied.

"I am always serious, Colonel! Look here at the results. See them for yourself. Positive test for blood types A-positive, O-negative, B-positive, and AB-negative. The DNA sample I took from him is an exact match... to more than *forty* people stationed here on Mars."

Collins bumped the bucket as he dipped the mop in again, grimacing as the sound broke the silence in the outer office area. The door to the doctor's office flew open. "Collins," the Colonel said.

"Sir?" he responded, snapping to attention.

The Colonel took in the scene quickly, noticing with some satisfaction that the cleaning was progressing nicely. He quickly wiped the smile off his face and said sternly, "Finish that section and get in here. There's more blood for you to mop up."

"Yes, sir."

COLD COMFORT

G host longed for the cold comfort of cryosleep. It had been a long time since she'd had the opportunity. Three years, by her rough estimate. Fireteam Zulu operated on a much faster pace than the military. The military had no problem putting you in a cryoberth and shipping you off to the other side of the solar system. A four-month journey to Pluto gone in the blink of an eye. A four-month nap, one you awoke from feeling more rested than any other sleep could ever give you.

How she longed for that feeling.

She'd found a cryotube, once, for sale in a small market in Bangladesh. But she was on the run, and had no place to actually use it. In retrospect, she realized that purchasing that unit would have been a bad idea. The cryotube was a consumer model, not nearly as large or as safe as the military berths she was used to. Too much chance of freezer burn.

She lay awake staring at the ceiling of the small cabin. Laying naked in bed with the air vents on full cold was a poor substitute for cryosleep, but she tried it every day nonetheless. Her armor was placed neatly on her table, her weapons placed just so beside it, skin-tight nano battle suit hanging in her small closet. She had a room to herself, not because she was a more special asset than the others, but simply because Sarge had said a woman should have her own space. Part chauvinism, part being nice. That was Sarge. But the reality was that she appreciated having her own room. It gave her a quiet place, a steel box to isolate her thoughts from others and meditate to gather strength.

She shifted to a sitting position, wrapped her legs beneath her, and started to meditate. If she couldn't sleep, she may as well do something that was both relaxing and productive at the same time. As she began to let go of her conscious thoughts, her body drifted into sleep.

*   *   *

Pluto. She couldn't believe her eyes. She considered pinching herself, but if it *was* a dream, she didn't want it to end. The planet was too beautiful for words. She wanted to spend a while admiring it.

The surface was a wasteland of ice, stretching off farther than she could see. Wisps of ice vapor floated like clouds above the surface, casting purple hues on the ground as they twirled around. She could see the structure that she assumed was the main base, nestled in a valley between two massive ridges of frozen nitrogen. From above it looked like a small city, three square kilometers of interconnected living quarters and training facilities. Beside the base was a chemical plant, built to create air and water from the gases in the atmosphere and the layers of ice beneath the surface, connected to the main base with a subterranean tunnel. Far in the distance she could see the small speck that was the Sun. The horizon was partially obscured by the enormous moon Charon, a body nearly half the size of Pluto itself. There was a base on Charon as well, a smaller installation devoted to making sure nobody came close without proper authorization. Even that base's staff didn't know for sure what went on at the Pluto base.

Shelly knew she was going somewhere special, but she never dreamed it would be Pluto. Of all the places in the solar system, the United Earth Federation had two that were deemed its highest military secrets. Just knowing about them was grounds for execution, so she made sure to pretend she had no clue. But she secretly longed to see the base on Pluto. And here she was.

It wasn't that she particularly liked the cold, or even knew what went on at this base. It was that Pluto was the farthest she could possibly go from Earth. If only she could tell her friends at the academy that she had actually seen Pluto. But her smile faded. She knew she could never tell. Telling meant termination.

The ship she was on tilted upward and started to descend, rocking in the thin atmosphere as it slowed. As the ship reached the proper pitch, Shelly could make out the shapes of Pluto's other natural satellites, Nix and Hydra. As far as she knew, they were still unpopulated, but in today's military there was no way to know for sure. If there were ores on there that could be used, the United Earth Federation would expand to it as soon as possible. The human race had nearly destroyed Earth with its insatiable consumption, and when they progressed beyond Earth they were still consuming resources as fast as they could find them. Some lessons were never learned.

Her thoughts were interrupted by the sound of a throat clearing behind her.

"Care to join us, private?"

Shelly turned from the window, twisting in her uncomfortable seat until she was once again in a normal sitting position. She tightened the straps that held her down. "Sorry sir," she said. She felt her cheeks flush as the other recruits stared at her. For a moment she felt like she had been caught daydreaming in school again. Except with this group, nobody would laugh at her. At least not now.

Lieutenant Withers sighed and tightened his own seat straps before continuing. "As I was saying, I can't speak about your training assignments. They, like this installation, are classified. You will be briefed when the time is right. For now, I will assist you in checking into your room at the dormitories in the main base. Feels like the transport is docked, so if you'll follow me..."

Shelly moved with the other recruits down the hallway into a large receiving area. She and eleven others had been selected for training in this facility. They couldn't discuss their assignments, or what they were being trained for. None of them knew. All they knew was that it was an honor to be selected for this base, and they were destined for greater things. She had tried to introduce herself to them when the trip started, but only one of them responded favorably to her sunny disposition -- a young man named Brigandine. His parents, he said, were big medieval history nuts, and named all their children after weapons or armor from the period. She had asked his siblings' names, but he just smirked and turned back to the window.

Lieutenant Withers led them to a window. "Form a line here. My orientation will be brief. Military discipline is to be maintained at all times. Yes, I know you have only enlisted a short time ago, but you have all gone through boot camp. You know the procedures. You understand rank and know how to obey orders. At this window, you will receive your room assignment and will be given your orders. Follow them. That is all."

Shelly waited her turn. She checked in and waited for the rest of the group to finish. They were escorted as a group to their rooms. The Lieutenant got to her room first. He opened the door and sent her in. Once alone, she tore open the small yellow envelope that contained her orders. Inside were strict instructions to only leave the room for meals or when ordered to leave.

Her room was small, sterile, and cold. There was a respectable collection of textbooks available in the computer in her room, which she exhausted quickly. That left her with many hours alone, staring out her small window at the surface of Pluto. Her thoughts drifted, occasionally, to Brigandine. He was handsome enough, she figured, but not very personable. She wasn't sure if she liked him or not. Every attempt she made to strike up another conversation with him in the mess hall resulted in another smirk from him and a superior officer's warning. Something in his eyes made her quiver. Something in his smirk made her wary. In her mind, left alone to wander, she'd been building him up into the perfect boyfriend. She knew it was happening, but couldn't stop herself. She needed some way to occupy herself during the long, lonely days. She tried to distract herself by reading all of the textbooks again, but they weren't any more exciting the second time around.

One morning, someone pushed a folded yellow paper under her door. Terse orders, printed in a faux typewriter font. She reported as instructed to a woman whose demeanor was as cold as her room had been. Major Cho. She would learn to loathe that name, some day, but at the time she was new to the station and hadn't begun her training yet.

"Private Michelle Seles, reporting for duty," she said to the instructor.

Major Cho looked her up and down, then said, "You were left in your room with no instructions. Do you know how long? Did you count the days?"

"No, ma'am."

"Forty-three Earth days," she said, watching Shelly's face intently for a reaction. She got none. "How did that make you feel?"

"Ma'am?"

"Did you get... lonely? Bored?"

Shelly tried to recall the days. Quiet. Serene. She had read, watched videos, did some studying on random topics. She never did mind being left alone during the day. The fabricated relationship with Brigandine she'd been working on made the nights more tolerable. "No ma'am," she said. A lie, a small one, for she *had* been a little lonely and a lot bored. But she had found ways to cope, so she figured this was one of those situations that called for a small lie.

Major Cho studied her again, then turned and walked to the window. Shelly watched as she stood before the window, watching another ship descending toward the surface. Her vision blurred a bit and she heard a voice say something. She turned around to look but she was alone in the room with the instructor. Then the voice repeated the words. *Tersus habenae.* Major Cho turned around and stared back at her, eyes narrowing. *Tersus habenae,* the voice echoed in her head again. The instructor's lips were pressed together, her gaze focused, her eyes vacant.

"Tersus habenae?" Shelly said, tentatively picking her way through the syllables.

Major Cho smiled and said, "You have been recommended for a new stealth soldier program. Top secret. If you mention this information to anyone, anywhere, you will be terminated. If you are ever captured by the enemy, you will be expected to escape or to terminate yourself. This program and their missions rely on you being invisible. Do you understand?"

Shelly nodded, slowly, not entirely sure what she was signing up for.

And that's how it all started -- the training, the years of mental, physical, and emotional torture. The instructors pushed her until they found her limits, and then they had pushed harder. They worked her body until it bled, then worked her mind until migraines forced her into unconsciousness. They let her sleep a while, then woke her up for more. Memories of her former life blurred. Thoughts of Brigandine and her imagined love affair with him vanished almost as quickly as he did -- there at lunch one day, and gone the next. She'd asked what happened to him, but her instructor either hadn't heard her or intentionally dodged the question. Training was especially demanding that day.

They pumped her full of nanotech, augmented everything from her hair to her blood. Every part of her was as lethal as the weapons they trained her to use. Her mind was honed into an instrument to aid her, turning her into a nanobot mage like the ones that roamed the Earth before the Great Solar Storm of 2096. At some point they declared her a graduate.

By then she had realized what her purpose was.

She was a killer. Stone cold, serene, invisible. An assassin. *Tersus habenae*, roughly translated from an archaic Latin dictionary she found on the Net, meant "clean the government."

They gave her the dirtiest jobs they could think of. They rewarded her work with cryosleep, while being shipped to her next target. She was the darling of the military. She killed on command, without question, and left no trace. Generals called on her for help, and when she arrived, they saluted her. She had no rank. She was so far above the normal ranks and rules that even knowledge of her existence was classified.

It wasn't long before the remaining rogue factions both on Earth and in her colonies fell in line. When the last threat fell, the military tried to make her disappear for good. Beijing, 2249, the final fall of the nation formerly known as China. Not the kind of day one forgets. They tried to put her in a cryoberth, to shoot her out somewhere and leave her. They had done as much with her counterparts. The most likely place was the station in orbit around Venus, the garbage planet. They'd revive her in a few decades if they needed her services again. She liked cryosleep, but not *that* much. The best part of cryo was waking up, and there was no guarantee that would happen this time. Nobody had ever attempted cryosleep for more than a few months at a time. There was no guarantee they would be able to revive her. Refusal meant termination.

And then pirates attacked the ship. *What kind of moron attacks a military vessel?* the Captain had cried. Crazy bastards. They tried to call on her to quell the threat, but she was gone, hidden from their view in the cargo hold, using the skills they had given her against them. She watched in silence as the pirates boarded the vessel and slaughtered most of the crew. The marines on the ship were better trained, but the pirates far outnumbered them.

When Fireteam Zulu showed up to salvage the ship, she recognized an acquaintance she had met about a decade ago while doing a job on Earth. Tex was in his early 20s at the time. He hadn't changed much. He didn't recognize her at first, and when he finally did he merely frowned. He said he saw action almost daily, and their reunion descended quickly into his summary of pirate hunting with Fireteam Zulu. It all sounded so exciting back then, and it felt more noble than what she had been doing. Plus she needed something to do. She couldn't keep running, and couldn't return to military service given the circumstances. She figured it was the best place to be -- just under the radar, just out of sight.

Like the ghost she was.

*   *   *

A buzz broke her trance. She opened her eyes and brushed fresh tears from her cheek. Her memories had triggered a realization. She liked cryosleep because it made her outside as cold as her inside had become. Somewhere deep inside her lived Shelly, the precocious teenager from New Seattle who liked puppies and ice cream. At least, that's what she tried to tell herself. The reality was far different. That Shelly had died during the training and was now nothing more than a distant dream. A dream she occasionally enjoyed in cryosleep, sleeping through birthdays, stored and shipped around like cargo. Just another military asset. Her last birthday was celebrated with Fireteam Zulu as her twenty-third, but she knew the truth was about sixty years off.

She turned to the com unit on the wall and saw the message from Weasel. They were near the ship that had called in the distress signal. Four hours gone by in a flash. She rose from her bed and started putting her armor back on.

SICK

ollins tried to clean the medical office, but once he got closer to the actual examination room, Dmitri had shooed him away. So he returned his cleaning supplies to the closet and went to the mess hall instead. His body was sore, muscles aching in protest with every movement. He'd developed a shooting pain in his left leg that pulsed with every step, and he'd started limping to lessen the shock. The other marines were still smart enough to refrain from teasing him about his manual labor.

He grabbed his meal and sat at a table, alone in the corner. The food was adequate, which in military terms meant it was barely edible. Some kind of meat product, browned and seared with grill marks yet inexplicably tasteless, slightly wrinkled from sitting on a hot plate all day. Yellowish slop that reeked of artificial butter; probably some sort of liquefied local vegetable. Brown specks on top that were probably cinnamon, but could have been anything. Healthy serving of greenish slop that he knew was a soy-based nutritionally-complete vitamin concoction. Someone could get an entire day's worth of nutrition from that green slop, but the military provided accouterments in an effort to increase morale. It wasn't working for the marines, but the local farmers who provided the other bits of food seemed happy. Collins forced the meal down as best he could, shoveling it into his mouth as fast as he could swallow, chasing the least appealing bits down with mostly purified water that held a slight taste of dirt.

Collins passed the Colonel on his way out. The Colonel studied the expression on Collins' face a moment before telling him to get some rest. The march across the quad toward the barracks was agony. He stopped once, not even halfway to his destination, and stood there, eyes closed, letting the sun shine on his face as he inhaled the warm Martian air. He was tempted to stand there like that all day, but knew that he had to get to his bed or face another round of administrative yelling. Things were bad enough already.

Collins entered his room in the barracks, an elongated hallway lined on two sides with bunk beds. As every soldier was part of a smaller group that had its own rotation, there was rarely a time when the dorms were empty. Several beds were occupied with off-duty soldiers, sounds of soft snoring echoing off the pristine walls. Collins sat on his bed and undid the laces of his boots, wincing as he noticed what the day's work had done to his morning polishing job. He closed his eyes and stretched his sore muscles. A cough from the bed above broke his trance.

O'Malley had been sick for days, some kind of mutated Martian influenza strain that the doctors hadn't been able to cure yet. They offered to pump him full of some nanobot antibodies, but O'Malley was already the most augmented soldier on the base. Adding anything else to the nano-cocktail that was his bloodstream could be catastrophic. O'Malley had wisely chosen to suffer through it. After all, a week or so of bed rest and delivered meals was worth a little coughing and stomach pain.

Collins stood and looked at O'Malley. On a good day O'Malley stood two meters tall, and was close to four hundred pounds of augmented muscle. His bunk bowed from the weight and shook with every cough. The military gave two choices when you enlisted: strength or speed. O'Malley had a large body frame and had chosen the strength augmentations. Most people chose strength. It was sort of an unwritten rule that only women took the speed choice, and even that unwritten rule was outdated. Most modern women went for strength augments. Speed augmentations were so rare they were almost non-existent with currently active marines. But O'Malley's body had acclimated to the strength augmentations with considerable ease. The doctors were so impressed, they gave him a second round of injections. It wasn't something they did often, for most people could only handle one injection. But O'Malley was a strong ox of a man to begin with, and his body took the second round without any problems. His muscles had expanded so much that the military had to special order his uniforms. Even now, years later, he was just as strong as he was in basic training. Last week he had bench-pressed the Colonel's jeep on a bet, doing three full extensions before collecting credits from those who thought he couldn't do it. Now he was relegated to bed rest, sickly and coughing the days away.

"Hey O'Malley," Collins said, trying to time his words between coughs, "you need anything before I bed down?"

"How 'bout a hooker?" O'Malley asked. He coughed again, launching a spurt of blood that stuck to the ceiling.

"You know me, O'Malley," Collins said, looking at the fresh blood stain with concern. There were others beside it that were already dried. "The only hookers I can get are ones *you* can't lift."

O'Malley laughed, which threw him into another coughing fit. He tried to say something else, but gave up and rolled to his side, facing away from Collins. Collins returned to his bunk and lay there, staring at the underside of the top bunk, where he had taped a faded photograph of Chrissie. She was standing in the shade of a tree in front of their high school, smiling and striking a pose. He'd asked her to the Prom, but she had refused. Some excuse about not wanting to go at all. He thought he was in love with her, but every time he worked up the courage to do something about it, she'd derail his train of thought with some random comment. She didn't love him back, couldn't, he knew that now. But there was still something comforting in that coquettish smile. With any luck, some day he'd meet another girl like her, one that did love him back. He frowned as he regarded the picture. He thought of Jane again, wondering if he already *had* met that someone. There was certainly something there, something he wanted to nurture. There was no guarantee that Jane felt the same way, or that she even could, but his relationship with her was already more real than anything he had ever had with Chrissie. It was at least a chance. He pulled the faded photograph down, looked at it one last time, and crumpled it into a little ball in his fist.

Another soldier coughed off to his left, a private who had arrived a month ago named Anya. Ugly girl with a dented nose and shaved head. She earned respect her first day by promptly punching another private who'd had the gall to tease her about her nose. Now she was laying in bed, struck down by the spreading disease. It was only a matter of time until Collins caught it. The only helpful thing he could think of doing was covering his nose and mouth with his sheets and getting as much rest as he could.

"Ain't that lovely," another soldier said from the bottom bunk beside him.

Collins turned his head to see Goddard, leaning on his elbow, looking his way and shaking his head. Goddard was well-known as being the most out-spoken of the small faction of soldiers who didn't want to be in the service. How he managed to get to be a corporal was beyond anyone's comprehension. He was one of the few marines who hadn't chosen the strength augmentations. He was a wiry man to begin with, and he decided that his speed was the best thing to augment. There had been some teasing, but when push came to shove, he was able to prove his choice was sound. Goddard had danced around a much stronger opponent, slowly whittling away at the man's stamina with quick jabs before darting away from his opponent's more powerful, yet slower swings. There were rumors that he, like O'Malley, had gone back for a second injection, making him as fast as O'Malley was strong.

At some point in his career, Goddard decided he didn't want to be a marine anymore. He spent most of his downtime trying to convert other marines to join his splinter faction. They didn't do anything about being in the service. They just complained about it. Collins usually found it was best to ignore Goddard, but something in his demeanor suggested that would be harder than usual today. Collins sighed and asked, "What's that?"

"Anotha one sick. First O'Malley, then Barnes, now Anya. Soon we all gonna get it."

"Pipe down and get some rest, Goddard."

"I'm jus' sayin' it ain't right. They should be bunkin' in medical. Ain't that right, Bryant?"

A meek voice from the bunk above Goddard confirmed assent. Bryant was a pushover, always falling in line with just about anything anybody asked him. How he got into the marines was a mystery that many soldiers discussed behind his back. The best explanation so far was Jane's: that some-one merely asked him if he wanted to be a marine. He lacked any sort of in-ternal drive, but made a good soldier. He'd follow any order, from anybody. Goddard had leeched onto him on the first day of basic training.

Goddard spat at the floor. "See? Ain't right, them sick ones bunkin' with us."

"Stow it, Corporal," Collins said. He said the words, knowing it was his duty to keep soldiers on his squad in line, but he knew deep down that he agreed with Goddard. A third private started a coughing fit from near the bathrooms. The infection was spreading.

"Alls I'm sayin', Sergeant, is the truth. Ain't that right, Bryant? Shit, I don't even wanna be here to begin with. Damn Martian air. It ain't right, us bein' here. Maybe I'll get sick next, get myself a medical discharge. Then I can get on with my life. Damned worst decision I ever made, comin' here. Ain't that right, Bryant?"- he waited until he heard another grunt of assent from above -"Damned right it is."

Collins rolled to the side, hoping to fall asleep before Goddard got into the second part of his almost nightly speech. He'd have to remember to report this later in the day, whenever it was he woke up. The Colonel didn't take kindly to this type of talk, and he'd tried more than he should have to keep it under wraps. Morale was already starting to falter with the influenza. The last thing this base needed was another infection.

BOARDING PARTY

Two ships hovered in the void before them, connected, floating with no indication of lights or power in either. Weasel ran every scan he had in his arsenal and came back with little of use. He'd already determined that there was no life aboard the smaller of the two ships, the one he had originally assumed was the ship that had sent the distress signal. Now he wasn't sure. Neither ship had any visible markings on it, which meant they were both illegal. Stolen, perhaps, or junked. There was a third possibility, but Weasel didn't want to consider that one. He knew Sarge would.

"What's it look like?" Sarge asked over the com channel.

Weasel flicked his eyes to the left and right, maximizing each ship readout, one for each eye. "Neither ship has markings. Neither ship registered. No response on any hailing frequency from either. Might be they're both pirate ships and this is a trap."

"Or," Sarge offered, "they're military, and it's a trap."

"Or it's a military ship that sent a distress signal because pirates attacked."

"Not much different from a planned trap. We're bound to get hosed either

81

way."

"So do we do this?"

"Well-" Sarge started to say, then stopped. A few moments later he added, "Can you get any more info from scanning before we go in?"

"Gotta connect to get a more reliable internal scan. Keep the hatch locked on our side and if you don't like the results, we disconnect. You ready for docking?"

"Always."

Weasel eased the throttle back slowly, firing a short correction burst that slowed the ship. A warning signal on his HUD flashed briefly then vanished. The distance counted down in blocky green characters. Closer, closer. He gritted his teeth just before contact, metal greeting metal with a brief scraping handshake. He had expected worse. He had a good amount of experience with docking two ships in space, but the process was a lot easier when both ships had power. A light turned on in his dash view indicating he had lock. He let out a sigh. That meant emergency systems on the ship were still functioning. He flipped a switch on his virtual dashboard and the atmospheres equalized, completing the transaction.

"We're docked," he said into the microphone.

"Security?" Sarge asked.

Weasel opened a command terminal and issued some standard commands to test the connection. No response. He tried again, with a general hailing frequency. Again, no response. He closed his eyes and initiated a direct connection to the Solar Net, sliding his mind into the ether. The disorientation was minimal. He'd been connected to Zulu Prime so long that the line between worlds was starting to blur. His avatar appeared on the digital representation of the empty bridge in the virtual world.

He took a deep breath to help orient himself before turning. He moved down the hallway, gliding to the aft cargo compartment where the airlock was. Punching a few buttons opened his side of the connection, revealing a short hallway and the outer airlock door of the other ship. Lifeless metal hatchway, closed and with no indication of a completed connection. He moved forward to examine the door. Before he could get to it, a small boy appeared in the air before him.

"Greetings," the boy said.

"Sarge, I'll be back in a minute." Weasel turned off his communication with Sarge and focused on the boy. "What ship is this?" he asked.

"I am sorry," the boy replied, "but we appear to have had a system reset recently. That information is no longer available."

"Security?"

"Offline. The ship log indicates a state of distress. Would you like me to open the hatch?"

"Life support?"

"Life support is an emergency system, and is currently active," the boy said. "I am showing twenty-six life signatures." He turned to the right and waved his arm, causing a schematic of the ship to appear in the air. Twenty-six red dots appeared on the schematic.

Weasel opened a communication channel with Sarge. "Sarge," he said, "life support is active. Looks like we got seven life signatures in the galley, up front near the bridge. Probably the crew. I'll try to patch through and talk to them later. Three others on the bridge, and sixteen scattered around the aft of the ship, cargo area mostly."

"Got it," Sarge replied. "We're opening the hatch."

"The ship's on emergency life support," Weasel said. "Adding your breathing requirements won't help things much..." he said, then opened a calculator window and ran some numbers. "You'll have about twenty minutes, by my calcs, before you start having breathing problems."

"Can you patch in an assist?"

"Negative. Zulu Prime can't support a ship that big."

"Jump?"

"Something's physically blocking the engines from starting. I can't do it from here."

"Copy that," Sarge said, "we'll have to restore power asap. Everyone ready?"

"Good hunting," Weasel said before logging off the com channel. He was used to their chatter and didn't really need to listen in on their mission again.

Besides, he had some potentially scared people in the galley that he had to try to reach.

"Alright," he said to the boy, who had remained silent and still. Just another computer prompt waiting for input. "I need to get a communication channel open to the galley."

"The communication lines are in place, but there is no power to support them."

"I know," Weasel said, "I'm going to have to hack a line to our electrical system for it. Are you equipped to accept wireless power transfer?"

"Yes, but turning on the apparatus will cost power."

"Of course, but you can siphon it from the life support system. As soon as I beam you some power, you can turn on the communication channel and route the excess back into the life support system."

"Understood," the boy said, "proceed with the transfer."

*   *   *

Tank leveled his pulse cannon, aiming at the center of the hatch, then lowered his aim a few degrees to compensate for kickback. Tex leaned against the wall on the left of the hatch, hand on the release lever, poised and ready for action. Ghost lingered in the shadows behind Tank, attention focused on the door. Sarge checked the charge on his pulse rifle one more time and nodded to Tex. Tex pushed the lever down and the door swung open to reveal darkness in the ship beyond.

"Check it," Sarge ordered.

Ghost slipped past Tank before any of the others could react, crouching her way into the other ship. She peered around the corners, studying each hallway for only a few seconds. "Clear," she announced.

"You and Tank go left. Tex, lead the way right."

Tex moved down the hall to the right with Sarge close behind. Tank stomped his way into the hallway and turned to the left. He blinked hard to clear his vision, selecting the green-tinted night vision in his optical implants to compensate for the dark hallway. He could see Ghost ahead, crouched and peering into a room on their right. She disappeared into the room and returned moments later, moving her hand to signal that the room was clear.

Tank shifted the heavy pulse cannon and continued his march down the hallway.

Something ahead caught his attention. He shifted his optics into heat vision mode, exposing a lone figure at the end of the long hallway. He zoomed in on the figure and analyzed it. The figure was leaning against the wall as if bored, idly scratching his groin. His plain clothing was tattered, layered denim and cloth, not a military uniform.

Tank called a challenge and the figure reacted by pushing away from the wall and shouting something into an open doorway beside him. He reached for a weapon tucked into his belt. *Wrong answer,* Tank thought. He pulled the trigger, causing his pulse cannon to warm up, the titanium barrels rotating with a soft whir. The pirate's friends emerged from the doorway, weapons ready as they scanned the dark hallway. One of them fired a shot into the darkness, missing Tank by several meters.

Tank's weapon finished its warming cycle and opened up, sending a thousand rounds a minute down the hallway. The pirates shook like they were dancing at a club, bodies gyrating to the bass beat of bullets thumping into the metal wall behind them. Tank released the trigger after several seconds and the corpses fell to the floor. He closed his eyes and inhaled the pungent stench of the propellant his pulse cannon released into the hallway. Ghost darted to the end of the hallway and inspected the carnage, careful to avoid the pooling blood lest she leave footprints as she continued into the open room.

Tank checked the other doors in the hallway, a series of empty crew rooms, simple metal and mattress beds. Personal lockers at the foot of each bed, still closed. Most had a musty smell, except one that had hints of artificial cinnamon in the air. He counted as he went, estimating the size of the crew that could sleep here at twenty. If this was a military ship, that meant as many as sixty could share the bunks in rotating shifts. Near the end of the hallway, an open doorway exposed a metal staircase leading down. A sign beside marked this as an exit to the cargo hold.

At the end of the hallway, Ghost slid into the room and looked around. She was in the engine room, which should have been alive with machinery, but was currently silent. She moved around the room quickly, darting from corner to corner as she checked for any additional threats. The room was empty. While inspecting, she noticed a panel near the floor that had been left open. She knelt and analyzed the exposed wiring. Tucked into the mass of electronics was a small box, wires patched into the existing circuitry with sloppy lengths of patch cable. She tapped the button on the inside of her cheek and spoke.

"Sarge?" she asked.

"Go ahead," came the reply.

"Got something here, looks patched into the engine room."

"What is it?"

"I'm no electrician," she said.

"Uplink it," Sarge said.

Ghost stared at the box and uplinked her optical output to the communication channel. She tilted her head so they could see it from several angles.

"Looks like an inhibitor," Tex said over the com channel. "Same type of thing the pirates used when we salvaged that ship last month near Venus. Probably why there's no power here. Should be safe to remove."

Ghost examined the wires carefully, tracing the patch lengths. "Looks like they cut the original wires to patch this in. Can't just rip it out, can I?"

"You gotta splice the originals back together, then it should be fine. Doesn't look like they had time to booby trap it like the last pirates did. Break *all* the connections first, then splice the black grounding wires, then the others."

"Okay, here goes."

Ghost removed the patch cables on one lead first, then the others. She carefully twisted the two original grounding wires back together. Tex watched the uplinked video and voiced his approval. Ghost proceeded with the other two sets of wires. The panel beeped, small LED lights springing to life as the machinery emitted a soft humming. She left the box and the open panel as they were and stepped back. The lights above her flickered to life, and a blast a cool air pushed out of the ceiling vent into the room. She started to announce that she'd done it, but figured it was obvious at this point. She headed for the room's exit and saw Tank outside, standing with his back to her, covering the hallway. The blood pool had expanded, surrounding Tank's boots, starting to seep into the engine room. Tank shouldered his weapon and held out his hands. Ghost jumped, he caught her, and ferried her to cleaner ground.

"Crew quarters and engine room clear," Tank reported. "We have one remaining exit on this side. It goes down to the cargo hold."

"Copy that," Sarge replied. "We've had negative contact so far in the starboard quarters. We're heading for the galley and bridge. You two go down to the cargo hold."

Tank confirmed his orders and turned just in time to see Ghost disappearing down the stairs to the cargo hold.

RECOGNITION

W oden reclined in the captain's chair as much as it would let him, leaning into the fake leather. Above him, a vent spewed artificial air in short bursts, metered for optimum efficiency, to keep the life support system active as long as possible. At first, he just sat there, counting the seconds between air bursts. But then the ship arrived. Zulu Prime. He felt the presence of the lives on board long before the computer terminal to his left announced the incoming ship. A smile cracked his lips as the ship docked. The scraping metal of two ships connecting was sure to alert the pirates. He couldn't hear the docking on the bridge, but anyone in the cargo hold was sure to know the sound.

Two pirates were on the bridge with him, surfing the Solar Net on the communication officer's console. They had a portable power pack on the floor between them with lengths of patch cables running to the three terminals. Woden could see the smut they were viewing, copying whatever they could find onto small memory sticks, hooting and hollering as they zoomed and panned the images they were viewing. He closed his eyes and did his best to block out the sounds.

He inhaled slowly, savoring the pristine artificial air. Something in the scent of it that wasn't on his ship. Probably the antiseptic they used, a different flavor than his own, not the tropical fruit scent he was growing bored of, but something simple, something mixed with vanilla.

He exhaled, and with his breath he let go of his body, floating with his conscious mind to the center of the bridge. Opening his eyes, he took in the bridge from this perspective, floating above the cold steel of the floor. His body was inert, nestled in the captain's chair and breathing in a slow, steady rhythm. Anyone who saw him would think he was sleeping. Woden floated through the door, down a hallway to the airlock where Fireteam Zulu was going to enter the ship. He could sense them on the other side of the door. Three members waiting for entry, a fourth seated in the pilot's chair, tethered and busy trying to finish the connection to the Orion.

Woden knew it would take at least a few minutes to negotiate the final connection, so he moved down the hall toward the cargo hold. The pirates were still struggling with some of the crates he had pointed out. They had set up portable lights so they could see what they were doing. Their Captain barked some commands but Woden couldn't hear them. He could project himself anywhere, see anything, but his powers did not extend to clairaudience. He stared at the Captain's lips, watching as they mouthed another command. *Hurry up you fools*, he seemed to say, *we have...* something... *time left. They're early.*

Captain Victor Wells didn't seem aware that he'd been screwed over. He thought Fireteam Zulu was early, or perhaps that his men were just slow. Woden would have laughed if his astral body would have allowed it.

The pirates were still avoiding the center crates he had warned them about, which was good. There was no need to let *that* cat out of the bag yet. It was bad enough they were stealing a wide array of terraforming equipment and several months' worth of food. Some colonists, somewhere, would have their plans delayed. That was an annoyance. But those center crates... that would be a catastrophe.

Woden let his astral body drift back along the corridors, returning to the airlock where Zulu Prime had docked. There was a little more of a delay, then the door opened. He quivered in anticipation. The best part of the pow-ers he'd been given and trained for was his ability to size up his opponents before a battle. By the way they looked and moved, he could tell a lot about them.

The first he saw was a huge mountain of a man who wielded an equally large pulse cannon. He stared into the ship, right through where Woden's as-tral body was floating, a permanent scowl etched on his lips. A soldier, rough around the edges, but he'd follow orders and would put up a fight.

Another member beside him had the look of a leader, brows furrowed in concentration, perhaps a bit of worry. He held his rifle casually as he was speaking. He started talking. *Tank go left*, his lips said. *Tex, lead the way right.* Woden knew little of the other team members, but he knew this man from the description he'd been given. Sarge. A cookie-cutter marine sergeant, like he was stamped out in a factory that made sergeants all day long. Short-cropped hair, military fatigues with insignia patches removed, calm confi-dence.

The big man stepped into the hallway and moved toward the aft of the ship. *Must be Tank*, Woden thought. *Appropriate name.*

Another man he hadn't noticed stepped into the hallway. *Tex.* Looked like he stepped out of a Western movie and into the hallway. Sarge followed him closely, heading toward the bridge. He'd meet them soon, but first he should see what Tank was planning to do by himself. Woden followed Tank down the hallway. He thought he saw something in the hallway ahead, dart-ing around in the shadows. Play of light? He stopped and concentrated on the movement.

Tank stopped, tilted his head back like he was shouting something, then shortly opened up with his pulse cannon. But Tank fired at something further down the hall, not at the movement he had seen. There, the ripple in the air moved again, sliding down the hallway toward the carnage the big man had created. Woden accelerated down the hall and followed the rippling air into the room at the end. He passed through the wall and came to a stop before a crouching woman, who was examining the black box he'd given the pirates. She turned the box over in her hands and moved her lips, talking. There was something...

Woden's vision twisted and fell, and with a violent rip he was pulled back into his body. His eyes shot open and he lurched forward, falling and planting his hands on the floor. He panted, felt fresh sweat beads roll down his face.

"Four?" he said out loud between breaths. The pirates were too busy watching a video to notice he'd spoken. He sneered at their backs. "No, *five*. The man on the ship is just the pilot. But who..."

He closed his eyes and concentrated on the image of the woman he'd seen. His body had responded to the sight of her, a recognition that had torn his link to his astral body and pulled him back into his conscious body. But who was she? Someone familiar, or he wouldn't have had that reaction. It didn't take him long to realize who she was. Some things she had changed, hair length and color for starters, and her demeanor had grown colder. But it was her, no mistaking those eyes. He'd always found them... enticing.

Woden sprinted from the bridge, running down the port corridor so as to avoid Sarge and Tex, who he knew were moving toward the bridge via the other side of the ship. He had to get to the cargo hold. He had to verify that it really was her, and not some trick. Five on a fireteam? And the fifth being a prize such as this...

He needed to be sure. And then he'd need to make a call.

SQUASH

After a few hours of sleep, Collins returned to cleaning duty. The pile of bloody dirt was where he had left it; only a third had been consumed by the microbes. He entered the janitorial closet and selected another bottle, with more powerful antibacterial agents. The bottle was almost empty, so he didn't bother measuring it, and emptied the contents on the dirt pile. While the bloody dirt was being consumed, he gave the mop a quick cleaning so it would be ready to tackle the remaining blood trail in the medical office.

This time when he entered the office, Dmitri didn't even acknowledge him. Collins tried to announce his presence and intentions, but the doctor waved his hand and told him to be quiet. Collins slapped the mop head on the floor and started to clean up the blood. The blood in here was resisting his efforts. Instead of being soaked up by the wet mop, it was merely being pushed around. *It should have dried by now*, he thought. Collins leaned in and put more effort into his scrubbing, trying in vain to get the blood off the floor, but the blood was just being relocated, like trying to mop up syrup. He propped the mop against the wall and went at the stain with a much smaller brush. The result was the same, but slower.

"Aren't you done with that yet?" the doctor barked.

"I'm trying, Doctor D. It's just not getting clean."

Dmitri sighed when he saw the frustration on Collins' face. "I'm sorry, Sergeant. I haven't gotten much sleep. This has been a rough case."

Collins nodded toward the corpse on the table, right where he had left it. "How's the patient, doc?"

"That's just it. He died quite a while ago. I can't figure out how he managed as long as he did."

Collins approached the examination table. The corpse was in slightly worse condition than he had left it. The doctor had made incisions and opened the body cavity wide. The inside was in even worse shape than the outside. Collins swallowed the lump in his throat. "What... what was his name?"

"Roger. Roger Bergeron. Farmer, like we suspected, from a colony not too far from here."

"A colony," the Colonel announced as he entered the room, "that is no longer active. We sent an aerial surveillance drone over it. Place is empty, not a soul in the fields or the streets. Collins, finish cleaning this mess for the doctor later. We're going in to get a closer look at that colony. Platoon's assembling in the quad, five minutes."

"Yes, sir." Collins saluted, gathered his cleaning supplies, and left. After returning the supplies, he ran to the armory, where his squad was already getting prepared. He hurried into his battle armor, slowing only to ensure that he was tightening the clasps correctly. Someone handed him a pulse rifle, which he checked quickly before grabbing a spare clip and running outside.

Collins joined the other soldiers assembled in the quad. The marines lined up at attention while the Colonel strolled in, muttering under his breath about the formation. He paused to count the soldiers present, realizing that the formation was wrong because they were short three soldiers.

"O'Malley, Naruga, and Barnes are sick, sir," one of the soldiers informed him.

"Damn," the Colonel replied, "damn it all. That's just what we *don't* need.

Good soldiers should be in bed from combat wounds, not disease." He frowned, considered correcting his statement, shook his head briefly, then returned to his usual vigor. "Alright marines, we're heading out to investigate the squash farming village north of here. Aerial surveillance shows nobody's there, but there should be a hundred farmers and their families, minus our uninvited guest in the medical office. High Command wants us to investigate and report back. Remember people, these are farmers, we're not here to engage an enemy. Your weapons are for protection and intimidation purposes only. Let's move out."

Collins herded with the other soldiers onto one of the two transports in the garage. Each transport was an armored bus, designed to carry half a platoon into any situation, over any terrain. Slits in the armor allowed the soldiers inside to fire their weapons from relative safety.

The vehicles started moving once everyone was on and set out into the Martian landscape. The ride was short and bumpy, giant red dust clouds kicked up in their wake, swirling in the morning air currents. Most of the soldiers chatted quietly for the duration, until one of them told a raunchy joke and was forced to repeat it louder. The soldiers smirked while they waited for the punchline, then most of them erupted into laughter. Red faces for those having trouble breathing and rage painted on the faces of the few who took silent offense. Collins tried his best to ignore both.

The vehicles skidded to a halt in the soft sand at the edge of the village. Soldiers filed off the transports, alert and scanning the horizon for threats. The Colonel barked a few orders, sending fireteams into the buildings. The more he sent, the more obvious it became that some teams were going to have to go in understaffed. By the time he ordered Collins into a nearby house, there were only two other marines left, Jane and Boris "Pav" Pavelovich, a new recruit from a secondary school outside Moscow. Collins firmly believed that Pav would be a good soldier, some day, but he was still a teenager and far too headstrong. He needed something to calm him down and make him fall in line. Perhaps the terror of actual combat, the exposure to death. That was something Collins didn't wish on anybody.

Collins knelt in the dirt in front of the building's door, taking aim at the portal. Pav pressed his back against the left flank of the door, looking far too excited for this mission. On the right side of the door, Jane leaned against the side of the building, gun poised and ready. Collins nodded. Pav opened the door and the three entered.

The building was a small family's home. The entry led directly into a family room with two simple wire-framed couches covered with some padding and a pale blue sheet. There was a comfortable looking chair beside them, next to a reading light. Small tablet book reader laying on a side table, still on but in a power-saving state. Telescreen set into a wall opposite one of the couches, one of the newer ones that could be rolled up for easier transport. There was an odd stench in the air, but Collins couldn't place it.

Pav looked over a short counter into the kitchen and dining area. Kitchen was dirty, red sand filtered in from a crack in the window. Large yellow squash on the counter, cut open, rotting. Places set at the table, plates clean and water poured into plastic cups. "Kitchen is clear," Pav said.

Collins proceeded into a connecting hallway with four doors. He motioned Pav and Jane to the end of the hall as he opened a door to his left. Bathroom, simple and clean, slight scent of vanilla in the air. Drops of water dripped in a steady rhythm from the shower head. Bar of soap on the sink had dried in a big, sticky clump. A towel, slung over the shower curtain rod, had dried and was slowly rippling in the current emitted by the air conditioning vent above it.

Pav went through one open doorway at the end of the hall into a master bedroom, bed made with neat corners and window shades open to the warm sunlight. He glanced into the closet then returned to the hallway to announce the room as clear.

Collins moved into the other room that Jane had entered. Child's room with unmade bed, clothing dropped on the floor. Jane was opposite the entry, inspecting a small desk in the corner with an open mathematics textbook next to a notebook with a half-solved problem written in pencil. Large blue plate beside that with a half-eaten piece of toast, cold and surrounded by crumbs. Purple tumbler, half-filled with warm milk that gave the room a sour stench. She looked at Collins, then indicated the desk.

"I guess two, three days," she said.

Collins was about to reply when Pav said from the hallway, "Basement. Stinks something awful."

Collins and Jane rejoined Pav in the hallway, where he was looking into the last door, down into darkness. The stench that wafted up from the dark depths was enough to turn all their stomachs. Pav reached and flipped the light switch. Nothing. He looked to Collins, who responded by turning on the flashlight built into his pulse rifle. Pav and Jane followed suit, and the three descended the stairs in single file, Pav leading the way.

Near the bottom, the stairs split to the left and right. Collins tapped Pav on the left shoulder. Pav nodded and moved down the left staircase. Collins went to the right. The stench grew more powerful with each step he took, slowly scanning the room with his flashlight. Storage boxes, stacked sandy floor to wooden ceiling, contents labeled in black marker. Billy's toys. Roger's files. Xmas tree. As he moved further into the maze of boxes, he heard Jane on the stairs behind him. They split in different directions, scanning the small room until they came face to face. Jane motioned that there was something to see behind him. She led Collins to a hallway she'd passed.

Collins took lead, moving slowly, shining his flashlight straight ahead while the beam from Jane's light danced around to expose the walls to his peripheral vision. The hallway opened slightly, a corner alcove with a ping-pong table. Paddles laying on the table, one of them holding down the ball. On the wall, posters of movies that were popular thirty years ago. A single light bulb above the center of the table. Small table and two chairs against the far wall.

"Sergeant?" Pav's voice, up ahead somewhere, laced with fear.

"Yeah Pav?"

"You... better see this, sir."

Collins moved to the other side of the alcove where the hallway continued. He stepped up the pace and turned a corner. He and Jane passed by a small power and heating unit and a workbench with a few essential tools. They moved into a larger area where the stench was threatening to yank the lunch right out of them. Pav stood at the bottom of the staircase, rifle pointed into a corner of the room that Collins couldn't see from where he was stand-ing. He moved closer, shining his light on Pav's face and trying to read the expression. It was familiar. He'd seen it before, in horror movies. He turned and added his light to the beam from Pav's rifle.

Bones.

Blood.

Tattered clothing, fragments of flesh, pieces of people.

This side of the basement was full of them.

VERY EX

Sarge watched the hallway from the small alcove he was tucked into, waiting for any signs of movement. The hallway was well-lit now, and they could see alcoves at regular intervals along the outside wall. Little vantage points that allowed off-duty personnel to watch the stars float by without obstructing movement through the hallway. Sarge was aiming at the door at the hallway's end. The schematic diagram in his left ocular implant said it was the bridge. Weasel had informed them of three people beyond, and he had said he was unable to contact them. That meant they were most likely pirates.

Sarge waved Tex past, and waited until he was beside the door to the galley before he moved from his vantage point. The galley had a single entrance on this side, and it was highly probable that another hallway mirrored this design on the port side of the ship.

Sarge was convinced that this ship was designed by the military.

Tex leaned against the galley door and listened, reporting that he could hear some sobbing inside. Sarge nodded and Tex tried the door. It wasn't locked, but wouldn't open. He pushed again, harder, making no progress but amplifying the sobs within. He was about to ask Sarge for orders when they both heard the clear sound of someone cocking an old pump-action shotgun from inside the galley.

"Whoa there partner," Tex said as he took a step to the side of the door, "we're not here to hurt you."

"You stay back!" a muffled voice cried from within. "Get off our ship!"

"We're here to help," Tex said. "We're Fireteam Zulu. You've probably already chatted with Weasel."

There was a pause. Some discussion within. Sarge moved to the other side of the door and waited, straining to hear what was being said inside. Sounds of metal scraping against metal and then the door slowly, tentatively opened inward. A face came into view in the open doorway, followed by a few frightened cries from further in. Tex was used to this and knew not to rush the room. He holstered his pistol and held up both hands. Sarge was out of the room's line of sight and ready for action.

"You don't look like pirates," the man said.

"We're not."

"We?"

Sarge stepped into view and started on his standard *we're here to help* speech, words flowing from his lips verbatim as if prerecorded. The man replied in kind, visibly relaxing and opening the door further. Sarge asked Tex to watch the hallway while he inspected the galley. The people were cowering in one corner of the room, seated at tables piled with food and drink. The lights illuminated far too well, showing that some of these people hadn't slept in days. Sarge examined the uniforms they wore, and though unkempt and in need of changing, they were obviously military in design. He couldn't tell which branch, and that bothered him. The man who had opened the door for him wore a uniform with an insignia that resembled a marine lieutenant. He was an older man, silvering hair and wrinkles on his face.

"You in charge here?" Sarge asked.

"Yes," he replied. "My name is Doctor Carter."

"Well Carter, give me a status update, quick as possible."

"A ship docked with us, about an hour ago-"

"Wait, *one* hour?" Sarge interrupted.

"Maybe two," Carter replied.

Tex scratched his head. "Didn't we get that distress signal before that, Sarge?"

"Yes, at least four hours ago," Sarge said. "And some of these people look like they've been in here for days."

"Some have been," Carter said. "Well, not here, but they've been awake for days. I'm afraid scientific research has big demands and no real time schedule."

"Anyway, that's not important. Continue. What happened after the ship docked?"

"They boarded," Carter said, "they cut off power, and took control. Captain Alvarez ordered me to hole up here to protect the personnel. There wasn't much we could do. Pirates outnumbered us and were very well armed. I'm afraid the only weapon we have is this shotgun, and that's just because the Captain kept it on the bridge-"

"And what about the bridge?"

"I don't know. Haven't heard from the Captain since we came in here."

"What's the nature of this ship?"

Carter coughed politely. "Scientific research. Beyond that, it's classified."

"Well the pirates probably already know," Sarge replied. He examined Carter's face. Determination etched in with weariness. He wasn't going to win this line of questioning. "All right, I understand. I need to know if there's anything here dangerous to my team."

"Dangerous? How?"

Sarge sighed. "We have live weapons, plastic projectiles and focused plasma. Will firing them compromise the ship or cargo in any way?"

"Not that I know of. Not any more than usual, at least. Except in the cargo hold. You must be very careful there, or... er..."

"Understood," Sarge interjected. He clicked his tongue on his cheek and turned his head away from Carter. "Ghost, Tank, come in. Check your fire in the cargo hold. Possible situation with cargo hold. Copy?"

Tank replied in the affirmative, curtly, and cut off transmission.

"How many of you are there?" Carter asked.

Sarge studied him and his uniform again. "Fireteam. Four. Not the kind of question a military man has to ask."

Carter looked him in the eyes and slowly shook his head. "I'm not military. Not exactly."

Sarge patted Carter's uniform. "Looks like a duck, quacks like a duck, it's a fucking duck."

"We're scientists. Military science, research vessel. Most of us haven't even learned our ranks yet, except the Captain and a few other officers. I'm in charge of the research team, that's all. But you talk like they do. Are you military?"

"Ex," Sarge replied, "very ex. Enough chit chat. We should get to the bridge and assess the situation."

"I'll come with you."

"Negative."

"I know the ship, I can fly it, and you won't be able to access the controls without me there."

"Negative," Sarge repeated in a tone of voice that made Carter stop talking. "We'll make sure the bridge is clear first, then send for you. For now, stay with these people and barricade the door again once we're out."

Carter nodded. "All right. Be careful."

"Always."

Mess

Collins, Pav, and Jane emerged from the basement, gasping for fresh air. The Colonel could see them through the open doorway, and watched them in silence. A few of the assembled marines snickered behind him. He heard Goddard's voice, starting to say something that sounded disparaging, judging by the tone of his voice, but a quick look from the Colonel silenced him.

The other teams had already returned from their sorties and were giving their reports. One after another, they announced the area as clear, while casting glances at Collins' team slowly regaining their composure. The Colonel sighed when the last report came in. He walked over to the open doorway and asked for a situation report.

"It's a mess, sir," Collins finally managed to say. He gagged and looked as if he were about to collapse.

"Oh God," Pav said, crumpling to his knees and clutching his stomach. He dry-heaved a few times before sitting, gulping down fresh air.

Jane stumbled to the couch and plopped down on it. She mumbled something the Colonel couldn't hear, but Collins nodded in response and placed a hand on her shoulder. He sat on the couch beside her and stared at the blank telescreen. The Colonel ordered the rest of the platoon to keep watch and entered the house. He surveyed the room and sighed again. Outside, one of the marines barked orders, and the rest moved off into patrolling patterns.

The Colonel took a few steps toward the kitchen. He saw the rotted squash on the counter and raised an eyebrow. "Well, Sergeant?" he said, turning back to face Collins. "Where exactly is this mess you speak of?"

"Basement," Collins said, "left side of the basement."

The Colonel approached the basement door and peered down the stairs, wrinkling his nose. He knew that stench. He'd smelled it once before and knew damn well what it came from. He marched down the stairs, pulled a small flashlight from his shirt pocket, and surveyed the mess in the basement with only minor twitches in his countenance. Thankfully, the soldiers who had already been down here had had the fortitude to leave the scene untainted. He was glad for that. Having to investigate something like this was tough enough without having to deal with weak stomachs at the same time. His stomach started to protest, so he walked back upstairs.

Collins and Jane were still seated on a couch in the living area. Pav was sitting on the floor beside them, looking like he had aimed for the couch but simply missed. The rest of the platoon was outside, milling around and keeping watch. Some were joking around, unaware of the situation inside the house. One of them saw the look on the Colonel's face and ordered the others into formation. The Colonel closed the door to the basement and approached the couch.

"Well," he said, "you certainly weren't kidding about finding a mess."

Collins stood and faced the Colonel. "No sir."

"None of the other squads reported any civilians. The town is vacant, except for here. Why here?" He paused and watched Pav, rocking back and forth, arms cradling his legs. He had seen reactions like this before and knew that Pav needed a job, or he was going to crack. "Private Pavelovich. Pav! Get up, son. Go out to the transport and tell Henderson to run a scan on this village. Find out who lived in this house and report back to me as soon as you know."

Pav started to say something, then stopped. "Ye... yes, sir." He stood, shaking, and shambled out of the door.

The Colonel watched as he left, then turned to Collins. "You and Jane gather the troops. Get some boards, find some nails. Dismantle another house if you have to. We're going to board up this house to prevent anyone else from stumbling on this."

The Colonel waited until they had left, took a deep breath, and waved a private over. He ordered the private to bring him a medkit from the transport. He waited until the private returned, then ordered him to guard the entrance. The Colonel opened the medkit on the kitchen counter and removed a surgical mask. He put it on, hoping it would block out at least most of the stench in the basement. Next he pulled on a pair of latex gloves. He closed the medkit, walked to the basement door, and started down the stairs.

He could have ordered someone else to do it, but that was one thing he didn't want to do. It was bad enough that anyone had to photograph and collect evidence from the scene. This was just one more dirty job he'd have to do. Besides, he'd seen grisly scenes before, like the riots in Cairo and Damascus. Some group of activists decided they wanted to be free of the world government, and they delivered their message with violence. The military responded with a bombing campaign to quell the insurgence. After the bombardment stopped, the ground troops were sent in to clean up the mess.

He remembered seeing the twisted bodies that burnt in the crumbled buildings, still clutching to their loved ones. Bombs had no conscience. Fire did not care what it burned -- men, women, children, animals. The innocent and the guilty both suffered equally. He was a young officer back then and the officer in charge of his platoon sent him in to do the dirty work of documenting the dead for later identification. He didn't want to be like that. He didn't want to subject more men to this horror than he had to. He'd order them to fight, to die if necessary, but this? Maybe he was being too soft on them. Maybe they could handle it. Hell, maybe they *needed* it. The experiences had certainly hardened him, prepared him for where he was today. For him, this would only be one more in a series of images that would haunt his dreams.

The Colonel placed the medkit on the step behind him and opened it. The medkit had ten vials he could use, and working as quickly as he could, he collected samples of blood from ten of the corpses. When finished, he closed the medkit and pulled a small camera from his breast pocket. The stench was starting to seep through his mask.

No, he thought, *I have chosen well. Nobody should see this. This is too much for any of them to handle well. This is not like the carnage of war. This is something else. Something worse.*

$C_{17}H_{19}NO_3$

Y ou hear that?" Tank whispered.

Ghost nodded, slowly, deliberately. She was pressed against the steel wall, hiding in the shadows provided by the staircase above her. Tank watched as she stepped to the door frame and peered into the cargo hold. She held up some fingers, closed her fist and repeated the gesture. Nine. Then she made another gesture with the same hand. Nine hostiles. She glanced at Tank and he shouldered his pulse cannon in response. She closed her eyes and slowly slipped away, her body fading to blend with the wall beside her. When Ghost's body had completely faded from view, she ran into the room. Tank waited the customary ten seconds before entering behind her.

The cargo hold was at least twice the size of Zulu Prime. Crates lined each wall with small breaks marking stairways and entry hatches, stacked to the ceiling in most places. A hatch on the far left side of the hold was open, showing a glimpse of another ship beyond. In the center of the hold was a pile of smaller crates, one of them opened and being examined by the nine pirates.

"I dunno," one of them said, "looks like medicine to me. Why the hell would that guy tell us not to take this?"

"Prolly worth a small fortune," the one beside him said.

"Who knows. Maybe wants it fer himself," another replied.

A tenth pirate poked his head out from the hatch on the connected ship. "I already grabbed two of the boxes, you idiots," he called out to them. "Figure out what it is and what it's worth later."

"Yeah, just grab the damn boxes and let's *go*," another one near the center of the room replied. "Lights are back on, and you heard the firing. They'll be here any-" He glanced over his shoulder, looking right at Tank, and froze.

It was then that the other pirates heard Tank's heavy footsteps. They whirled and stared at him as he stopped and the barrel of his gun started to whir. Before they could draw their weapons, his gun started pelting them with rounds. Three of the pirates in the center of the group dropped instantly in pools of expanding blood. One of the pirates on the left side dove for the hatchway leading to his ship, barely making it through intact. The pirate on the far right took aim at Tank. Before he could pull the trigger, his neck sliced open. He dropped his weapon and grasped his throat, warm blood spurting forth as he collapsed in slow motion.

The remaining pirates split their attention between hunting for the phantom that had killed their friend and shooting at Tank. Several rounds hit Tank's body, focused plasma from pulse rifles hitting in the shoulder where his armor didn't cover, old plastic projectiles pinging off his battle armor. One of the pirates aimed a small pistol and fired. A blob of blue plasma sailed across the cargo hold and hit Tank in the chest, penetrating his armor, and forcing a cry of pain from him. He sank to his knees and his aim faltered, rounds hitting the crates and breaking small vials open, white liquid spilling onto the floor. As his rounds shot around wildly, another two pirates fell. Another pirate screamed in pain as his chest opened in a shower of blood. The last pirate ran for the hatchway, which closed as he reached it. With a sad face he turned back to the carnage. He started to say something but was cut short as Ghost faded back into view, her serrated blade already embedded in his abdomen. She removed her blade and he collapsed.

The ship rocked as the pirate ship disengaged from the Orion. Ghost watched through the port hole in the hatchway.

"They're getting away," she said.

She turned to inspect the room, tongue moving toward the button in her cheek so she could announce their progress. Her gaze paused on Tank, tongue poised but no longer interested in the button. Tank was on his knees, pulse cannon dangling from one arm as he panted like a winded dog. His face slowly tilted upward, pain etched in its features. She ran to him and inspected his wounds, several scattered around his torso, a mixture of old style projectiles and focused plasma burns. His armor had deflected a few of them, but at least ten rounds had penetrated his flesh. The troublesome wound was where the blob of plasma had hit. It had already eaten through his armor and his shirt, and was starting to eat through his chest. He grunted as she inspected the wounds.

"C'mon," she said, "we gotta get you back to the ship."

Tank gritted his teeth and shook his head vigorously. "Don't think I'm gonna make it this time. Didn't expect them fuckers to have plasma." He glanced down at his chest, reaching for the hole in his armor but careful not to touch it. He couldn't see the plasma eating into his chest, but he could feel it. "Shit burns," he said.

"Don't touch it. You can make it. It's almost done, anyway. Your armor slowed it down enough. Might eat a rib or two, but should stop there. Just gotta get you something for the pain." She rummaged through his pockets, wincing as she was obviously aggravating his wounds. He dropped the pulse cannon and fell onto his back. "Morphine. Don't you always have morphine you stupid grunt?"

"Fresh... out," he responded, having trouble forcing the words out.

She knew his time was short. The plasma would go further than his ribs. There was still too much of the gyrating blue gel left, and no way to remove it once it bonded with its target. His ribs would be next. Painful, but not lethal. Beyond them, his lungs. That would be the end of him.

She ran to the pirates, searched one of the corpses with shaking fingers, looking in the most likely place one would store morphine tablets. Pirates weren't likely to carry painkillers, she knew, but there was always hope that one would. She had to hope. It was all she could do. She checked another, and another, and found nothing of the sort.

And then she saw it, like an oasis, amongst the shattered crates in the center of the cargo hold. Small glass vials of white liquid. $C_{17}H_{19}NO_3$ written on the splintered wooden side of one crate's remains. She'd been in the military long enough to know that meant morphine. There was some other text beside it but she didn't know enough about chemistry to understand it. All she knew was that it said morphine. Tank was dying, but at least he could go without pain.

She grabbed a vial and ran to Tank, pausing only to open the top of it. This wasn't in tablet form, and she didn't have a needle to administer it the proper way, so there was no telling what this would do. She hoped it would ease the pain somewhat. She knelt beside him and lifted his head. Between his labored breaths, she forced him to drink the vial. The effects were almost immediate. His body started convulsing rapidly. He coughed up a spat of blood, then fell back to the floor. Ghost stared, horrified, wondering how badly she'd acted and how she was going to live with this. Killing people was her job, sure, but not like this. Tank was her comrade, her friend. She averted her eyes from his convulsions, a single tear winding its way down her cheek as she concentrated on breathing and blocking out the gasping behind her.

And then the gasping stopped.

Silence fell on the cargo hold, quiet as the woods on a snowy night. Her legs failed her and she fell into a sitting position. Another tear joined the first, then another. She buried her face in her hands, trying to wipe the tears, but for every one she wiped away there were two more in its place. Before she realized it, she was crying full force, something she hadn't done in years. She gave up on trying to hide it and let the grief overtake her, shoulders quivering with the sobs that wracked her body. A voice, sort of like Sarge's but muffled by her crying, said something in her ear. She couldn't make out the words and didn't want to hit the communication button in her cheek. She had to compose herself first. Sarge would assume she was busy with combat. If he wanted a report, he'd get one when she was ready. If he had something to say, he'd repeat it later if it was important. Either way, she was busy. She wasn't sure how much time had passed since she started crying, but for the first time in years, she was wide awake and once more feeling like Shelly, the girl she used to be.

"I wasn't entirely sure it was you, until you started crying," came a man's voice from behind her. "Now I'm positive. It's good to see you again, Shelly."

Ghost wiped the tears from her eyes and glanced around. "Wha-" she said. "Who?" Her gaze fell on a man who stood behind her, looking down with arms clasped behind him. "Brig? Brigandine Owens?"

"It's 'Woden' now, actually."

"Woden?"

"It means-"

"I know what it means."

"Ah yes, I'd almost forgotten about all the research you must have done on me while we were having that fake relationship."

"Wha-"

"Oh I'm sure you remember, Shelly. All those kisses you planted on your pillow, wishing it was me. All the fake conversations we had. The dates I never took you on. Yes, yes, I know all about the things that went on in your head."

"You knew... back then?"

"I did."

"Why didn't you ever say-"

"Say what, exactly? Hmm?" Woden arched an eyebrow as he looked down at Ghost. "I knew perfectly well how much you'd built me up, Shelly. I also knew myself, quite well. There was no way I was ever going to live up to the man you had created in your mind."

Her cheeks burned momentarily, but she hid the red tinge by wiping tears from her eyes again. "You could have been him. I wanted you to be him."

Woden's visage softened. He nodded. "I know."

"What happened to you?" Ghost asked. "You were there, every day in the cafeteria, and then one day-"

"Leukemia," Woden interrupted. "They thought it was the flu at first, but

I wasn't getting better no matter what drugs they pumped into me. Turned out that chronic sickness was just a symptom. They said I had four months to live. No point in staying in the program they had planned out for me. And considering my condition, they released me from the obligation."

"Just like that?" she asked. Another sniffle, another attempt to wipe the grief from her face. "And then what? It's been far longer than four months-"

"Oh, I know. Believe me, I know. They said I was an advanced case. No cure. No hope. But I'm a fighter. I wasn't going to take that laying down. On my way out of the base, I met a scientist, a doctor. He had a top secret research vessel, lots of funding, and needed some volunteer patients. So I left with him. He gave me... something... and I got better. He was concerned, at first, but it appears my training has had some benefits."

"How so?"

Woden's cheek crinkled in a sly smile. "Let's just say I was able to do what none of his other patients were capable of. Anyway, it cured my leukemia, and I continued my training on my own."

"What are you doing here? Working with the pirates?"

"Military scientists gave me four months to live. Doctor Carter gave me more. You think I'd waste that gift with this scum?" Woden kicked a corpse beside him. "I'm a mercenary. Freelance. Sort of a locate-and-retrieval specialist. I came here to capture the legendary Fireteam Zulu. Imagine my surprise when I saw you here, Shelly. Or I believe it is 'Ghost' now? That was your code name back then, wasn't it? Usually, I know everything that goes on around me. It's really quite surprising that my employer neglected to mention *you* were a member of this group."

"So you intend to capture me?" Ghost blinked away the last of her tears, the training starting to take over as she recognized the threat. She shifted her weight, poised and ready to spring, left hand already casually making its way to one of her blades.

"Oh, no," Woden said, holding his hands before him. "Not anymore, anyway. Having you here is like an early Christmas. But I have no intention of expending any energy on capturing you until I've negotiated a new price with my employer. And capturing your friend Tank now would be trivial. Where's the fun in that?"

"Tank's dead."

"Hardly," Woden replied. "He'll live. Even now he stirs."

A meaty hand pressed down on her shoulder and she tensed. Turning her head, she looked down on Tank's groggy face. Fresh tears welled up in her eyes. She wiped at them and turned back to Woden, but he was gone.

"Hey," Tank said, "that was some fight, wasn't... hey, what's wrong? Why are you crying?"

She turned back, tried to blink the tears from her eyes. She reached out, fingers touching his chest to ensure he was really there. The hole where the plasma had eaten through his armor was still there, and so was his chest. The skin was clean and smooth, not a hair or a scratch on it. Her fingers continued probing to the edges of his armor, inspecting his wounds. He'd stopped bleeding and was looking at her with a worried expression. She pulled aside the coverings from one wound. Then another. Another.

They were all completely gone.

FARMER ZERO

The Colonel finished his grim job and returned outside. He watched in silence as Collins and Jane were jogging back to the house, the rest of the platoon behind them, all carrying boards from other houses. He walked to a good vantage point and watched the marines work. They worked quickly, boarding windows in sync with each other. Collins finished the window he was boarding up and approached the Colonel. As he got closer, Pav ran to his side and addressed the Colonel.

"Sir," Pav said, "I've run a check on the residence. It belongs to Roger Bergeron and his family."

"Family?" the Colonel asked.

"Three, sir. Roger, his wife, and son."

"Roger Bergeron," the Colonel repeated. "Sound familiar, Collins? No? He was your previous mess. The farmer with the railgun fetish. Take this medkit, Collins, we'll give it to Doctor Dmitri when we get back to the base. Private Pavelovich, finish sealing off this building. We're done with our investigation, for now. Be on the truck in ten minutes."

Pav ran to the building to help the soldiers boarding the front door. One

115

of the other sergeants spray-painted a military symbol on the front door's boards along with a warning to anyone who would see it. The chances were slim that anyone would come to this village intentionally, but it was possible. The Colonel watched the last of the soldiers board the transports before climbing into the front seat.

The transports accelerated over the landscape, back toward the base. The marines were their usual jovial selves until one made the mistake of asking why Pav looked so pale. In broken sentences, he told them what he had seen. The soldiers stopped talking, and remained silent for the remainder of the return trip, nobody quite knowing what to say. No jokes were told. No boasts. Quiet as a funeral detail should be.

Collins sat beside Pav, medkit balanced on his lap, held in place by quivering hands. He closed his eyes and saw visions of the basement. He had seen combat before but this was a different type of carnage. Even cleaning up Roger's body and blood trail didn't compare. At least Roger was still mostly in one piece. Collins opened his eyes to see Jane, sitting across from him, shock still on her face. A single tear left her eye and snaked its way down her cheek. When it reached her chin and fell, her whole body quaked. He placed a hand on her knee. Silent comfort. She'd seen the carnage too. She gave no response to his touch.

The transports slowed and entered the base's garage. The Colonel ordered everyone to return to their previous duties. Collins waited by the transports until the others had left, then approached the Colonel. Without saying a word, the Colonel grabbed Collins' rifle and motioned for him to follow. They walked to the medical office, where they found Dmitri still busy at work on Roger's corpse. The Colonel gave Dmitri an abbreviated form of their discovery as he connected the rifle to the viewscreen on the wall. He typed in an access code and the rifle's built-in video recorder displayed the entire encounter, starting from the moment Collins turned on his rifle in the back of the transport. Dmitri stared at the screen in silence.

"You can fast forward past this part, sir," Collins said.

"How far?"

"I turn on the light as we head into the basement."

The Colonel advanced the video until he could see the extra light on the screen, as Collins was descending into the basement. The three men watched the feed as Collins met up with Jane and turned down the back hallway. When Collins turned the last corner and focused his rifle on the pile of villagers, Dmitri casually covered his mouth and looked as if he might retch. Collins had maintained his composure enough for his rifle to scan the entire scene, focusing on several faces in the mass of bodies. The video stream concluded when Collins turned off his rifle after sitting on Roger's couch.

"We brought you blood samples from the bodies," the Colonel said after a short pause. "I also took some high-res still photos with my camera. I don't know if they'll help. I just want to know what the hell happened there."

"I'll find out what I can, Colonel."

Collins handed the medkit to Dmitri and turned to follow the Colonel. He noticed a huge corpse, covered with a single white sheet, was on the table beside Roger. "O'Malley?" he asked. He already knew it was; nobody else on base was that big.

Dmitri shrugged in response. "Died earlier today."

The Colonel stopped when he heard this. "Damn it all. He was a good soldier. Strong lad. Damn it."

Collins frowned. "How'd you get him all the way in here without help, Doc?"

"He came on his own," Dmitri said. "Showed up after you all had left. Said he was feeling better and wanted something to do. Started cleaning up the rest of the mess you had left before I could say anything. He seemed okay and wouldn't let me examine him, so I let him be. Then he collapsed. Fell face-first into the blood he was trying to scrub off the floor. I heard the crash from my office and ran out here. He was starting to get up. Had a cut on his cheek and a bunch of Roger's blood smeared on his face, and he said he was feeling dizzy. I helped him to the table as best as I could. Few minutes later he started convulsing, then... that was it. He stopped. He was dead before I could even finish hooking him up to our diagnostic equipment."

"Damn it," the Colonel repeated. "That damned Martian flu again? When are you going to have that cured, Doctor?"

"I've doubled vitamin rations for the other infected soldiers," Dmitri said, hurt. He pointed to an adjoining examination room and added, "Sandra and Kevin have been working on a vaccine for three days now. We hope to have this under control soon. We're doing all we can with the staff and equipment we have."

"I know, I know," the Colonel replied. He took a deep breath and shook his head. "I'm sorry Dmitri. You know how I feel about these marines. We'll have funeral detail for O'Malley later. Right now I need those blood samples from the farming colony looked at."

"Yes, Colonel," Dmitri replied.

Collins followed the Colonel outside, where he was ordered to get some rest. Collins went for another meal in the mess, but took one look at the mountain of pureed squash in the serving trays and decided against it. Squash no longer held any appeal for him. Not after seeing those farmers in the basement.

He returned to his bunk, now eerily quiet without O'Malley above him. He pulled off his boots and laid down in his uniform. A cough from his left was echoed by another on his right. The air was stale in the barracks and a tad on the warm side. Footsteps and coughing echoed off the walls in regular intervals. He could hear Goddard's voice, spouting his usual tirade of dissent, but it was a stream of words that he couldn't piece together this time. He was grateful for that. Collins stared at the underside of O'Malley's bunk and slowly fell asleep.

BRIDGE

Tex worked on the controls beside the door, clipping wires and re-routing them to override the door's locking mechanism. The tangled mass was the worst he'd ever seen. "It's almost like someone *tried* to make it this bad," he said. "Security through obfuscation, ya know? Pure chaos, Sarge." Fifteen minutes had gone by since he'd started, and Sarge was starting to get impatient. Another set re-routed, then another, and still there was no sense to what he was doing. The door wasn't responding.

"Maybe I should get Carter," Sarge said.

"Aww, Sarge, c'mon. I can do it. Besides, someone already mucked with the locking mechanism. Look at this bunch of wires here. No way it's supposed to be this way."

Sarge tapped the button in his cheek. "Hey, Weasel, any chance you can help Tex with this door?"

There was a pause. "Try the green wires," Weasel said. "Mint green, two sets."

Tex pushed the mass of wires around and found one of the mint green wires. He clipped it, stripped the insulation off, and patched around them.

The door whirred to life, but remained locked. He found and clipped the second mint green wire and the door beeped in response, changing a light set into the side of the frame from red to green.

"Thanks, Weasel," Sarge said.

"Thanks *Weasel*?" Tex balked. "Bah. I did all the work..." he put his tools away and pulled out one of his pistols. "Alright, let's do this."

Sarge tapped the door with his foot and it slid to the right.

The bridge was rather small, but with plenty of consoles and chairs to hide behind. Bug hunt. He stepped into the room and to the right, wedging most of his body behind the ship's navigation console, rifle poised as he surveyed the room. Someone moved on the other side, near the captain's chair. Sarge fired a round and the impact scorched the chair, sending the smell of burnt plastic into the air. Another figure to the right of the first returned fire, forcing Sarge to crouch behind the console.

Tex slid into the room on the finely polished floor and shot twice, both projectiles ricocheting off machinery. Someone cursed and the other entrance to the bridge opened. Sarge and Tex both opened fire in the direction of the door, pelting the area with rounds until the door had closed. They waited half a minute, quietly, waiting for any indication that they were not alone. A quick inspection showed they were alone now. Bloodstain near the other doorway, single projectile crushed against the hull in the center of it. Tex congratulated himself while reloading his pistols.

"We clear?" Sarge asked. "Check the door."

Tex opened the other doorway. He scanned the hallway and waited for any signs of movement. "Looks clear," he said.

Sarge tapped the button inside his cheek. "Ghost, Tank, look alive. Two pirates ran from the bridge. One's wounded."

"Copy that," came Tank's reply. "Cargo hold clear, one of the pirates that was here got away and took his ship with him."

Sarge acknowledged, closed the communication channel, and returned his attention to the bridge. He inspected the machinery that had taken hits from the short firefight. Everything looked serviceable. Definitely a military ship. Nobody else would think of protecting machinery from small arms fire.

Three corpses were piled in the corner, away from the bulk of the machinery. Sarge checked and announced them as dead, then moved on.

The pirates had attempted to access the flight computer but it was still on a login screen, with a small window opened in the corner filled with error commands. He sent Tex to retrieve Carter, who entered the bridge and immediately started to complain about the scorch marks on the computer equipment. While complaining, his gaze fell on the corpses in the corner. His voice faltered, his face fell. Sarge ordered him to patch in a connection to Zulu Prime. Carter nodded, dazed, and sat in one of the chairs. He logged into the ship's computer. It didn't take him long to establish the connection.

"Weasel?" Sarge asked.

"Yeah, I'm here."

"What's our status?"

Short pause. "I show three life forms on the bridge, two in the cargo hold, two approaching the cargo hold quickly, and the rest in the galley."

"That's it?"

"Yes. Wait... two running for the cargo hold departed."

"Good. Guess our work here is done."

Tank's voice cut into the conversation, announcing the two pirates were terminated. Sarge replied by curtly ordering them to the bridge. He launched into his standard speech about their work being done and was about to ask if they could acquire some spare ammunition or food when Ghost and Tank entered the bridge. Sarge glanced at them and did a double take. Even from the other side of the bridge, he could see where holes had been punched through Tank's armor. The most obvious was the size of a fist, exposing his bare skin. There was blood around the holes, but Tank was moving as if unhurt.

"What happened, soldier? You okay?"

"Yes, sir."

"He took several hits," Ghost said, voice shakier than he'd ever heard it before. When Sarge didn't reply, she cleared her throat and continued. "He was fatally wounded, sir. Plasma to the chest. Ate right through his armor. I tried to give him some morphine. At least to dull the pain, you know? But he was out."

"Fresh out," Tank said. "We ran out last month on Ceres colony, sir."

"Then I found some," Ghost said, "in the hold."

Carter stood so fast he hit his knee on the console. "Oh God," he said.

"Some crates were busted in the cargo hold," Ghost said, undisturbed by Carter's interruption.

"Oh God no," Carter said. "You didn't... you... gave it to him?"

"Yes," Ghost said, "$C_{17}H_{19}NO_3$... morphine. That's what the crates said. I just wanted to ease the pain for him."

"That was not morphine, you dolt!" Carter held a shaking hand in front of his mouth, as if trying to keep more words from spilling out.

Sarge turned on Carter and cast a threatening gaze. "Every grunt in UEF's military knows what morphine is."

"True," Ghost said, "but it wasn't morphine, Sarge. It didn't ease the pain. It erased it, and the wounds, in minutes."

"What the hell was it?" Sarge asked. "Carter, what was it?"

Carter took a step back and shook his head. "I... I can't... it's classified."

"One of my men was injected with something, and you're going to tell me what."

Surrounded, outnumbered, Carter caved in quickly. "You didn't read the rest of the crate," he said. "It's an experimental form of morphine. Nanobots, programmed to work in conjunction with morphine to kill pain and repair the body."

"Doesn't sound so bad," Tank said.

Carter shook his head. "No, sure, but they don't work quite right yet. There have been... experiments. Things have gone wrong. The nanos don't stop. They *never* stop. They will always be in you, always repairing damage, always killing pain, always fabricating more morphine. It dulls the nerves so much that you'll stop feeling everything. No more touching, no more tasting, nothing."

"So," Sarge said, "it's like he's invincible or something?"

"I want some too, Sarge," Tex said, suddenly interested.

"No, God no," Carter said. "He can die. In fact he will die. Hours, days, maybe, weeks at the most. Depends on a lot of factors, like the extent of your wounds, and presence or absence of other nanobots in your system. Our latest subject lasted about three weeks, even with very advanced cancer in his system, then he died. His brain was numbed so much by the nanobots that it just gave out and he dropped dead."

"I don't wanna die, Sarge," Tank said. "Not like that."

"Is there a cure?" Sarge asked.

"It gets worse..." Carter replied, concern creeping into his face.

"How can dying slowly get worse?" Tank nearly shouted.

"The brain is killed by the numbing of the nerve endings, but the nanos don't die. There's still electrical current, and they feed off that and keep working. The... subject... the latest one. We were monitoring video feeds of his house remotely. We saw his movement slowing before he collapsed and died. We didn't expect... he... he rose again. When he did, he started to eat. The nanos keep the body going. That's what they're programmed to do. They know that the body needs food and drink, and they keep pursuing it in whatever form they can find."

"What do you mean, whatever form?" Sarge asked.

"Food, leftovers, waste products, plants, weeds. Any organic material, really. Including p... pe..." Carter's voice faltered. He shivered and closed his eyes before whispering, "people." He swallowed hard and took a few deep breaths before continuing. "By the time we realized what was going on, we plotted a return trip to his home as quickly as we could."

"And?" Sarge asked when Carter had paused. "What happened when you got there?"

"We didn't. We were on our way when the pirates docked with us."

"I don't wanna die like that," Tank repeated. "I wanna die like a soldier, Sarge, just me and a few dozen pirates. That's all I ask. Unless you can find some big fucking space alien, with weird tentacles and gigantic eyes or some shit like that. That would work too."

"Is there a cure?" Sarge asked.

Carter shrugged. "One. Only one way we have found to stop the nanos. EMP blast. We have a chamber on this ship that we constructed once we figured out what was happening with the Nano-Morphine. The procedure lasts seconds, but..."

"But what?"

"He's a marine," Carter said, as if that was explanation enough.

"And?" Sarge asked.

"Most marines are augmented. Pretty standard in today's military. Only a few die-hard Norms are allowed to avoid the procedures, and only then with the right political connections. Depending on the extent of his augments, the procedure could produce any number of side effects."

"Shit," Sarge replied, then turned to face Tank. "Report. What's the extent of your augments?"

Tank scratched the nape of his neck while he ran down the list. "Optical augments, with zoom and vision enhancement features, as well as optical display for superimposing data and targeting reticle assistance. Muscle augments, standard issue, with power and stamina enhancements. Implanted communications and wireless networking access. Bone structure reinforcement nanos to prevent breakage. Brain augmentation with data drive for tactical maps and orders. Anti-toxin nanos, with immunization for all known common illnesses-"

"That's quite a list," Carter interrupted.

"Well, those are the ones I know about," Tank said.

Sarge turned back to Carter. "Well?"

"In all honesty, we'd be looking at a total system failure. The data drive and networking equipment in his head would be fried. Failure of the optical implants would most likely render him blind. Muscle augments would backfire, leaving him weakened, probably confined to bed for at least a few months. Combine that with a shock to his bone enhancements and you're looking at possibly years of bed rest. And that's assuming he even survives the system shock of the EMP blast."

"Would it be possible to do this procedure, then reinstall all the augmentations?"

"To fix damage to that extent?" Carter frowned as he thought it over. "If he survives the initial system shock, it might be possible. But we'd have to proceed slowly, or risk losing him with every operation or injection. You'd still be looking at years of recovery time. It should be possible, though."

Sarge started to say something and then decided to keep quiet. This was Tank's decision. He could issue an order, and Tank would follow it, whatever it was. But this was one order he didn't want to give, regardless of which way he thought was most promising. He looked at Tank and could see the expression on his face. Despair. It was mirrored in Ghost's face. He turned to see it in Tex's face as well. He didn't like it one bit. "Your decision, Tank. What do we do?"

"Some fucking decision, Sarge. Take an EMP to kill one threat and either die or become a vegetable. Or, wait, and die and become some fucking... re-animated... zombie thing."

"I know, Tank. Wish there was a third option."

"There is, Sarge. Find some pirate ship and let me run in and pick a fight. Take a few bastards with me and die like a soldier should."

Sarge nodded, knowing that he would choose the same thing.

"There's... more..." Carter said. All eyes turned on him. "The nanos are not linked directly to him. Any nanos they come in contact with will be conscripted. They're already converting the other nanos in his body to do their work. And anyone who mixes blood with him will acquire the... infection."

"Fuck a duck," Sarge said.

"We only learned of this possibility recently, in our test lab. I'm afraid I have no way of knowing what it will do to the augmentations already in his system. Once the nanobots are conscripted, they may continue their primary functions until needed, or they may convert totally and leave him with partially functioning or completely dead augmentations. There's really no way for me to know. I can have the other scientists prep the EMP chamber, just in case. But I need to get the communications back online. We have to check on our previous subject. Since he physically died, anyone he comes into contact with is in danger." Carter moved back to the console and started typing commands.

"You said you had a video feed on his house? Where was that?" Sarge asked.

"Mars. Some squash farming colony. I don't remember which offhand."

"A farmer?"

"Yes," Carter said. "We found him through his doctor. Cancer had spread to most of his major organs and they couldn't do anything for him. So I contacted him, and told him a little about what we were doing. He volunteered without hesitation. We installed some equipment in his house to monitor his recovery from the procedure. But just in his house. If the infection has spread-"

Tex gulped. "Shit, Sarge, there's about two and a half million people on Mars."

"More like three million," Sarge replied, "once you include the military bases. Carter, can these... reanimated people be killed? I mean, again?"

Carter paused and turned to face Sarge. "An EMP blast would stop them. Theoretically speaking, any targeted electronic pulse to the brain would do it. Anything to overload the electrical circuits and kill off the Nano-Morphine's power source."

"What about plasma? Like a pulse rifle round, to the head?" Sarge asked.

"Plasma, definitely. A well-placed shot would eat through just about anything. But a focused burst from a pulse rifle? Same ammunition, but smaller amount- it *is* ionized gas... if you consider... well, it *might* work. It might carry enough of an electrical charge to do it."

Tank shouldered his pulse cannon and grinned widely. "Looks like I might get my wish of death by combat after all, Sarge. Any chance that Mars is already covered with these re-peeps?"

Carter turned his attention back to the communications console. "God, I hope not."

WHAT'S THE BOUNTY FOR A GHOST?

N estled amongst the asteroids, a small ship waited, silent and dark. For all intents and purposes, anyone who approached would assume the ship was a derelict, abandoned years ago. From the outside, it had the appearance of a ship that had already been stripped for parts. The fuselage had gaping holes, missing panels, exposed wiring. All strategically placed to mislead anyone who saw it, while at the same time avoiding any sensitive parts that would prevent functional usage or compromise hull integrity.

Inside, the ship was pristine, kept clean around the clock by a small army of robotic cleaners. The ship had only three rooms, but every room had at least a dozen cleaners. The latrine was the most spotless of the lot. Every time the toilet was flushed or the sink was returned to its upright docking position, a cleaner would be dispatched to scrub the soap and water away. Every time the light was turned off, another cleaner would polish the mirror.

Next was the single berth, more of a sleeping alcove than a room. Still, half a dozen robotic helpers worked diligently here, sanitizing the sheets and smoothing out any wrinkles the moment the owner stood from the bed. Even waking in the middle of the night to use the bathroom, he would return to a clean bed.

Across from the bed was a food station, small appliances needed for meal preparation and cupboards full of military meals, individually packaged and all mostly ready to eat. The few that required heating to be palatable were stacked on the opposite side, so he wouldn't make that mistake again.

The main cabin required more work, due to its size. There were robots to scrub the floors, robots to clean the display screens, even robots to ensure the console chair was well-oiled and at just the right height. Nanobots flew around the interior, just in case someone might sneeze, to insure the air was kept clean of any infections. At first, he was unsure of them, worrying that he'd accidentally swallow one while walking across the ship. Now he didn't even think about them. They were smart enough to avoid collisions.

The air in the main cabin shimmered a moment, then was still. Machines detected the life presence and whirred in response, pumping freshly recycled air into the space. The air shimmered again and Woden appeared, standing perfectly still, arms crossed in front of his chest, looking for a moment like a scandalously dressed mummy. His body solidified, and a moment later he collapsed on the cold floor of his ship. His body rocked, shaking violently with the exertion. Blood poured from his nostrils in a steady stream as he coughed, expelling all the air in his lungs and sending him into another round of convulsions.

A small robotic cleaner slid across the floor, silently mopping up the blood. It started to return to its docking station, but Woden sneezed another spat of blood on the floor. The cleaner detected this and returned for another round of scrubbing. Woden opened his eyes and watched as the cleaner sprayed a thin film of disinfectant on the floor, polished it to a slight shine, then returned to its dock. Woden glanced around the cabin of his ship, then looked out the viewport. The ship was still where he had left it, parked amongst the asteroids with a clear line of sight to 8 Flora. The screens on his control deck showed all functions normal. He shuddered again, then collapsed.

*   *   *

Hours later, Woden awoke on the floor, sore from head to toes. He stretched without attempting to rise. Cracks from sore ligaments echoed around the small cabin. Slowly he rose, and stretched his back, hearing several pops. He walked into the bathroom. The light turned on when he crossed the threshold. Woden snatched a towel from the rack, wet it, and wiped at the caked up blood under his nose. He dropped the towel into a small clothes hamper, where more robots waited for things to clean.

Woden glanced at his food station momentarily, but decided against eating. The last time he'd teleported home and tried to eat, the end result was not very pleasant. He'd try to give himself at least a couple of hours of awake time before attempting to eat anything.

He sat in his console chair and double-checked the readouts. Everything normal. He tapped the screen and began issuing commands to create an encrypted channel. The program filled the screen with random characters, then returned the display to its previous state. A single line of text appeared in his console window, announcing the encryption key it had chosen. Woden dragged that key to another window and opened a secure call to one of many memorized numbers.

A young woman answered the call, filling his screen with her finely coifed blond hair. "Anderton Enterprises. How may I direct your call?"

"Gabrielle Anderton."

"I'm sorry, sir, that line is-"

"Security override," Woden said. "Clearance code papa november niner three niner two seven whiskey. Code name Hunter."

"One moment please," she responded. Her eyes went blank, then pigment returned. "Clearance code accepted. User 'Hunter' identified and confirmed. Please hold while the call is connected."

The screen went blank. Woden tapped his fingers on his console and stared out of his viewscreen. In his peripheral vision, he saw Gabrielle's face appear on his screen. "Woden," she said, "have you captured them?"

"Not yet," he said, returning his gaze to the screen.

"Then why are you contacting me?" she said, agitated. "Do you have any idea-"

"My price has gone up."

"You-"

"You failed to tell me that there are *five* members of Fireteam Zulu."

Gabrielle Anderton sighed. "This is news to me. But what does one more matter? What do you want, Woden? Sixty million instead of fifty?"

"Three hundred million."

"You- What?!"

Woden stared at the screen and silently counted to five. "Mrs. Anderton," he said, slowly, calmly picking his way through the syllables. "The fifth and final member is someone who, shall we say, is going to be quite some extra effort. So if you think an extra two hundred and fifty million is too much, then you tell me -- what is the bounty for a ghost?"

"A ghost?" she asked, then she squinted and leaned in. "You mean you found Ghost?"

"Michelle Seles, a-k-a Ghost. She's working with Fireteam Zulu."

"You're sure it's her?" Gabrielle asked, excitement evident.

"Positive."

"I'll have to get back to you."

"You do that," Woden said, then cut off the transmission.

He leaned back in his chair and smirked. "Indeed," he said to the cleaning robot that was busy cleaning fingerprints off his keyboard. "What *is* the bounty for a ghost?"

Contamination

C ollins awoke to the sharp, high-pitched crack of a pulse rifle. He sat and looked around the barracks to see his fellow soldiers had responded similarly. The younger soldiers scanned the room, some looking out the windows to see what was going on, others gripping at their bed sheets while sweat poured down their faces. Scared like a bunch of kids away at camp, awakened by a thunderclap. The veterans were already lacing their boots, preparing to move out. Collins pulled his boots on and laced them, slowly, methodically.

Another crack echoed through the camp, then another. Pulse rifles were unmistakable, even when muffled by distance and concrete. Higher pitched than the old-style weapons, but louder, and the echo always lingered a little bit longer. By now the green soldiers were panicking, starting to say things but disciplined enough to know they were better off silent. Collins stood and scanned the room, quickly assessing that he was the most senior marine present. He saw Pav at his bunk, dressed for the day and standing at attention. Collins walked into the center of the barracks.

"Ten-SHUN!" he shouted. He glanced around the barracks. His exclamation had gained him some attention, but they still looked scared. "Settle down, marines. Get your boots on and prepare to move out. Pav, check the path to the armory."

"Is... is this a drill?" asked a private that Collins hadn't met yet.

"Unknown."

"But... do we... I mean-"

Collins made a hand signal indicating silence. "We are marines. We'll respond to this the way we've been trained to. Pav?"

"Looks clear," Pav announced.

"We'll proceed to the armory," Collins said. "Stay low. Check your flanks. Get armor and a rifle, then assemble in the quad in two minutes. Got it? Move out!"

The soldiers filed out of the barracks and ran the short distance to the armory. Another crack of pulse rifle fire made most of the new recruits flinch and duck lower as they ran. Collins paused outside of the armory and listened, scanning the base for signs of activity. Someone shouted, then another three loud cracks of gunfire emanated from the vicinity of the medical office. Collins went into the armory, pleased to see Pav and Jane motivating the others to get their armor on. He pulled on combat armor as quickly as he could and followed the others outside, grabbing a rifle from Pav on his way. More shouting and gunfire from the medical office. Collins turned on the troops in the quad to see them standing at attention, ready for action.

The door to the medical office flew open. The Colonel ran out, tripped on something and fell to the ground in a puff of red dust. He scrambled to his knees and started crawling toward the barracks, shouting something Collins couldn't hear, sound drowned out by more gunfire from within. Collins shouted and the Colonel turned his head, blood-streaked face filled with fear. He noticed the soldiers, armed and ready, and the sight seemed to calm him somewhat. He pointed at the medical office. Collins ordered the marines to follow him and jogged to the building.

As they got closer, the sounds of shouting grew. Someone screamed, sharp terror cut short with a crack of pulse rifle fire. Collins entered the building and aimed his rifle down the hallway. The hall was well-lit with the morning sunshine. Stench of blood and charred flesh filled the air. The marines filed into the building and took up defensive positions near the door. Collins picked four of the marines at random and sent them to the supply closets at the end of the hall. He sent another team outside, to circle around the building and cover the alternate exit.

That done, he took a deep breath and looked over the remaining marines under his command. It was times like this that Collins found himself wishing he wasn't a Norm. Any other soldier would just call up a tactical map of the building on their HUD and plan the mission. Scanning the nearby faces would provide him with a detailed list of soldiers and capabilities. Some of the newer officers had tactical planning augments that would even automatically generate logical groupings based on common tasks. He had to rely on memory. But he knew the layout of the building well, having cleaned it recently. As for the soldiers, he knew some of them. The rest would have to deal with random assignments.

He knew that the teams covering the supply closets and alternate exit would take care of anyone getting out of the examination rooms. So most of the building was already covered. All that remained were four areas: Exam Room A was near the supply closets, and Exam Room C was on the opposite side of the building. Both rooms had only two entrances -- one with this hallway and one adjoining doorway into Exam Room B. That made Exam Room B the hardest to secure, as it was nestled in the center of the building and had the most entrances to cover. There was an office on the other side of Exam Room B that Doctor Dmitri used. Anyone trapped in the exam rooms would be most likely to retreat to that office if they couldn't make it outside. Collins felt it was up to him to take the dirty job, but securing Exam Room B would be impossible without sending capable soldiers to first secure rooms A and C. The worst part was that any threat retreating from rooms A and C would be chased into the team trying to clear room B.

He wanted to take Pav and Jane with him to clear room B, and almost issued the order until he saw the look on the other soldiers' faces. They needed leadership, or at the very least they needed someone with combat experience to lead them into this mess. He had Pav and Jane, and knew their capabilities well. He also had Goddard, who was thankfully quiet for once, and Bryant. They could handle themselves in a fight. At least they wouldn't have grounds to complain if they were busy shooting things. They'd do their jobs. He just didn't want to put them in charge of anything. Unfortunately, Goddard was the second-highest rank in the group. The rest of his collection were frightened privates, barely out of boot camp. There was only one logical choice for him to make.

"Corporal Goddard," he said, "take Pav, Topaya, and Costanza. Circle to Exam Room A. Jane, take Bryant..."- he paused to read their name tags -"Smith and Troy. Clear Exam Room C. Both teams, flank B once cleared, I'll meet you in the middle." They acknowledged his order and departed, leaving him with three very scared looking privates under his direct command: Olsen, Konrad, and Templeton. Collins swallowed a deep breath and flipped the safety off his weapon. "Take a deep breath, boys. Calm your nerves a moment. Check your fire. Watch your flanks and our backs. Stay close to me. Let's go."

Without further ado, Collins approached the double doors labeled 'Exam Room B'. He crouched in front of the door and motioned for Olsen to crouch beside him so both could cover the opening. He motioned for Konrad and Templeton to flank the doors and open them on his command. They complied and when he heard a pause in gunfire, he ordered them to open the doors.

The room was coated in blood and scorch marks from pulse rifle fire. Exam tables overturned, medical instruments scattered around the room. Anya lay in a pool of blood near the door, body twisted unnaturally, large scorched hole in her face where her dented nose should have been. The rest of her body was littered with pulse burns, thin cotton examination gown burnt and torn, leaving her nearly naked corpse exposed. Beyond her, another corpse, another new recruit Collins didn't recognize because most of his head was missing.

At the far end of the room, two figures wrestled around the entry to Doctor Dmitri Vladlodikov's office as he used the communication station within. One of the men was a marine in fatigues, the other a naked man, large hulking frame in a tattered examination gown. There was only one marine that could have been. *O'Malley,* Collins thought. *But what is he doing? Wasn't he... dead?*

Collins moved cautiously into the room, nearing the pair, trying to line up a shot but not getting the chance. He shouted a challenge, but neither of the two responded. The pair staggered side to side, looking more like inexperienced preteens dancing than warriors locked in a mortal struggle. O'Malley gained the upper hand and the other marine fell to the ground with a gasp.

"O'Malley! Stand down!" Collins yelled as he aimed his rifle. But he couldn't take a shot without endangering Doctor Dmitri. O'Malley shambled into the office and Collins had no choice. He fired, the blast from his rifle tearing through the man's chest and showering Doctor Dmitri with blood. O'Malley paused but didn't fall, and a moment later the gaping wound in his chest closed, flesh stitching together like ice forming in a time-lapsed video. O'Malley took another step forward and grasped Dmitri, pushing him out of view of the doorway.

"Move!" Collins shouted, leading his team across the examination room.

Sounds of pulse rifles firing from the other two examination rooms. Doctor Dmitri cried out, his scream trailing into a gurgle as Collins entered the small office. Doctor Dmitri lay crumpled against the wall, neck ripped open, hands clawing at the back of the naked man crouched over him. Collins aimed his rifle and fired. The figure shook with the impact, then the wound closed itself like the other had. He fired again, and again the wound closed itself. His third shot ripped through O'Malley's abdomen into Doctor Dmitri's prone body. This one appeared to aggravate him. He rose in response and turned on Collins. His jaw was slack and dripping with blood, his eyes vacant and glazed over. Even with the paleness his skin had taken on, he was unmistakable. Collins had known him for long enough to recognize him in any condition.

"O'Malley?" he said.

O'Malley let out a tired groan in response, a primal and guttural moan that described a desperate urge. "Kaaaawwww..." he said. "Liiiinnnssss." He took a step toward Collins and reached out both arms. "Heeehpp-"

Collins fell back and tripped, falling onto his backside. The other marines on his team reacted instantly, training overtaking their fear. They pulled their triggers and sent a barrage of pulse rifle blasts into O'Malley's body, shaking him and sending him back against the wall. Collins turned his head in a daze from side to side. *No*, he thought, *it can't... he can't...*

O'Malley leaned against the wall and groaned again, wounds stitching themselves closed as quickly as they were created. One of the privates paused to reload his rifle, dropping the spent clip to the ground. Collins watched it hit the floor tiles, bounce once, then come to rest. He looked from O'Malley's dancing to the clip, which quickly became two, then three. His friend, his bunk mate, now some other creature, locked in a constant shake as his body was ripped apart and repaired repeatedly. As the pile of spent clips grew to four, his gaze drifted to Anya, with the hole in her face. Then the other soldier with half his head missing. Collins looked back at O'Malley and watched the pulse rifle fire ripping apart his arms, legs, and torso, wounds closing almost instantly. Collins aimed his rifle from his position on the floor and fired, sending a single shot through O'Malley's extended hand and into his left eye. O'Malley collapsed to the floor and lay motionless.

The silence that followed was eerie, broken only by the familiar stomping of well-polished boots as the other teams converged on Exam Room B. Someone said something but Collins couldn't make out any of the words. The constant pounding of his heart drowned out the rest. Pav helped him to his feet and gave him a quick check to ensure he was unharmed.

The Colonel entered and surveyed the marines present. A lot of tired faces, many splattered with blood. He ordered everyone to sweep the rest of the base. Goddard, looking quite a bit more chipper than usual, saluted the Colonel and started barking orders to the rest. The Colonel watched them leave, then entered the office. He crouched before Doctor Dmitri and sighed.

"You did good, Collins," he said. "As good as could be expected."

Collins swallowed the lump in his throat and tried his best to accept the compliment gracefully. He stumbled over the words a few times, sighed, and finally replied, "Thank you sir."

"I lost my lieutenant," he said. "That makes you my second in command.

Stay close to me."

Collins nodded, still slightly dazed from the encounter with O'Malley.

The Colonel stood and walked to the communication station. It was dead. Stray rounds had penetrated several components of the console and fried the electronics. "Damn it all. I hope he got through. The only other communication station on the base is in my office. Let's go."

Collins led the way to the Colonel's office, keeping careful watch for any hostile movements. He saw Pav approaching the barracks with a squad, giving orders and leading the way. He couldn't see Jane, but assumed she was acting the same way. He had taught them both what he'd learned from the officers he admired. There were too many gutless officers who didn't see anything wrong with ordering good soldiers to their deaths while they waited in safety.

Good soldiers, Collins had told all the privates placed under his command, *should be led by good officers.*

Pav and Jane had been the only ones who seemed to have understood the lesson. He'd recommend either one for sergeant in a heartbeat. He was assuming that the Colonel's short speech was indicative of his considering Collins for lieutenant. Part of him wouldn't mind, but the rest of him didn't want the responsibility. Some days were hard enough just being a soldier and taking orders. On the other hand, he was due for retirement soon, and a last-minute bump in pay grade wouldn't be unwelcome.

The Colonel pushed his way past Collins and entered his office. He made his way to the communication station and turned it on. Collins darted around to inspect the other rooms in the Colonel's office. The adjutant's desk and the bathroom were empty. He returned to the building's only entrance. While Collins waited, watching the quad for any signs of movement, the Colonel worked at the console. "That damned fool!" he said, pounding his fist into the mud brick wall. "Why the hell would he call a research vessel instead of High Command?!"

"Sir," Collins said, "our communications dish was broken by last week's sand storm. All we got is the emergency backup dish. Can't reach High Command on that."

"I'll try Fleet, then."

"Dish hasn't got enough power to send that far either, sir."

"I just heard from Fleet yesterday!"

"Emergency dishes can receive almost anything," Collins responded, "but transmission range is limited."

"Damn it! What about the other bases?"

Collins shrugged. "What other bases, sir?"

"There are fourteen other military bases on this planet."

"News to me, sir. Must be classified, like this one."

The Colonel kicked the trash tin by the station. "Damned short-sighted bastards. What about the station in orbit around the planet?" He pressed buttons on the communication station and watched the screen for a response. An image of the planet rendered on the screen, showing the base's location with a little gold star. None of the other bases were marked. The space station was not marked either. He knew the bases were there, and that the station was there, but they were all classified. He clenched his fists and shook with rage. "Assholes!"

"Sir?"

The only other landmark on his map was a civilian recreation station in high orbit. That meant his only viable alternative was to try to get them to relay a message, and that could take a while. Or he could try to reproduce what Dmitri had done. The Colonel brought up the record of Dmitri's connection with the research vessel and examined it. The ship was classified as well, but he could patch in a connection based on what Dmitri had done. That was at least something. He opened the message header and started reading it as sounds of gunfire erupted outside. Collins looked out into the quad. Jane was backing out of the barracks with two other soldiers, firing into the building on full auto.

"You might wanna hurry, sir," Collins said.

"I know, Sergeant, I know."

DISTRESS

Sarge watched the screen as the man who introduced himself as Doctor Dmitri Vladlodikov tried in vain to speak above the roar of gunfire behind him. Carter stared in horror at the shambling forms outside the room, tearing at the marines who were trying to protect the doctor. Tank, Tex, and Ghost stood behind, silently watching the screen.

"Shoot them in the *head*," Carter screamed into the microphone.

"What was that?" Dmitri replied. "Repeat?"

A flash of light nearby disrupted the video feed momentarily. The audio cut out, leaving the rest of the conversation to a combination of Carter doing his best impression of shooting for the head and Dmitri talking and glancing around in a panic. The last soldier behind him fell under the weight of a large naked man. After the soldier hit the floor, the large man straightened and stumbled in Dmitri's direction. A rifle blast tore through the man's chest and the video feed went black.

"Well," Sarge said, "guess it's too late to help him."

Carter turned on him. "Dammit, that man just died there. They all did. We have to help them."

"Not our problem. Besides, who says anyone's still alive down there?"

Tank cleared his throat. "Sarge, I wanna help them."

"You just want to go down fighting."

"Hell yeah."

"Well stow it, marine," Sarge said, then paused and let out a sigh. He wasn't too keen on helping in what looked like a hopeless situation, yet they were marines. Even though he wasn't one any longer, he still saw them as brothers. "All right, we'll help them. But I doubt it will be easy. I was at a classified base on Mars before. Damn automatic snipers will railgun the shit out of our ship before we can get anywhere close. We'll have to land a few klicks outside the base and walk it."

"This ship can bypass their security and get us through," Carter said.

"No dice."

"This is a military research vessel, Sergeant, we're authorized to be there. We're authorized-"

"No dice," Sarge repeated. "We go in with Zulu Prime, land about two klicks out and walk it. Ghost can disable the automatic snipers once we're on the ground."

Carter's face turned slightly red. "Dammit Sarge, landing in the base is going to be the fastest way to help those people!"

"I know how you feel, Carter, but you got a ship full of scientists here. Stay in orbit, in case we need help, but we go in alone." Sarge studied the look on Carter's face and interrupted him before his next round of protests could be spoken. "I'm not taking a bunch of noncombatants into a hostile situation. That's final."

Carter turned back to the console and typed on the keyboard. "Fine," he said. "At least let me see if I can start a landing sequence with this ship. That might disable the defenses and allow you to land closer."

"Good idea. Ghost, Tex, get back on Zulu Prime and get Weasel up to speed. See where we can land and get a course plotted. Tank, take care of the weapon reloads. I want full battle readiness as soon as we hit dirt."

"Yes, sir!" Tank beamed. He collected everyone's weapons and followed Ghost and Tex into the hallway.

Sarge looked back and watched Carter typing on the console. The screen was showing his words, but it was a language Sarge couldn't decipher. He'd seen Weasel do similar magic on the computers on Zulu Prime's bridge. It wasn't anything that normally interested him, until now. Now he was worried that Carter's magic commands would initiate some landing sequence he didn't want to happen. Sarge made a mental note to learn at least enough of these computer systems to understand what someone was *really* doing. Hopefully Carter would not realize Sarge had no idea what he was doing and would shy away from anything against his orders out of fear alone.

Carter stopped typing and focused his attention on a second rectangle that had appeared on his screen. He leaned in closer to the screen and studied the text there. "Huh," he said.

"What's that?"

"Incoming connection attempt. Well, sort of, packet looks forged. Like someone took an earlier message header and fudged the timestamp."

Sarge frowned, but nodded his head as if he knew what that meant. "Where's it coming from?"

"Packet header says Mars. MP-2184. Same base," Carter said. He typed a few commands and added, "And my trace confirms the origin."

"Can you establish the connection?"

"Sure," Carter said. "Although I'm not sure that I want to talk to someone who forges connection packets to classified ships."

"Right now," Sarge said, "I'm interested in *any* communication from that base."

Carter tapped the screen where the new window was and typed on his keyboard. The machine beeped and a small video window appeared on top of the text. Carter put two fingers on the screen and spread them apart. The video feed expanded to fill the screen, showing more detail on a very tired face. The man leaned into the screen and smiled.

"I think I've got it," he said.

"You have," Carter replied. "This is a secure channel for military use only. Please authenticate."

The man on the screen's smile faded, replaced with furrowed brows and a scowl. "I know it's a secure channel you dolt!" He leaned away from the screen, showing the top of his uniform. Colonel's insignia and an impressive rack of medals. "I'm Colonel Gerald Robbins, UEF Marine Corps."

Carter hit something on his keyboard and the other text window appeared on top of the video feed. He typed a command and added the Colonel's name as a parameter. The machine whirred and responded with a full printout of the Colonel's file. "Acknowledged, Colonel. I'm Doctor Thomas Carter. I was in-"

"Never mind that. I need you to relay a message to High Command immediately. Requesting immediate assistance against unknown threat. I can't even begin to describe it..." his voice trailed off as he hung his head.

Sarge stepped behind Carter and crossed his arms. "Let me try. People died. Then they came back to life and started killing."

The Colonel looked up at the screen. "And who the hell are you?"

"They call me 'Sarge'."

"You look familiar. Marine?"

"Ex. Very ex."

The Colonel stared at the screen a moment, his scowl widening. "Yes, I know you, *Sarge*," he spat. "And let me tell you, we don't need any help from a vigilante paramilitary group. Why don't you just go hunt some fucking pirates. I need soldiers, *real* soldiers."

"Colonel, you're getting my help whether you like it or not."

"Doctor Carter, relay my message to High Command as follows-"

Sarge placed a hand on Carter's shoulder and squeezed. "Colonel," he said, staring directly in the Colonel's eyes, "you and I both know a signal to High Command from here will take at least a half hour round trip. If they deploy soldiers to assist you that could take weeks. If they notify the other bases on Mars to assist you, they could still take days to mobilize and reach your position. My team can be there in one hour, two tops. Maybe we can help. Maybe we can't. But we're willing to try. Relay the message if you still want to, but my team will arrive and assist in the meantime."

The Colonel leaned back in his chair, exposing the background of his office. Sarge could see a marine standing in the doorway, firing his weapon at something outside. He said something and the Colonel barked at him before returning his attention on the screen. "All right, all right. Doctor Carter, relay my message to High Command. In the meantime, Sarge, you and your team come down and help. I'll turn off the base defenses but you damn well better hurry."

"Sitrep?"

The Colonel exhaled. "People have been getting sick, and dying. Seven of them were in the morgue when they got up and starting killing the doctors in the medical office. That's when Doctor Vladlodikov called you, I suppose. Total population of Mars MP-2184 is eighty persons. Seventy marines, rest are, or were, medical personnel. Current population unknown. Infection unknown. Surviving marines... unknown."

"What happened to the conversion taking days or weeks?" Sarge asked.

Carter frowned. "I... I don't know. I've never heard of this happening so quickly. You said the marines were getting *sick*, Colonel?"

"Some kind of influenza," the Colonel said. "Some new strain that started hitting us about a week or two ago. Doctor Vladlodikov referred to it as 'interesting'. In my experience, it's a bad sign when a doctor thinks you're interesting."

"I'll have to confer with my team-" Carter said, stopping when Sarge nudged him in the back. He cleared his throat. "Er, but for now, Colonel, let me get you up to speed while Sarge and his men head there."

"Thank you, Doctor," the Colonel said. He started to say something else but stopped. He looked up at Sarge and then shook his head. "I can't fucking believe I just contracted Fireteam Zulu for help."

"Got a shit-fest? Send in the best," Sarge replied, grinning mischievously. "We can bullshit later over a couple beers, sir."

"You're on."

Carter started relaying details about the Nano-Morphine to the Colonel. Sarge stood in the doorway and listened for a moment. People had learned to not rely so heavily on technology back in 2096. Or, rather, they should have. And here they were again, screwed over by themselves in their pursuit to fix what nature had created. Life moved in cycles. You lived, you died. It was the natural order of things in the universe. Scientists constantly tried to interrupt that order, to bend nature to their will. They always came up with a more clever way to circumvent the inevitable end of life. First it was the physical augmentations to make soldiers faster and stronger. Then came the mental augmentations to make soldiers braver and more alert. Now they were trying to cheat death with overzealous nanobots fixing wounds within seconds and removing pain from the equation completely. You sign up, you fight, and if you're lucky then you live to fight another day. When you're too old to fight, you get a desk or a discharge. It was the natural order of things in the military.

Next they'll probably find a way to cure the aging process too. Sarge smirked at his joke, smile slowly fading as the full effect of his thought hit him. *Soldiers who live forever. Soldiers who fight forever.*

He left the bridge and walked to the docking hatch. As he entered Zulu Prime, he ordered Tex to close the hatch so they could depart. They had work to do.

THE QUIET PLACE

J ane squeezed the trigger again, sending a round into Private Yuri's shoulder. She had liked him, once. He had a sly smile and told the dirtiest jokes. There was something downright honest about him, a tenacious attitude toward life that she found interesting. Now here he was, still clinging onto that life, somehow. She fired again, hitting him in the throat. That made him stumble back, but he regained his composure. When his throat had closed again he groaned, and took another step forward. She shot him again in the shoulder, which snapped. His left arm fell to the ground with a thud. He paused and glanced down at it.

"Stop," she pleaded. "Please... just... stop."

Tears were starting to well up in her eyes. She blinked hard and they dripped down her cheeks. She signed up to be a marine, to protect her world and fellow humans. This wasn't at all what she imagined her job to be. Killing her friends was not part of the contract she'd signed on her first day of basic training.

She had gone into the barracks with two other soldiers. Now she was alone, backed against the side of the medical building, and out of ammunition. She slumped to a sitting position as Yuri started walking to her again, reaching out with his one remaining arm. She could hear gunfire from the barracks still, and beyond. Yuri paused before her, groaned again. She covered her ears and buried her face in her knees.

Please, God, let me die and escape this horror, she pleaded. She closed her eyes. *Please make it quick.*

Two shots rang out from her right, a pulse rifle burst. Both rounds hit Yuri in the side of the head, sending him to the dirt in a cloud of red dust. She opened her eyes and stared. He lay there, on his side, glazed eyes staring back at her. She shuddered as blood pooled beneath his head.

"Hey, get up Private. You hurt?"

Of all the damned luck, Jane thought, turning her head to see Goddard looking down at her.

"C'mon, Jane, get up, we still got work to do."

"Damn right!" Bryant chimed in. "You see that fuckin' shot? Hells yeah!"

"Just cover us, Bryant. Don't need your commentary," Goddard said as he held out his hand. "Get up, Jane. You hurt?"

She shook her head, took his hand, and stood with his help. "Ran out of ammo," she said.

"Well shit, that ain't no reason to give up," he said. He leaned in close to whisper, "Wipe yer eyes." Then he pulled back and said louder, "Bryant, give her some ammo."

Bryant handed over two clips. Jane ejected her spent cartridge and loaded a fresh one. The pulse rifle registered the new clip and updated its display. This clip was only half-full, but it was still better than the one she had.

"C'mon," Goddard said, "we gotta help out who we can in the barracks."

He took off at a light jog, moving to flank the barracks entrance on the right. Jane instinctively moved to cover the left. When they got closer, Bryant knelt directly in front of the door and announced that he couldn't see anybody inside. Goddard moved in with Jane and Bryant close behind.

"See this shit? I knew I shouldn't have come to this fucking backwater planet," Goddard said.

Movement, a quick flash, at the end of the hall. Bryant fired at it before

Jane could say anything. She took a deep breath and raised her weapon, examining the movement, trying to make out who it was. *What,* she told herself. *What it is. These aren't my friends anymore. They're... something else.*

She fired at the movement and soon it stopped. Goddard called out a challenge and fired a shot of his own. Jane saw something else move on her left. She swung to aim but it was too close. Something heavy hit her in the shoulder and she heard bone crack, felt an overwhelming spike of pain. She yelped but Goddard and Bryant were both firing their rifles. She spun around, strong hands gripping her, pinning her arms to her side. Something pressed on her abdomen and forced her backward, driving the breath out of her. The other hand moved and started clawing at her breast. Warm breath bathed her neck, then a sharp pain. She yelped again and this time Goddard turned.

"Fuck!" he shouted.

Bryant turned and took a step back.

Jane felt warm blood pouring down her neck as the teeth bit further into her flesh. Goddard raised his weapon and took aim. Bryant spouted some blasphemy and backed into a bunk, nearly dropping his weapon. Goddard squeezed the trigger but Jane couldn't even hear the gunshot. All she could hear was her own heart beating and what sounded like a panting dog. Then the teeth were ripped out of her neck and the arms let go. She crumpled to the floor, eyes half-closed.

She could feel the life draining out of her. Time seemed to slow, the sound of her pulse took over all others. She had heard of this before, once, in a legend. The Quiet Place, her mother had said it was called. That eerie place between life and death, when you knew you were crossing, when all you could hear was your own heart beating its last. *You know the end is near,* she had claimed, *and all you can do is listen to the last beats of your heart and wait for death to take you away.*

Thump, thump.

She felt strong hands grip her. Someone was shouting but she couldn't make out the words. A hazy face moved in front of her, but it could have been anybody. Then the feeling of moving. Her eyelids fluttered. The barracks ceiling moved. No, someone dragging her, across the floor, but without any feeling of friction, like falling sideways. *Your senses become hazy,* her mother had said, *but a lot of other things will become clear.*

Thump, thump.

The movement stopped. *It is in this place that you become truly aware of your spiritual self,* her mother had said. *You will finally understand how precious life is.*

Precious. Jane's eyes opened again, for a second, then closed. Goddard and Bryant were in front of her, firing their weapons. She was sitting now, probably propped against a wall. She wasn't a spiritual person, never had been, but she was finally starting to realize something. All the time she spent talking with Collins and she had never admitted to herself that she loved him. She had kept him at a distance, on purpose, with the hope that one day they'd both be out of the military and able to be with each other without having to worry about what their superiors would say. *Many things will become clear, in The Quiet Place.*

Thump, thump.

She felt herself exhale, involuntary contractions in her body. All she could think of was Collins. She knew then that she did indeed love him. But she had no idea how he felt. She had her suspicions. Things he did. Looks he cast her way. Some of his actions, like the way he'd sometimes place a hand on her knee while they talked. If only she hadn't kept him at a distance. If only she had let him in closer. If only she had taken a chance, and asked the one question she had never let herself ask. If... only...

Thump.

A Matter of Trust

Woden had finished a light meal and was contemplating sleep when the call came in. It came a lot earlier than he had expected. Longer deliberations usually ended in more favorable responses, at least in his experience. A quick response like this couldn't be that good of a result. He could ignore the call, but the answer wouldn't change. A lesser person might get nervous and change their answer. Not this woman. She'd reach a decision and stick with it.

Woden cleaned his mouth with a hand towel and tossed it at one of his cleaner robots. He sat at his console and checked the call before answering it. Just as he suspected, it was a direct call from Anderton Enterprises, heavily encrypted with a cipher key he'd given exclusively to Gabrielle Anderton. He tapped his screen to answer the call and waited until the transmission completed the initial handshake. Her face appeared on the screen and he could almost see the unfavorable response etched in her bored expression.

"Mrs. Anderton," he said. "I trust you have a response to my inquiry."

"Woden. I do."

He studied her face and nodded. "And I take it that my price will *not* be met."

"Ghost is not worth all that you thought, I'm afraid. The military did want her captured, once."

"And now?"

Gabrielle shrugged. "Now they can't trust her. She fled them once, and they can't risk that happening again. Now they want her terminated. They are, however, willing to pay for that service. And for the discretion of not letting her be associated with Fireteam Zulu. If she went on trial along with the rest, there'd be a chance of exposing the Psi-Ops program. They don't want that. They want her dealt with as quietly as possible."

"How much?" Woden asked, staring into Gabrielle's eyes as best he could. She was dodging his attempts. Probably still unsure of herself after discovering the hard way that he could affect her remotely.

"Fifty million," she replied. "But they want solid proof of her death. A corpse, nothing less."

Woden counted to five again, silently. "All right," he said. "Fifty for her corpse, fifty for capturing the rest. One hundred million credits, total."

"Correct."

"I'll be in touch." Woden hit the button to sever the connection.

He stared out into the blackness, watching distant stars drift by. He knew perfectly well the fate that awaited Ghost, or at least the fate that *had been* awaiting her. It would have been his own fate, if he had stayed in the program all those years ago. The other Psionic Operations soldiers were trained and deployed. When their tasks had been completed, they were collected and shipped to the space station in orbit around Venus. Deep within, on a floor hidden in the center, was a room that acted as the central gravity pull for the rest of the station, but had none itself. Cryotubes lined the walls in this room, and in each one was a Psi-Ops soldier, frozen and preserved in case their unique services were needed again some day. He had projected himself there, once, and the image in his mind was one of the few things that chilled him.

There were still empty cryoberths on Venus Station. One for him. One for Ghost. A few more for... who? The others he recognized from the program were already there. Still, he had departed early, and there was a chance that others came to replace him afterward. But this business with Ghost was an unexpected turn. He had never seen the military so casual about discarding such an expensive asset.

Trust. That's what it all came down to. Hard to earn. Easy to lose. Impossible to regain.

Woden turned to his other console, where he had an image of Mars on the screen. A blip beside the planet marked the location of the Orion Research Vessel. Another marked Ghost. Probably on Zulu Prime, considering that it was moving away from the Orion. Placing a tracer on her was easy, as distracted as she had been while mourning her friend. Catching up with her would be easy. Fighting her... that would be interesting. The only hard part so far was accepting the money he'd been offered. He was hoping for so much more.

PLANETFALL

Weasel ran a scan on the base's perimeter defenses and reported his result as negative. The base defenses were currently on-line, but the ship identifier for Zulu Prime was listed as an authorized ship now, and the railguns would let the ship land. That was a good thing, because even a single railgun shot into the ship's hull would render it useless in the vacuum of space.

"Well?" Sarge asked from beside him.

"Looks safe," Weasel replied. "We'll be down in ten minutes. Tell everyone to strap in."

Sarge left the bridge and walked down the hallway. He entered the crew quarters and ordered everyone to strap in. They moved to the far end of the hall, where ten chairs waited, built into the hull of the ship so that anyone properly strapped in would experience only minimal vibrations during re-entry. Sarge sat in one of the seats and strapped himself in. It had been a while since any of them had made planetfall, but it wasn't a new experience to them by any means. He tightened the straps and hung his head forward. Most novices leaned their heads back, but Sarge knew that would amplify the shaking by absorbing more impact from the hull itself. Not to mention the headaches from skull impact with the hull. He closed his eyes and said a silent prayer. Taking off and landing from a planet. That's the only time he ever prayed anymore. Never found much use for religion in his line of work. Killing always seemed to get in the way.

Ghost grit her teeth, like she always did, pulling her straps taut with her eyes closed. She knew the routine. She'd done this hundreds of times, on Earth and Mars. Planetfall on Pluto and Luna was a different story, no atmosphere to buffet the ship. She took a deep breath and held it, counted to ten, then silently mouthed the words to her mantra as she exhaled, lulling herself into a relaxed meditative state.

Tex had rummaged through his locker to find his signature hat -- the stetson he had acquired in New Texas -- and was ready to wave it in the air during their descent. It was part of his charm, the image of a cowboy born four hundred years too late. He refused to allow landing on any planet if he didn't have his stetson in hand. Not that anyone paid attention to his orders, but he gave them nonetheless.

Tank was looking more subdued than usual. He strapped himself in and sat there, silent, waiting for the shaking to set in. His body shuddered. Too early, the ship hadn't even entered the atmosphere yet. He opened his eyes and realized he was sweating. It wasn't the ship that was shaking. Tank shook his head to clear the fogginess that was setting in. *Just have to hold on a little longer*, he thought.

The ship rumbled as it hit atmosphere, shaking violently as Weasel fought the controls to keep the speed and attitude within acceptable parameters. His adjustments were instantaneous and precise, until the ship jerked so hard to port he felt his body slide in the chair. The cabin temperature soared into what he considered desert ranges. He issued a corrective burst and righted the ship, narrowly averting disaster. The ship rocked with a new wave of turbulence.

"Yeeeee-haaaaaw!" Tex screamed, throwing his hat above him. The hat floated a second then slowly drifted toward the aft of the ship.

Sarge smirked. It wasn't just routine with Tex, it was expected at this point. As quickly as the buffeting had begun, it was over. The ship slowed and the cabin cooled off. Weasel calculated the best route to the military base and set the ship on autopilot.

Sarge was the first to unstrap himself. He tapped the communication button in his cheek and said, "ETA?"

"Two minutes," Weasel replied.

"Get armed and armored," he said to the others. "We hit the ground in two minutes. We'll exit via the loading bay. I want you all combat ready as soon as we hit dirt."

Ghost unstrapped herself and retreated to her quarters to get her armor. Tex ran to recover his hat before suiting up. Sarge watched with growing concern as Tank shambled to his locker. He'd lost soldiers before, but usually in combat, when death collected them with the alacrity a good soldier deserved. Seeing his friend and comrade deteriorate like this was unfair. He turned from Tank, not able to bear it anymore, and reached for his armor.

The ship screamed above the Martian dirt. Weasel circled the base from a good distance to see what he could. The area between the buildings was empty, but he could see the light pulses from small arms fire all around it. Setting the ship down there could cause problems. The last thing they needed was to deal with a hot landing zone. He circled again and chose to put the ship down a short distance north of the base.

As soon as the ship touched down, Sarge flipped the switch to open the loading bay. A siren wailed and a synthetic voice announced that the cargo doors would open in five seconds. Before the voice could complete instructions on how to stop the procedure, the cargo ramp cracked open and started its journey. A blast of fresh terraformed air flooded the cargo hold of Zulu Prime. The team inhaled deeply, savoring the departure from the recycled synthetic air they'd been breathing for the past few months. It wasn't Earth air, but it was better than recycled air. At least this air had a scent of something in it besides metal and antiseptic.

Sarge motioned for the others to follow him and took off at a light jog to the base. The first building they approached was the mess hall. They entered through a back door into the kitchen, where they heard some shouting and gunfire coming from the main hall. Sarge motioned for Ghost to enter, but before she had the chance, an unusually excited Tank charged into the room.

"Well... so much for stealth," Sarge said.

Inside the mess hall, two marines were quite startled to see the four of them charge in. They paused their firing, focusing on the new arrivals. Behind them, several unarmed men and women moved toward them, shambling their way along the floor, holes burnt in their clothing. In the dim interior light, anyone without ocular augmentations would have mistaken them for regular people. But Tank zoomed in and there was nothing regular about the images he saw.

"Re-peeps!" Tank shouted. "Get down!"

The marines watched in horror as Tank aimed his giant pulse cannon in their direction, then, taking the hint, they dropped to the floor. Tank pulled the trigger and the great cannon warmed up. The cannon roared as it filled the reanimated marines with shot after shot of charged energy, ripping what remained of their clothing to shreds. They attempted to continue forward, not seeming to mind the assault, but under the constant barrage of energy pulses, they were unable to make any progress.

Tex took aim and fired a round from his pistol into the nearest one's head. The thing's head recoiled from the impact, then the hole sealed itself. Sarge fired his pulse rifle, hitting another reanimated marine in the head, sending it crashing to the floor. Tex fired again, and again the hole sealed itself. "What the hell?"

"Shoot for the head," Sarge offered.

"I am!"

"Guess your plastic bullets are useless then. Needs to be an energy pulse to kill 'em. Gotta start using a real weapon."

"Fuck," Tex said. "Well at least this is a good place to go shopping for one."

Sarge agreed, and shot another reanimated marine in the head, sending it to the floor. Tank leaned back and peppered the remaining three reanimated marines in the head with his pulse cannon fire, killing two of them instantly. He released the trigger as his gun started to beep an overheat warning.

The last reanimated marine paused and regarded them with sad eyes. Its jaw went slack and it moaned. "Paaaa..." it said. Then the side of its head ripped open from a focused plasma round from behind them.

"Looks like this room is clear," Ghost said.

"Hey Sarge," Tank said, "we got time for some of this chow? I'm starving."

"Job first, marine," Sarge replied. He knelt before the two marines they had saved. "Where's the Colonel?"

They told him, and he ordered Ghost to make contact. She slowly faded from view and left the building. Sarge helped the marines to their feet and started to give his standard *you're saved* speech but thought better of it. This situation called for something a little more familiar.

"Saddle up, marines," Sarge started, "we got work to do."

"Yes sir," they replied, not missing a beat. They snapped to attention, then their will faltered as they scanned his combat armor for any sign of rank.

"I'm Sarge. We're Fireteam Zulu. Your Colonel asked us to pop by and help with some cleanup duties."

"Hey," Tank interrupted as he pocketed a bread roll from a nearby serving tray, "any chance you have some ammo we can borrow? I'm almost out."

"I could use a spare pulse rifle," Tex said with a bit of sadness in his voice. "Not that I plan to make a habit out of it."

"Armory," one of the marines said. "We got all that stuff in the armory."

"Sounds good," Sarge said. "What're your names, marines?"

"Private Olsen," one said.

"Private Pavelovich," the other said, "but they just call me 'Pav'."

"Let's go. Stay alert."

They left the mess hall through the front entrance and ran straight for the armory. The quad was empty, quiet save for occasional pulse rifle firing from inside another building. The armory was dark. Not even the emergency porch lights were on. The front entrance, usually well guarded around the clock, was closed and locked. Olsen banged on the door and shouted, eliciting no response. He banged again. Pav stepped forward and banged his fist on the door, as if that would help get it open faster, as if the other marine was just doing it wrong. The two of them started an argument which Sarge had to separate when it looked like it was about to turn physical.

"Now is not the time for this," Sarge said in the best stern-father voice he could muster. "Keep the tension in check, marines. Now is the time to focus on the task at hand. You'll have plenty of time to argue and be scared later. Now, Olsen, is there a back door?"

"No," Olsen replied. "One entrance, one exit. Secure."

"Windows?"

"Yeah," Pav said, "there are a few. Barred, but they're there."

"Okay," Sarge said. "Tex, see if you can climb up that pipe and gain access through the roof. I'll circle around with you two and see if we can get in through a window."

"What about me, Sarge?" Tank asked.

Sarge looked Tank up and down, trying to judge his condition. He looked tired but alert, the recent combat having given him some measure of vigor. There was no telling how much trouble he was in, or how close he was to giving in to the Nano-Morphine. Might as well make use of his talents while they had them. "Front door," he said.

"But... but it's locked."

"And?"

"Yes, sir!" Tank said, stepping up to the door. He swung his pulse cannon like a battering ram, striking the door in the center of mass. The metal door shuddered from the impact but held. He inspected the pulse cannon and found it had gained a few scratches but was otherwise unharmed. He swung again, hitting hard enough to make Tex lose part of his grip on the large pipe that ran up the side of the building. Tex cursed and hurried up as Sarge led the other two marines around to the side. Tank took aim and fired the rest of his rounds into the door but the rounds didn't penetrate. The next swing shattered the warmed cannon's barrel with a loud crack. Tank dropped the broken weapon on the ground and cursed his stupidity. The area around the building was cleared, nothing that he could use to batter the door with. He attempted to strike it with his shoulder, got a single quick stab of pain when he struck, then he felt nothing. The door didn't budge.

Tank glanced to his left and saw a lookout post, a single-man station with an automatic sniper. He sprinted to the station and grabbed the giant railgun with eager hands, yanking it from its base with a shower of sparks and screeching of metal. The railgun beeped a warning signal and the operator's monitor filled with error messages. Tank snorted, kicked the monitor over and into the dirt. The railgun was quite heavy but his muscle augments were up to the task. He reached down with one hand and ripped out the remainder of the cabling that connected the railgun to its monitoring station. He walked back to the armory, now too encumbered to run. The railgun powered up when he hit the manual switch on the side. Tank aimed the railgun in the direction of the door and fired. The roar of the weapon filled the quad, bouncing from building to building in a recursive echo. The round punched straight through the door's locking mechanism, removing it completely and ripping the door off one of its hinges. The recoil nearly sprained his shoulder.

"What the hell was that?" Sarge barked over the com.

"New toy, sir," Tank replied. "Front door is open."

PULSE

J ane lay on the floor of the barracks, shuddering as blood leaked from the gaping wound in her neck. Goddard knelt beside her, aiming his pulse rifle at a reanimated soldier that was shambling toward them. Bryant stood behind him, firing wildly and babbling. One of his shots grazed the reanimated soldier. The momentum of the shot turned the creature, but didn't slow its progress. It moaned in response, took a step in the wrong direction, then turned back to them.

Goddard paused to reload and glanced at Jane. Her eyes were open but staring right past him. Pupils dilated, breathing coming in short gasps. "Dammit," he said. He pressed two fingers to the side of her neck, the side that was still there, and frowned. It was a weak pulse, but it was there. For now.

"This ain't right," Bryant said. He fired another round. "They ain't dyin'."

Goddard looked up and saw several more reanimated soldiers joining the first. "Shoot them in the head, Bryant. The head!"

Bryant fired a round and missed. He pulled the trigger again and his gun clicked in response. "I'm out," he said. "Shit, I'm out."

161

"Last one," Goddard said as he tossed a fresh clip to Bryant. "We gotta move. Way to the mess looks blocked. I can't see the other way."

Bryant inserted the fresh clip and looked in the opposite direction. "No way, Goddard. Other exit's blocked."

Goddard pivoted and looked behind him. The bathroom. Currently empty, but it was a last stand. Nowhere to run. A few windows, but nothing big enough to fit through. Dead end. But still, it was either wait for death here or in the bathroom. At least the bathroom had only one entrance to watch. "Bathroom," he said. "Grab her other arm. Let's move."

Goddard grabbed one of Jane's arms as Bryant grabbed the other. Together they dragged her across the floor into the bathroom, leaving a trail of blood across the tiles. They propped her against the outer wall of one of the stalls. Goddard knelt beside her and trained his rifle on the bathroom door. He checked the readout on his rifle. Forty-one rounds left. Barely more than two-thirds of a clip.

Bryant looked around the bathroom as if seeing it for the first time. "Shit. Shit! We can't fit through them windows!"

Goddard took a deep breath to calm his nerves. "I know, Bryant. This is it. The only choice we have. Cover the entrance. If they get in, pop the pin on your grenade. I ain't gonna be eaten like Jane."

Bryant swallowed hard and nodded. He looked down at Jane and traced the path of blood with his eyes. He knelt beside her and looked into her vacant eyes. Reaching out, he pressed two fingers against the side of her neck. "Can't feel it. She ain't got no pulse."

"Good," Goddard said. "Always thought she was a good soldier. I'd hate to have her see this shitstorm coming."

The groaning in the barracks grew in volume as the hazy shapes stumbled toward the bathroom entrance.

CLEARANCE

The Colonel had tried every access code he knew to establish a connection, any connection, to someone other than Carter's research vessel. He didn't want to relay a message through a science vessel. That was a breach of protocol he wasn't prepared to make. He had asked, and Carter was willing to relay the message, but after learning what he had about the Nano-Morphine, the Colonel decided to try contacting High Command on his own. That meant the space station. There wasn't much chance of getting a message to High Command any other way. He knew the station was there, but it was only responding on civilian frequencies, and everybody he talked to there was useless. He needed either a relayed connection to the military space station or he needed someone at this civilian one with the authorization to contact High Command or the military station on his behalf.

He was staring at an older man on his screen now, a man who had said he was the director of the station. Small office that barely fit the screen. Nobody to listen in on the conversation, unlike the other rooms he had seen behind the other personnel he'd talked to. This was definitely someone with a higher rank. And yet he was spewing the same nonsense. The lies were obvious and predictable, yet there was little he could do. The Colonel laced his fingers together to keep them from shaking with the rage growing inside him.

"I'm sorry, Colonel, but I really don't know what you are talking about," the director said, sly grin growing wide on his face, showing finely polished white teeth. "CrossWorlds is just a recreational station. The only military presence on this station is a single platoon to keep order and protect from pirates. Their highest ranking officer is a lieutenant. I don't know what else to tell you."

"*I* know they are there. *You* know they are there. I need you to relay a message to the military station that is also in orbit." The Colonel ground his teeth and looked away from the screen. "I just don't have the clearance. Is that it?"

"I'm sorry, Colonel, but I really don't know what you are talking about."

"Look, tell that lieutenant in charge of your security force that I need him to relay a message to the military station. You can do that can't you?"

"I can ask him, but I really don't know about any other stations in orbit around Mars."

Collins tried to keep his focus on the quad. He had overheard several conversations like this and was growing weary of them. A group of marines ran out of the mess hall toward the armory. There was some debate amongst them and then they separated. Three went around the side of the building. One started climbing a drainage pipe. The last, a giant of a man, attempted to use his pulse cannon as a battering ram. He took a few swipes, fired several shots, then dropped the weapon. At first, Collins thought he was O'Malley, but that wasn't possible. Just another marine jacked up on augmentations and turned into a beast.

Another group of marines exited the barracks, walking backward and concentrating their fire on the doorway. They weren't watching their backs and were getting dangerously close to a group of unarmed figures approaching from their rear. More of those soldiers stricken by the strange plague. Collins took aim at the group and fired a few shots. The marines whirled, now hearing the commotion behind them. They were almost surrounded and started firing wildly. Collins took careful aim again, sighting the old way down the barrel of the rifle. He squeezed the trigger and sent a single round. The round whistled through the air and struck one of the reanimated soldiers in the head, killing it instantly. The marines got the idea and started aiming for head shots, quickly gaining control over the situation.

A cold breeze swept past Collins, chilling his left side briefly. He looked back at the Colonel, still arguing with the man on the screen. As he watched, another person slowly materialized in the room beside the Colonel. Collins whirled and took quick aim with his rifle. The Colonel took a step away from her, pulse pounding from the unexpected intrusion. Collins could see the man on the screen casually turn his head to focus on the new person in the room, regarding her with mild amusement.

The new figure raised her hand and glanced at Collins. "Don't fire," she said. "I am with Fireteam Zulu. Sarge wanted me to inform you that we've liberated the mess hall and are proceeding to the armory."

"The armory is locked," the Colonel replied, "no need to go in there."

The loud report of a railgun echoed through the quad. Collins glanced back to see the large marine holding a sparking automatic sniper in his bare hands. The door to the armory had been ripped open by the blast. The rest of his comrades rushed to his side and they entered through the doorway. "Too late," Collins said.

"We were low on ammunition," Ghost offered.

The Colonel nodded. "I see. I guess that's alright. Least of my troubles at this point."

Ghost glanced at the video screen. "Do you need any assistance here, Colonel? Or should I return to my team?"

"No," the Colonel spat, then chuckled. "Not unless you have sufficient security clearance to get this guy to admit that there's a military station in or-bit around Mars."

"Alpha charlie seven seven four three niner alpha. Code name Ghost."

The man on the screen's face dropped. He turned to his left. "Please hold, authorizing," he said. Ten seconds later his eyes grew wide. He turned and refocused his attention on the screen. "Identity confirmed. How can I be of assistance, Agent Ghost?"

"What?" the Colonel said. "Are you fucking serious?"

Ghost cleared her throat and said, "Please provide what assistance you can to the Colonel."

"Of course, Agent Ghost. Colonel," the man replied, "I'm General Smith Hanson."

"So it *was* all a lie?" the Colonel said.

"Not entirely," the General responded. "There is only one station in orbit around Mars. CrossWorlds Station is both a civilian recreational facility and a military installation." He tapped a few keys on his computer and the facade of civilian clothing vanished, revealing his military uniform. "Now, Colonel, if Agent Ghost is involved, then I assume this is a *very* serious matter. Give me your report."

The Colonel summoned what dignity he still retained after his series of conversations and stood tall. "General, sir, we have a situation." He explained what he knew of the outbreak, and Ghost filled in what she knew above and beyond that. The General took it all in with only a few changes in his countenance. When he had finished, the Colonel asked Collins for a report.

"Quad looks clear, sir. I can hear gunfire, sporadic, near the barracks I'd guess."

"I'm aware of the Nano-Morphine project, Colonel," the General said. "But these side effects are news to me. I'll pass it up to High Command and will get back to you when I can. In the meantime, I'll mobilize a few squads. If you do not have the situation under control when I call back, I'll send them down to assist."

"Thank you, General," the Colonel replied with a salute.

The General saluted and cut the transmission.

Ghost started for the door. The Colonel, still standing at attention, turned his head to look over his shoulder at her. "Any chance you'll explain how an ex-marine has higher clearance than an active duty colonel?"

Ghost paused but didn't turn around. "There's only one person alive now who has the authority to revoke my clearance, and he's been busy running the solar system." She didn't wait for a response or any further questions. She willed herself invisible and quickly faded to transparency.

"Strange girl," the Colonel said.

Collins nodded absently, attention still focused on the quad, gun poised as he scanned the area for threats.

COMPLICATIONS

Tex exhaled and focused his pulse rifle sights on the thing's head. It wore a uniform with the insignia of a private on its shoulder. But now it was something else, flesh dripping from its face, roaring in fury as rounds tore open its chest. The rifle felt foreign in his hands. He tried to tell himself it was a Winchester, like the one he used to have back home. He squeezed the trigger and a single charged round shot forth and split the thing's head open. It crumpled to the floor of the barracks with a squishy thud.

"Good shot," Sarge said. "Maybe you should hang onto that thing."

"Not a chance," Tex replied. "Switching back to my six-shooters as soon as this is done."

"It was worth a shot, Sarge," Tank said. He took a step forward and pulled the trigger on the giant railgun he held. The round struck another rean-imated marine in the chest, sending him flying through the air and slamming into the opposite wall. The same round continued its journey into another re-animated marine, piercing its neck and removing the thing's head cleanly from its shoulders. "I, on the other hand, am totally keeping this fucking thing!" He fired again, the round tearing the left cheek off another of the re-animated marines before hitting one of the bunk beds, sending it screeching across the floor. The thing stood there a second, exposed jaw falling slack in a silent scream, then it took a shaky step forward.

Sarge laughed as he aimed his rifle and took a quick shot, dropping the reanimated marine. "Good luck clearing that one with the Colonel."

"Aww, you ain't gonna put in a good word for me, sir?"

"Government property," Sarge said. "You remember how that is."

Tank faltered and almost dropped the railgun. He recovered it with only a minor shift in his balance. He sighed loudly, trying to cover up the fumble with the exaggerated expression. "Yeah, sir, I remember."

Sarge noticed Tank's fumble and eyed him with growing concern. "Carry on, soldier, clear this building."

Tex and Tank acknowledged the order and moved forward together, firing and covering each other in a standard formation. The barracks were almost clear at this point, a short trail of bodies marked their entrance and the only place left to check were the bathrooms. They moved to the bathroom entrance and flanked the doorway. Sarge marched between them and entered the bathrooms.

Two marines stood near the far wall by a row of urinals, pulse rifles raised and ready to fire. A third was crumpled on the floor near them in an expanding pool of blood. She breathed in short gasps and coughed up a spatter of blood. Sarge lowered his rifle and the two marines followed suit. He examined their uniforms, two privates and a corporal. He asked for a report and the corporal stepped forward.

"Corporal Goddard... sir?" Goddard said, eying Sarge suspiciously.

"I'm Sarge, we're Fireteam Zulu. Your Colonel asked us to pop in to help out. What's your situation here?"

"We were clearing out these barracks. Started running low on ammo and were forced to retreat to the bathrooms. Had to drag Jane in with us. One of them things bit her, strangest fuckin' thing I ever seen."

"It *bit* her?"

"Yes, sir. Just grabbed her and started scratching and biting."

"Jane was dead," Bryant interjected, "um, sir. I felt no pulse. She was *dead*."

Jane coughed and moaned in response.

"What about you? They bite either of you?" Sarge asked, eyes focused on Jane.

Goddard frowned and continued, "One of 'em scratched me, but I'll be okay. See? Already stopped bleeding."

Sarge nodded and looked at Bryant, who sniffled and shrugged. Sarge glanced around the bathroom. Urinals, toilet stalls, open shower, large mirror along one wall with four sinks. Large trash can. Three windows. "Looks secure. No other exits?"

"Correct, sir."

"All right. Barracks are secure. We'll move her out to a bed and regroup."

The two marines slung their rifles over their shoulders and followed Sarge out, carrying Jane between them. After laying Jane on a bed, they turned back to face Sarge, Tex, and Tank. Tex and Tank had overheard the conversation in the bathroom and knew what was coming. Sarge sighed, genuine regret written all over his face. "I'm sorry, but we've got a serious problem." The marines tensed but didn't reach for their guns. Sarge looked over their uniforms again. Corporal Goddard. Private Bryant. Private Moashamanididajad, the one they called 'Jane'. He started to explain about the Nano-Morphine and the reanimated soldiers, but it was obvious that the information wasn't sinking in. Their expressions were similar to those he saw when giving his standard *sorry we couldn't get here on time* speech. When he'd finished, he stood there, staring at them.

"So," Goddard said after a long pause, "she's gonna turn into one o' them reanimated soldiers?"

"I've been callin' 'em 're-peeps'," Tank added, a little too cheerfully.

"Yes," Sarge said, "she will. And you as well."

Bryant swore. "Me too then, if it's transmitted by blood." He looked at his exposed arm, where a smear of blood was drying. He wiped at it and inspected the underlying area. "Hey, it already healed."

"So what do we do?" Goddard asked. He could read the despair on

Sarge's face. "Die?"

"There's a chance you can live, depending on a lot of factors. How badly you were hurt. How long it's been since you were hurt. How quickly we can get you to Doctor Carter. And, we're told, a lot depends on how augmented you already are."

It was Goddard's turn to swear. "We're stock soldiers. Nanos regulate everything from sight to speech to shit." He glanced at Jane's convulsing body, shivering in the warmth of the barracks. She didn't have much longer to live without some serious help. But if Bryant was right, she had already died, technically. As he watched her with growing sadness, the large bite mark on her neck sealed itself. Alarmed now, he called attention to it. All eyes focused on Jane as her other wounds closed. She sat up and shook the fogginess from her vision. "Holy shit! You call that somethin' bad?"

"You don't understand," Sarge said. "The Nano-Morphine will kill you. Then it will reanimate you. You might have a couple hours, or days at most, before it's too late. Unless you've had this Martian influenza. That seems to accelerate the effects. The Nano-Morphine has to be neutralized."

"You mean *we* have to be neutralized." Bryant said. He nudged Goddard and added, "Fuck that." He pulled a grenade from his belt with his other hand and deftly popped the pin. The small fragmentation device whirred to life and armed itself with a quiet tone.

Sarge slowly slung his rifle over his shoulder and held out both hands. "Woah, son, hold on there. Don't do anything stupid."

"I ain't dyin' easy," Bryant said.

Goddard unslung his rifle and pointed it at Sarge. "Me neither. We ain't just gonna let you shoot us. We're gettin' outta here."

"We can't let you leave," Tank said. "This Nano-Morphine can't leave this base."

Tank took a step forward and slowly raised the railgun. Goddard swung his rifle to honor the threat and pulled the trigger. The rifle roared and pumped rounds into Tank's chest, sending him staggering backward against the wall. The railgun clattered to the floor. Tank's armor stopped the bulk of the rounds, but several struck him in his arms and sent splatters of blood against the wall behind him. Goddard took a step back and stopped firing. He ordered Bryant to help Jane, but she was already on her feet and moving with them, frightened look on her face not coupled with any hesitation on her actions.

Tex aimed his pulse rifle, but Sarge pushed it down. "No, hold your fire."

Goddard took another step back and was about to say something when he noticed Tank flexing his unharmed arms. "Mother-*fuckers*!" he shouted. "You're all jacked up on this shit too!"

"No," Sarge said, "it's not like that."

"Damned liars, trying to keep this Nano-Morphine to yourselves, huh? You're no better than the pirates you claim to fight!" Goddard said, continuing to back up. He fired another volley into Tank, aiming to put as many rounds around Tank's armor as possible. Another shower of blood erupted from Tank's body and splattered over the floor and wall. Tank fell to one knee and grunted, the quick drop in altitude the only thing that saved his head from taking the last few rounds.

Tex raised his rifle and fired a burst, hitting Bryant in the arm, sending a spray of blood over Goddard. Bryant faltered, but Jane grabbed him and pulled him along. Sarge unslung his rifle, and with a sad look on his face, he took aim.

Goddard backed up all the way to the exit door, fired a final shot that struck Tank in the neck as he was trying to rise, and called for Bryant and Jane to hurry up. Sarge fired a round into Goddard's thigh. Goddard grunted, then looked at his own leg and watched as the hole slowly stitched itself closed. Jane ducked past Goddard and started running from the building. Bryant tossed the grenade onto the floor and fled out the side door, with Goddard following.

Sarge and Tex dove into the bathroom, with Tank close behind them. The grenade exploded, shaking the building and overloading their augmented hearing. The explosion ripped a hole in the ceiling and shattered several nearby bunks, sending a shower of shrapnel into the bathroom after them. Tank was only halfway through the door when the grenade detonated. He screamed and fell to the floor, large pieces of metal protruding through the armor on his back, blood soaking his shirt. He rose to his arms, shaking, blood dripping from his ears. He convulsed and his shredded armor fell off, taking the sopping wet shirt with it. Sarge and Tex scrambled to him and started pulling the shrapnel from his back. Tank moaned with each piece they extracted, shaking on knees and unsteady hands, until there were no more pieces they could see.

"Dammit, don't you die on me!" Sarge shouted over the ringing in his ears.

Tank moaned. The wounds in his back started to close, paused, spewed out another batch of blood, then resumed closing. The worst of the wounds closed itself as they watched, but the rest stayed open. Then another started to close and stopped. Tank groaned again as a wave of pain flooded his senses. "Shit that burns," he said. He shook his head and winced as his forearms gave out and sent him face first into the floor.

"You feel that?"

"Yes... sir, it..." his voice trailed off into another groan as he clenched his jaw. His body shuddered as Sarge pressed lightly on a scorch mark on his lower back.

Tex felt for Tank's pulse and nodded. "We should get him to the infirmary, Sarge."

Sarge agreed, and together they picked up Tank and carried him out of the barracks.

BLIP

I t wasn't more than a cursory notice on the Solar Net. If he wasn't actively tracking her, he probably wouldn't have even seen the message.
But Woden was tracking Ghost now, and the blip that got sent out on
the Net was very noticeable to him.

Ghost clearance, MP-2184

That's all it said, but it was enough to inform anyone who was looking
for Ghost that she was alive, well, and currently on Mars. Anyone with the
proper clearance, at least. One had to have enough clearance to know where
the bases on Mars were. Woden had a rough idea, but trying to land there to
pursue her would probably be suicide. If not for him, then certainly for his
ship.

Woden had his ship on autopilot, cruising its way to Mars to meet up
with Ghost and Fireteam Zulu. He didn't need this annoyance thrown on top
of his already daunting task. He double-checked the navigation coordinates
in his computer, then turned his full attention to his Solar Net console. With a

slight sigh and a mild expletive, he plugged the data cable into the base of his skull.

*   *   *

Woden's avatar appeared in the Solar Net near the construct for Mars, as that was the node he was currently closest to. The connection was terrible. Every two virtual steps forward resulted in him warping back one. Another complication to slow him down. There were several notes he'd left himself to upgrade the network interface card in his ship, but he connected to the Solar Net so seldom that he never got around to taking care of the issue. It was only times like this that reminded him; and he usually left himself yet another note to get the work done.

He staggered to a more secluded spot, away from the other people currently logged into the node. That helped a little, reducing his lag to one back-warp per every three steps. Not a huge change, but it would have to do. It at least made typing less annoying, and that was all he needed for the moment.

He opened a command window and issued a command to filter out all the non-encrypted traffic. Most of the civilian chatter disappeared with that. His connection was now almost at a speed he considered to be normal. He glanced around the building he was hiding behind. From there, he could see a few AI constructs waiting for connections. The frame rate was not as good as what he'd get on Earth, but it was better than a normal connection on Mars. But he wasn't here for surfing.

He returned his attention to his command window, and searched for a checksum that matched the message he'd seen. He found the message and analyzed the encryption header. Military, of course. The origin was a bit of a surprise. He was expecting the message to have been sent from the Mars base, but it was instead sent by a general on CrossWorlds Station.

The message was being broadcast to the UEF fleet, the bulk of which was currently in orbit near Luna. Woden traced the message to a dispatcher node on Deimos, where it was waiting for the next data pulse to be sent back to Earth. He floated up into the virtual air and accelerated toward the node.

While he worked his way there, he contemplated his next action. He could issue a fake response to the packet. But the General would probably see through that. If nothing else, the response would be too soon, raising suspicion. Checking some of the internals of the forged message might reveal something about the sender. He could schedule the fake response to appear at a later time, but why bother with that deception? Simply deleting the message would accomplish the same thing, without exposing any of Woden's location information. The General wouldn't even realize anything went wrong. His computer would detect the message deletion, but would assume it was lost in transmission and re-send it. The message would be delayed long enough for Woden to take out Ghost, or at the very least would give her enough time to be somewhere else.

He reached the node and circled around to the side of the virtual dispatch building. His trace indicated the message was inside, somewhere, waiting for the timed relay to Earth. He fumbled through his list of programs, looking for the right tools for hacking into the node. A message indicator slid into his view, announcing that his ship was nearing Mars. The dispatch node was warming up to dispatch the messages. A single tone emanated from the structure and a countdown timer appeared in the air beside it.

Out of time, he thought. *Time for the nuclear option.*

Scrolling down his list of programs, he found the one he wanted, tucked all the way at the bottom of the list, with his own warnings etched side-by-side with the big red warning from the programmer who had made it. Woden had never tested it. Never had a reason to. The programmer who posted it in one of the few remaining illicit corners of the Solar Net had posted a video showing the virus taking down a server in Korea. News reports the following day proved it wasn't a hoax. That was good enough for Woden. He launched it at the node.

*   *   *

Half a second later, Woden was sitting in his chair, once more conscious and staring at his Solar Net console. He detached the cable to his skull with a trembling hand and dropped it to the floor. A cleaning robot worked its way to him and sanitized the cable as it slowly wound its way back into his chair. The console screen was solid black, a single white line blinking in the upper left corner. The machine beeped, the screen cleared, and the Home screen ap-

peared, welcoming him to the Mars node. Deimos, it said, was currently having a networking problem, and the connection to Earth was currently down.

RUNNING

G oddard pointed to the ground transports as the three of them ran out of the barracks. The explosion behind them shook the ground and caused Bryant to stumble. He fell face-first into the soil. Jane helped him to his feet and the three resumed running. When they reached the transport, Bryant jumped into the front seat and started the engine. Jane and Goddard got into the back and reloaded their weapons with spare clips from the transport's munitions locker.

Bryant shifted the transmission and pressed on the accelerator. "Where we going, sir?" he asked.

"There's a space ship in the squash colony we raided earlier," Goddard replied. "Looked like it's been there a while, but should still fly. Could take that to orbit."

"Then what?" Jane asked. She motioned for Goddard to turn around and yanked a large piece of shrapnel from his back. When he saw it he burst out laughing.

"Who cares!" Goddard replied. "We can do whatever we want. In-fuck-ing-vincible. I'm loving this shit. I guess Fireteam Zulu ain't gonna be the only game in town anymore. You ever see the outer solar system? Maybe hang out there a while, fight some pirates, shit like that."

"We'll be heroes," Bryant shouted over the sound of the engine.

"Don't give a shit 'bout that," Goddard said. "Let the pirates do the dirty work, then take the shit from the pirates."

Jane sat on one of the seats and looked up at Goddard. "What about what they said? We feel nothing, then die."

"You believe those assholes? You saw what happened to that big guy when I shot him? They were lying-"

"They weren't lying Goddard, not entirely," Jane said. "I... I died back there. I know I did."

"Really?" asked Goddard. "I figured Bryant was shitting me. So, what was it like?"

Jane shivered. "Nothing. Just emptiness. I had a lot of thoughts go through my head, then it all just sort of... ended."

Goddard pursed his lips and nodded slowly. "So... then you just sort of... woke up from it?"

"Yeah."

"Sounds like a dream to me."

Bryant started to voice his agreement, then cursed and jerked the steering wheel to avoid a small ditch.

Jane clenched her fists and punched the seat. "No, not like that, not at all."

"Riiiight... anyway, I still say they were lying, probably didn't want any competition. I bet those fuckers are rich, that's why they didn't want us to compete with them. We should get another person and have our own vigilante fireteam. Screw this marine salary bullshit."

"Damn right," Bryant agreed and pushed the accelerator down more. He knew the route to the squash colony, having driven this same vehicle there on their last mission. The colony grew in the distance as they neared it. He could see the space ship on the landing pad and steered for it. "Hey Goddard, you think you can fly that thing?"

Goddard looked out the viewport at the transport ship. It was big enough

to bring the whole colony here, all the way from Earth. Probably reconfig-
ured as a cargo ship after they landed but that wouldn't change the maneuverability much. He knew he could fly it. He would have preferred a combat
ship, but this would have to do. He was tired of living by the military's rules
and regulations. Things might have been different if he had volunteered, but
when his parents passed away days before his eighteenth birthday, the government drafted him into the marines. One more day of forced drills and
barked orders would have driven him over the edge anyway. This gift of im-
mortality was too good to be true, and came at just the right time.

"Yeah I can fly it," Goddard said. "We should swing by CrossWorlds
Station. My brother's there. He's pissed at the military too." He bit his tongue.
He wasn't sure of how his brother felt about the military. He was a year
younger and seemed to acclimate to the service more easily than he had.
Maybe he truly liked being a marine and wouldn't dream of deserting.

Goddard had to try. He was family.

Bryant brought the ground transport to a halt, kicking up a dust cloud
that obscured their vision for half a minute. When the bulk of it had cleared,
Jane hit the switch to open the back hatch. They filed out and sprinted to the
cargo ship. They boarded and soon were strapped into the chairs on the
bridge.

Goddard swiveled in his pilot's chair and punched at the controls, flipping switches and hitting buttons in the right sequence. The engines came to
life and purred during their warm-up routine. He ran his fingers over the console, feeling the whirring controls like a lover's body. *My ship*, he thought.
This is now my ship.

"What do we call ourselves?" Bryant asked.

"What?" Goddard snapped.

"I mean, are we going to be another fireteam or something? Fight
pirates? What are we going to call ourselves?"

Goddard mulled the question as he instructed the navigation controls to
plot a course to CrossWorlds Station. "We'll call ourselves..." he said then
paused. It was a ludicrous question, but Bryant was staring at him anyway,
waiting for some kind of response. He didn't really care about fighting pi-

rates, and certainly wasn't going to spend his life looking out for anyone else, not in that way at least. Pirates could do what they wanted. It didn't matter much to him, except that it seemed the pirates were the richest of them all. Raid the pirates, amass some wealth, keep the ship flying. That's all that really mattered at this point -- to keep going. To keep being free from the controlling military. Goddard looked at Bryant, who was still patiently awaiting a response. He shrugged and said, "We'll call ourselves free."

"Goddard, damn it, you *will* respond," the Colonel's voice barked over the communication channel of the ship. "Go-"

Goddard flipped a switch and the Colonel's voice was silenced. He continued working at the controls as if nothing were wrong.

"They'll come after us," Jane said.

"Who? Fireteam Zulu? Bah, let them come. Let them try."

Jane sulked. She wasn't thinking of Fireteam Zulu. She was thinking of the military. They didn't look too kindly on deserters. She had regrets, sure, but her most ambitious plan to date was to serve the rest of her term and take a discharge. She never planned anything like this.

SURVEILLANCE

G host leaned against the wall of the Colonel's office and waited. In all her training, one thing she had learned was that the most valuable bits of information usually came when people thought they were alone. It was just a matter of time for something important to be said. No amount of interrogation or torture could substitute. People often said what they were thinking, talking to themselves if need be, anything to find someone willing to listen. It was one of those strange but true maxims that she had learned to accept long ago.

"Strange girl," the Colonel said.

She turned her gaze, waiting for Collins' response, but he just nodded, attention focused outside. He raised his pulse rifle, aiming at something she couldn't see from her location. Finger poised over the trigger but not constricting. She considered moving, but he lowered the barrel before his action became interesting enough to warrant movement. Still, he had seen something, and reacted instantly. She'd seen him handle the reanimated marines earlier, and seeing him not fire his weapon was almost as interesting as seeing how well he had handled it in combat.

Sound of small arms fire in the distance and something that sounded like a railgun, muffled slightly by the confines of a building. She'd heard more than her fair share of combat. This was just one more war. There was another railgun shot, and then a pause. She watched and waited, but neither of the two men moved a muscle. After several long, tense minutes, another round of small arms fire started in the barracks. Short bursts of pulse rifle fire. Then an explosion, small yield, probably a fragmentation grenade.

"Sir!" Collins, startled, pointing out toward the barracks.

"What is it, Sergeant?"

"Three figures running toward the garage, sir."

Ghost leaned and looked out the window. She squinted and zoomed in, framing each face in turn. She didn't recognize them but knew that Collins and the Colonel would. She recorded an image of each face, as well as she could frame it. One of them stumbled, and as she focused on him she could see a large gash on his shoulder seal itself. She turned back to Collins and the Colonel and studied their faces. No sign of recognition.

"Times like this make me wish I had some of those bionic eyes," the Colonel said with a sigh.

"Me too, sir."

Norms? Ghost thought. *Both of them... but how could a Norm have made those shots earlier?*

The Colonel turned back to his adjutant's console and typed some commands. Ghost had a clear line of sight over his shoulder. He typed commands and a window opened, local surveillance program linked to cameras all over the base. A progress bar started moving across the window. When it had filled, the machine beeped and displayed a profile. She confirmed the face match. Goddard, a corporal. Another face appeared, Bryant, the one who had stumbled. And then a name that made Ghost wince, but the image matched the third person she had seen running. She snapped a shot of each personnel record. It was only the first page of each, barely more than name, rank, serial number, and a picture. It was enough to know who they were, but not enough to really know how dangerous they were going to be. Or what they would do. She needed more information.

"Jane?" Collins asked.

The Colonel hit another key and said, "Goddard, what's going on, soldier?"

No response.

"Goddard! Damn it, what are- what the hell is he doing?"

"Bad communication, sir?" Collins asked.

"Looks like it was cut off."

Collins glanced back outside. He shifted to his other foot, hands starting to shake. Sunlight glinting off fresh sweat on his forehead. He clenched and relaxed his free hand several times. Ghost smirked, hidden in the shadows, invisible to both. *Now for the payoff*, she thought.

"Sir, I... I need to tell you something," Collins started. "I should have said something... I mean, earlier, I should have-"

"Spit it out, marine."

"Goddard has been saying a lot of anti-military things lately, sir. At night, mostly, in the barracks. Going on about how upset he was, how it wasn't what he signed up for, things like that."

"You're right, Collins."

"Sir?"

"You should have said something earlier. That kind of talk needs to be quelled the moment it happens."

"I know sir. Every time he started, I'd make him stop. I'm sorry I didn't say anything earlier."

"Well it's too late to do anything about that now," the Colonel said. He hit another command key on the computer console and a map of the local area appeared. A bright green dot blipped and moved to the North. "Looks like they're going to that squash colony. Damn it all, probably heading for the cargo ship there. I'll have to mark the lot of them as deserters. It's the only way we'll be able to stop them at this point. Who knows what pilots we have remaining from this mess."

"Deserters?" Collins asked. "Jane..."

The Colonel didn't look like he picked up on her name, but Ghost did. She could see the pain in Collins' face. She'd seen that look before, mostly in the mirror when she was a much younger and more naive girl named Shelly. Then once in South Africa, on the face of a young politician pleading for the life of a homely girl standing behind him. Love. But there was something else mixed in with it, a sort of indecision, reluctance, something holding him back. *The worst kind of love*, she thought.

Ghost turned her gaze back to the Colonel, who was staring at his console screen. He tapped out another sequence and a new window opened. He leaned in closer and studied the lines as they scrolled by.

"The cargo transport's life support system is registering three occupants," he said.

"Can you prevent it from taking off?" Collins asked.

"No, ship's too old."

"Where are they going?"

The Colonel watched the data feed scroll by on his screen. "Oh God," he said, fingers on his hands clutching at the table as if he were about to fall out of his chair. "The navigation system reports a direct course for CrossWorlds Station."

Ghost slipped out and ran across the quad. Behind her, she heard the Colonel shouting Goddard's name again. She had to get to Sarge. He had to know what was going on.

When she was far enough from the Colonel's building, she stopped and focused. She could feel familiar presences in the medical offices. Tex and Sarge, strong feelings clouding their minds, overloading any attempt she could possibly make to read what they were thinking. Tank was there too, but his thoughts were faint, staggered. Something was wrong. She opened her eyes and hurried into the medical office.

OVERLOADED

Tank lay as still as he could on the examination table nearest the doctor's office. Sarge and Tex had plopped him down on his rear end and forced him onto his stomach, which had sent a fresh wave of pain through him. He hadn't been injected with Nano-Morphine very long ago but he had already grown accustomed to not feeling pain. Something felt right about that, like he was a more effective soldier because he could fight without the distraction of pain. He was back to normal now though, complete with all the aches and pains from the combat he had spent most of his life participating in. Now the others wanted him to lay there on his stomach while they connected him to the automated examination equipment. His bare back was exposed to the air, his body shuddering with every breath as his wounds leaked blood in small streams that pooled on the table beside him. Walking wasn't so bad, but laying down was brutal. The pain was so intense, he was fighting to hold back from crying.

"What the hell does this crap mean?" Tex asked. He pointed at the machine's readout and tapped the screen. His touch expanded a list, showing more statistics. "Seriously, Sarge, what the hell does this all mean?"

"I don't know. See if you can patch me into Carter's ship," Sarge said.

"Will do." Tex moved to the console and worked at the connections. The system was off, and wouldn't turn on. He examined the pulse rifle burns and traced a circle around one with his finger. "Looks like the power supply took a hit."

"There a spare?" Sarge asked.

Tex explored the cabinets beneath the communications equipment and rummaged through the cables and boxes. He pulled one box out, read the label, and blew a cloud of dust off its surface. "Yeah, there's a spare. Been here a while, but it's in better shape than *that* one."

Tex opened the door covering the previous power supply and detached the cables from the box. After replacing the shot unit with the new one, he reattached the cables and flipped a switch. The communication console whirred to life. Tex reviewed the recent call list and found an entry for Doctor Carter on his research ship. He patched together a forged packet based on the same encryption key and transmitted it.

Tank stirred, trying to lift himself at least partly off the table. Sarge pressed down on his shoulder, forcing him back to the cold steel. A fresh wave of pain ripped through his backside and he yelped involuntarily, then bit down to keep further outbursts in check.

An image of the research vessel's bridge shimmered into view on the screen. Carter moved into view and started talking but there was no audio. Tex dropped to the floor and climbed under the computer console. He worked with steady hands in the low light to patch the audio cable to a working node. A spark lit up his field of view when he found a live wire. He patched the audio to it and a speaker in the ceiling crackled to life.

"-the Colonel? Sarge?" Carter asked.

"We're here," Sarge said. "Having problems with audio, missed most of that. Can I patch exam computer data to you?"

Carter flinched. "Um. Sure, I guess." He explained the procedure, a simple combination of buttons to press on the automated examiner. Tex followed his instructions and soon Carter was viewing the data, eyes looking at another screen, slowly scanning side to side. "Looks fine to me. Extensive trauma to the back but the patient should live. A single tube of patching gel should suffice."

"Nothing... unusual?" Sarge asked, taking a glance back to Tank. His heart lurched when he saw the grimace on Tank's face.

"No. Why?"

"That's from Tank."

Carter blinked, shook his head, blinked again. "Wait. Your teammate who was infected with the Nano-Morphine?"

"Yes."

"What happened?" Carter asked, leaning in closer to the screen.

"What do you mean?"

"How..." he started, then turned and typed something, fingers loudly punching the keys on his old keyboard. "How did you remove the nanos without injuring him?"

"That's just it, Doc," Sarge said. "We didn't do anything. Crazy marine shot him for a while and then a grenade blew up behind him. The wounds in his back are mostly from shrapnel."

"Interesting," Carter said, leaning back in his chair. He turned completely around and said something Sarge couldn't hear. He nodded and turned back to Sarge. "I'll check," he said, typing commands on his keyboard. He turned his head to inspect another screen on his side of the connection. A hand appeared in the window, pointing. "You're right!" Carter said. "Yes, it makes sense."

"What makes sense?" Sarge asked.

"Sarge, my colleagues think that the trauma he sustained to his back shorted out the Nano-Morphine. It's the only thing that makes sense given what we're seeing."

"Come again?"

Carter sighed. "Tank sustained so much trauma in such a short time that the Nano-Morphine couldn't keep up. In a word, we think they were overloaded. Burnt out. They are only machines, after all."

Sarge took a few steps toward the screen, stopping at the entrance to the small office. "What about his other augmentations? You had mentioned the

Nano-Morphine bots exerting control and conscripting others to do their job?"

Carter was silent for a few moments, scanning something else on his screen. "All of this looks normal to me, Sarge. Overloading them must have broken the connection they had with the other systems in his body, assuming they had even been in there long enough to conscript others."

Tank planted his palms on the table and pushed himself up, rotating to a sitting position, sweat pouring down his face from the exertion. He took a few staggered breaths, then opened his eyes. "You mean... I'm gonna... be fine?" he said between back spasms.

"Well, yes, I'd say so. There's no trace of active Nano-Morphine in the reports we're receiving. I'm afraid I'm not that well-versed in military augmentations. But the machine you're hooked up to should have a routine for diagnostics. What?" He glanced over his shoulder for a moment. "My colleague says there's a green button, probably labeled 'diag'."

Tank looked at the machine next to the table he was sitting on. "Yes, I see it." He pressed the button. "Hey," he said. "I'm blind! My vision's gone... wait... well this is strange. All I can see is black, with green text. This okay. That okay. Now it says, 'Augmentations operational.' Has a blinking warning about blood loss, but it says that's being corrected."

"Thanks, Carter," Sarge said. "That's good news, but we got work to do. Three marines, all of them infected, jumped a ground transport out of here before we could stop them. We have-"

"It gets worse," Ghost's voice interrupted as she slowly materialized in the room behind Sarge. "Those marines went to a local farming colony and jumped on a ship. They've plotted a course."

Sarge took the bad news with no more than a slight nod of his head. "Where to?"

"CrossWorlds."

Carter moved closer to the console and said something rude to the people behind him. "Wait, what? Can you repeat that?"

Ghost did.

"Jesus," Carter said. "There's at least ten thousand civilians on that station at any given time, and only a platoon of soldiers to protect them."

"Quite a few more soldiers than that, actually," Ghost said. "I've made contact with General Hanson on CrossWorlds. We will have his full cooperation." Ghost glanced at Sarge, who nodded in response. Carter started to protest but Ghost held up her hand to silence him. "Those people," she said, "will have Fireteam Zulu to help protect them as well."

"You really think another four marines will make a difference?"

"Always," Sarge replied. "Carter, see if you can call the General and tell him how to kill these things, should an outbreak happen there. If there are any other procedures for containment that he or the Colonel here need to know, take care of it." Carter nodded and the screen went black. Sarge turned to Ghost and asked, "Did you get any intel on those three marines?"

"I saw their files, but only a glance, and only the first pages," replied Ghost.

"Tex," Sarge said. "Go to the Colonel. I need personnel reports on Bryant, Goddard, and some name I can't pronounce. They called her 'Jane'. Need to know who we're dealing with."

Tex acknowledged the order and sprinted outside.

"Yeah," Tank said, sliding off the table and planting his feet on the floor with a grunt. He winced briefly but stood tall, clenching his teeth as he flexed his massive muscles. "Cause they obviously don't know who *they're* dealing with. Fuckers should know it takes more than a grenade to stop a tank!"

"Ghost," Sarge said, "see what you can do about Tank's wounds, then meet us back on Zulu Prime. I'm gonna see about resupplying our ship."

Ghost searched nearby drawers and located a tube of patching gel, which she squirted onto Tank's wounds. The gel adhered to his skin and stopped the bleeding immediately. Tank sighed with relief as the painkillers numbed the nerves in his back. The gel worked wonders, but was in short supply in most battle groups and used sparingly. She emptied an entire tube on his back and pocketed a second one she found beside it in the drawer.

She wrapped an arm around Tank, but he gently removed it. They exited the medical offices and started the long walk back to Zulu Prime. They saw Sarge walking out of the armory with a new suit of armor and a pulse cannon, gifts for his recently fixed soldier. Tank accepted them with a wide smile and carried them onto the ship.

Sarge started a return trip to the armory but stopped after only two steps. He saw Tex walking toward them with two other figures.

"The Colonel," Ghost offered, "and a sergeant who was with him."

Sarge approached the trio and extended his hand to the Colonel.

"You must be Sarge," the Colonel said with a scowl. "Normally I expect salutes, but since you aren't active military..." He accepted Sarge's hand with a firm grip, slight tremble. It had been a rough day.

"What's the sitrep?" Sarge said. "Seems quiet, we assumed we were done here."

"Base is cleared, far as I know," the Colonel said. "I have two squads of soldiers left. I've tasked them with patrolling and cleanup for now. Doctor Carter mailed us some procedures for neutralizing the remaining Nano-Morphine to prevent further infection. I doubt we have enough supplies to deal with all the blood laying around this base, but... but we have a bigger problem."

"Three marines deserted and jumped a transport to CrossWorlds," Sarge said.

The Colonel blinked, mouth falling open. "How did you-"

"We have our ways," Sarge interrupted. "Just need to know who we're up against."

"I'm afraid I only have standard records on most recruits. I hadn't had much time to get to know them. But Sergeant Collins knew them. I want him to go with you."

"Sir?" Sarge and Collins objected in unison.

"Collins commanded Jane, and has spoken with both Bryant and Goddard, and has acted as leader for all three. He knows them, what they look like, maybe even some insight on who they are and what they'll do. I'm afraid the only intel I can offer is that Goddard has a younger brother stationed on CrossWorlds."

"Well at least that's something," Sarge said. He looked over Collins, sizing him up. He was used to working with only his team, but Collins looked like he could hold his own in combat. He was a sergeant, after all, and after today he was definitely a veteran of at least one combat. "No time to argue the point... All right, we'll take him along. He can brief us on the way."

"Besides," the Colonel added, "Collins is up for retirement next week anyway. Unless he chooses to re-enlist... Didn't think so. After these last few hours, can't say I blame you. Might as well stay on CrossWorlds a bit. Take a vacation. I know I could use one."

Collins turned and saluted the Colonel, crisp and perfect. Sarge watched and waited. He knew a good soldier when he saw one.

Sarge took Collins and Tex into the armory to gather more ammunition and supplies, which the Colonel agreed to. He frowned at the broken armory door but figured that was the least of his worries at this point. High Command would have to resupply their base. With all the dead marines laying about, some missing supplies and a broken door were barely anything worth making a fuss over. The Colonel was going to give the idiots in High Command ten rations of shit over this Nano-Morphine project.

Sarge led Collins back to the ship carrying what useful materials they could find. He closed the hatch on Zulu Prime and ordered Tex to strap in for liftoff. Sarge directed Collins to his chair, figuring it was central to the others, and would make conversation a little easier for him. There were plenty of other empty chairs left, but Sarge opted to strap himself into a bunk instead. He needed a quick rest anyway. He looked at his bunk, and almost went to it, but realized that he needed some time alone. There was too much noise in here. It was rare times like this that he wished he had kept the sergeant's cabin for himself. He cast a glance at Ghost, and nodded toward what was now her room. She responded with a curt nod. Sarge left the room and went into Ghost's room. He climbed into her berth, strapped in, and closed his eyes. He listened absently to the rest of his team and Collins making introductions, followed by several minutes of idle chatter. The engines roared and drowned out the conversations, giving Sarge a moment of peace.

The calm before the storm.

CROSSWORLDS

G oddard watched as CrossWorlds Station grew in the viewport ahead of them. Bryant made some comment but he wasn't paying attention. Probably overwhelmed by the size of the place. Goddard had seen it before, once, and wasn't that eager to return. The place was always overcrowded. He didn't care much for games anyway. There were more important things to do than plug into a video game for a week.

"All right," he said, "here's how it's gonna be. We're here on shore leave. Shouldn't be that hard to make them think someone lost the paperwork, 'specially with all the chaos down in that base at the moment. We get in, get to my little brother, and get out before they have a chance to verify our orders."

"Damn right," Bryant added.

Jane squirmed in her seat, feeling an itch in her lower back that usually indicated something going terribly wrong. The last time she felt that was two days ago, the night before all this started. She found herself thinking of Collins, wondering how she was ever going to explain this or if she'd even see him again. She sighed and slouched in her seat as best she could, choosing instead to focus her thoughts on the space station that was slowly filling the viewport.

CrossWorlds Station was built shortly after Mars terraforming began. Someone at Anderton Enterprises had the idea for what they considered to be the ultimate resort -- a place where you could relax, play games, socialize, or detach from reality completely if you chose. The designer wasn't far from the mark. The Station was the most popular destination in the entire solar system. Everyone who could afford a vacation on CrossWorlds Station bought one. Everyone who couldn't tried their hardest to figure out how to get there anyway.

The Station was the size of a small moon. Two central spires of living quarters stretching parallel to each other half a mile in each direction from the center rings, massive constructs that wrapped around the spires like a belt the size of a small city. The central area held four docking bays and all of the Station's recreation. There were essentially four sections of CrossWorlds Station that visitors had access to.

First were the living quarters, varying from basic rooms the size of a roomy coffin to deluxe quarters fit for royalty. Where you stayed depended entirely upon how much money you had. It wasn't uncommon for security to find a dozen or more people sleeping in a room meant for two, usually rotating their sleep schedules to cut down on costs.

Second were the public spa sections, modeled after what the Romans had created, where visitors could relax and be pampered in any way that modern science allowed. The robotic masseurs were widely regarded as the best in the solar system, and the Station also offered services from psionic adjutants who could *really* clear your mind and wipe all thoughts of your day job away. The mind wipe wasn't a permanent change, but it lasted long enough for a typical vacation. There was no finer way to spend a vacation than to completely detach from the life you were taking a break from. But the most popular amenity by far was the zero gravity aerobics chambers, especially at night when couples could rent them for private sessions.

Third were the gaming decks, where visitors could play a variety of games against each other. Everything from chess to checkers to card games and almost everything in between. The Station had regular tournaments that often drew the attention of crowds on Earth and Mars, who would tune in on subspace television channels to watch their favorite competitors play. The players in the top ten of the tournament ladders always won CrossWorlds prizes -- usually room upgrades and extra time to stay on the Station. The top five players were regulars who won prizes so highly valued that they were able to live on the Station full time.

Finally were the virtual worlds, everything from prehistoric to medieval to futuristic. At any given time, up to two-thirds of the Station's visitors would be plugged into the virtual worlds, brain first, living their ultimate role-playing fantasies together. Many people had Turina Jacks installed specifically for playing in these games. The Station employed a staff of over three hundred programmers dedicated to crafting new content for the virtual worlds. CrossWorlds had gained its name from this feature, as players could take the skills and items they had gained in one world into another, with minor adjustments. A powerful sword in a fantasy realm would become a powerful rifle in a modern one, for instance. CrossWorlds Station also employed a staff of forty psychologists to help deal with problems related to game addiction. They were the most overworked people on the Station.

But escaping reality was only part of the Station. Beneath the facade of virtualized entertainment were miles of twisting corridors, barracks, and a completely hidden docking bay filled with warships. A dedicated crew worked around the clock to maintain the ships and keep them armed and ready for action at a moment's notice. CrossWorlds had been attacked by pirates once, and the current CEO of Anderton Enterprises vowed it would never happen again. Such attacks, after all, were quite bad for business. The trillions she spent on military contracts and hardware paled in comparison. The next attempted attack was repelled with extreme prejudice. That was years ago, but the soldiers and crew on the Station were still paid well to be vigilant.

Goddard was worried that that vigilance would be a problem.

Whether they managed to convince his brother to tag along or not, once the military figured out they weren't really on leave, some of those warships would undoubtedly be deployed to capture or neutralize them. And they were in a transport without weapons of any kind. As he saw it, the only solution was an even riskier proposition: they had to steal a warship. Only then would they be able to defend themselves, or, with any measure of luck, accelerate fast enough to evade pursuit altogether.

Either way, he knew that they would always have to run.

"Unidentified civilian transport, please acknowledge," came a voice over the communication channel.

"Transport one three," Goddard said, reading the ID tag off the console in front of him, "uh.. niner niner four zulu alpha one."

There was a pause. "You aren't registered. Last minute vacation?"

"Something like that. We're marines, on leave." He hated having to divulge their military status, but he knew unregistered transports would not be allowed to land at the Station. His brother once told him over a video message that his primary duty was turning back passengers who hadn't made reservations. Goddard and the others couldn't afford tickets at their pay grade, so the only way onto the base was as a marine. Free shore leave for up to a week, once every two years -- one of the few perks of the service. But using this perk meant they had to enter as military personnel.

Another pause on the com channel. "Proceed to Docking Bay Five, land, and wait for contact."

"Roger," Goddard said with a wince. Docking Bay Five -- the military hangar -- was both a blessing and a curse. He knew that was the only way they could get onto CrossWorlds. It was their only chance at acquiring a better ship when leaving. But it was also going to be the most watched, most protected part of the Station. He flipped off the com channel and grasped the controls. No turning back now. "Alright," he said, "here we go."

FAIR WARNING

The shakes hadn't lasted as long as Collins had expected. They usually hit him during the whole takeoff, but today they were less pronounced than usual. Something with the excitement, perhaps. Too many things to focus on at once. Collins was dreading the impending confrontation. It wasn't Goddard or Bryant. Dealing with assholes didn't bother him much. He was more senior than them so he didn't have any problem pushing them around. If push came to shove, well, he'd seen their scores on the firing range. Even against their augments, he knew he could take out at least one of them by himself. But Jane was a different story. And he was starting to admit to himself that he loved her. That complicated things.

When the ship stopped shaking, he opened his eyes. A small window to his left showed the vast black sea around them. His body lifted a little then held when it hit the tension of the straps. The artificial gravity kicked in and pulled him back to his seat.

Tank unstrapped first, standing and stretching like he had just awakened. He watched Collins pull at the straps and moved to help. "It sticks. You have to twist it, like this," he said, twisting the buckle almost sideways before pulling. The clasp opened with a sharp ping.

"Thanks," Collins said.

"So what's your deal?" Tex asked. "That Colonel said you were due for retirement? You don't look old enough for that."

"Twelve years active service," Collins said.

"That's a far cry from the thirty required to retire," Tex replied.

"Last two terms were on Mars, and you can retire after twenty years now if you get enough time off Earth."

"Ah," Tank said, "I remember them talking about the Remote Outpost Bonus. I think they implemented it right after I discharged. My kind of luck."

"News to me," Tex said. "I served four and got out. I had enough fun."

Ghost walked into the room, silent as a cat. She stopped behind Collins and placed her hands on her hips, waiting for a lull in the conversation.

"Well," Collins said, "I barely hit twenty with the bonus, and I'm due for a break. I thought about going career at one point, but-"

"Damn re-peeps?" Tank interrupted.

Collins sighed, thinking of Jane. "Yeah. Something like that."

"What can you tell us about Goddard and the others?" Ghost said.

Collins shook briefly, obviously startled by the undetected intrusion. He whirled to face Ghost and tried to force himself to relax. "Goddard? Well, he's a career asshole," he said, "with a capital A. Self-centered, narcissistic. Not so much evil as totally indifferent to others. He doesn't care what it takes to get what he wants, and when backed into a corner he'll complain loudly. He's got a touch of charisma there, like a politician. He complains in ways that gets people to listen. Then he persuades them to join his cause, whatever that is at the moment.

"Bryant is kind of his lackey. Latched onto him early on and follows his orders. Bryant doesn't have much of a sense of politics, wrong or right, or anything else for that matter. He does what Goddard says, agrees with Goddard, follows him like a puppy. Repeats his words and agrees with them like they're scripture. If Goddard were a pirate, Bryant would be his parrot."

Tex squawked. "Bryant wanna crackah?"

Tank and Collins laughed. Ghost, stone-faced, waited for them to recover before asking, "How dangerous are they?"

"Well," Collins said, "Goddard's a corporal. Trained marine, skilled in all standard-issued weapons. Pretty good tactical skills and marksmanship."

"Standard marine augment mix?" Tank asked. "I'm stronger than-"

"No," Collins replied, "no, he went for speed, agility. He was a wiry guy to begin with and now he can move like lightning if he deems it necessary. There were rumors that he had a second round of augmenting, so don't even count on that description. I've seen him on the practice mats, and in a few fist fights after duty hours, before he made corporal. He'll surprise you. Still, the most dangerous thing about him is probably that the people he does lead, like Bryant, don't question his orders. I'd say he was born to be a leader, but lacked the drive to really pull it off. Charisma mixed with insanity."

"And the parrot?" Tex asked, barely suppressing a chuckle.

Collins shrugged. "Bryant's a tool. Standard marine as far as augmenting and training. My advice is to keep an eye on him, but don't concentrate too much effort. Take down Goddard, and Bryant will fall in line."

"That may have been true before," Ghost said. "Things are different now. Nano-Morphine changes the equation. Bryant's standard augments will probably make him just as dangerous as the other marines we encountered in your base. But an infected speed-augmented marine could be something entirely different."

"True," Collins said. "Speed augmenting is rather rare to begin with, these days. And if he really *did* have twice the issued dose..."

"They never offered me a second dose," Tank said, sounding sad.

"What about the other?" Ghost asked. "The girl they called 'Jane'?"

Before Collins could even form the words, Ghost could already see the answer on his face. "Well," he said, "she's... a good soldier, a good woman. No idea what she's doing with them, except she wasn't too keen on finishing her term of service. I knew she had regrets, but... I never thought she'd desert. Never thought she'd..."

"Alright," Ghost said. "I'll relay the intel to Sarge. You guys get ready. Weasel says we'll dock in twenty minutes."

She left and turned up the hallway toward her room. Behind her, echoes of squawking and laughter. She rolled her eyes and took a deep breath as she stopped before her room. She rapped on the door and entered. Sarge was sitting on her berth, as close to relaxed as she had ever seen him. The door slid shut behind her as she began relaying what Collins had said. Sarge sat there, staring at the floor, breathing slowly and remaining silent through her whole report. When she finished, she stood at attention. For a moment, she thought that maybe he was asleep with his eyes open, for he made no movement. She was about to verbally nudge him when he looked up.

"Sounds like we have two problems to deal with when we encounter them," Sarge said. "Goddard and Bryant."

"Goddard should not be a problem. I'm sure I can move faster than he can, even if he does have a double dose of speed augments. And I believe Collins will be right about Bryant once we've neutralized Goddard. Even with Nano-Morphine in his system, neutralizing him should not be any more difficult than the other marines at that base. Sarge, I believe the real problem is Jane."

"Why?"

"She's an unknown. Without knowing her motivation, she could be a major wild card. And worse..."

"Yes?"

"Collins is in love with her."

Sarge stood and walked to the window, leaned against the hull as he stared out into the black. "That *is* worse," he agreed. "Love certainly complicates our job. Always does," he said, glancing at Ghost's reflection, looking for a reaction but getting none. "Would've been so much easier to just shoot the bastards and bring their bodies back. The military certainly wouldn't mind." He sighed and watched stars drift by for several moments. "All right," he said. "We'll-"

"Hey, Ghost?" came Weasel's voice over the com channel set into the wall. "You there?"

"I'm here," she responded.

"There's a call coming in, for you."

Sarge turned and looked at her. "Who's it from?" he asked.

"Dunno," Weasel replied. "It's encrypted, heavily."

"Put it on screen," Ghost said.

There was a pause while the screen activated, then it filled with static. A burst of white noise, then a beep. The image came into focus and the screen filled with what appeared to be the interior of a small ship. A man sat in the center of the image, looking rather pleased with himself.

"Woden," Ghost said.

"Hello again, Ghost," Woden said. "And *Sarge*, nice to see you too."

Sarge stared at the screen, cold. "You two want a moment alone?"

"No," Ghost said. "Anything he has to say to me, you can hear."

"Are you sure, Shelly dear?" Woden replied.

"Anything you have to say, Woden, I'll repeat to him later anyway."

Woden nodded. "All right. And here I thought you were still pining over me. I'm just giving you a quick call to say I'm nearby."

Sarge nudged Ghost.

"Oh, she hasn't told you yet?" Woden said, arched eyebrow. "How interesting. So much for repeating things to him later."

"We were busy with the military base. Didn't want to cloud his thinking before combat. Woden was sent to capture us," Ghost explained.

"Not... quite..." Woden said, a little too cheerfully. "You see, Shelly dear, there's been a slight miscalculation on my part. I *thought* they wanted you. You know, for Venus Station. Nice little cozy accommodations for one. But, alas, it appears they no longer require your services."

Ghost took a deep breath before responding. "You think-"

"I *know*," Woden interrupted, his face dropping all semblance of cheerfulness. He leaned forward. "They no longer *trust* you. Oh, they still want your friends alive, but they're paying me just as much to bring you to them in a zipper-bag. Thought I'd give you fair warning. The next time we meet, one of us will die."

Ghost reached for the communication panel. "So be it," she said, flipping a switch and ending the conversation.

Sarge returned to his seat on Ghost's berth. "Care to tell me what's going on?"

Ghost continued to stare at the screen. "His name is, or was, Brigandine Owens. I called him 'Brig'. He was being trained at the same facility that trained me to be what I am. Originally, his code name was 'Hunter'."

"Ghost and Hunter. Sounds like the people running that place lacked originality."

"Not really," Ghost said. "They chose simple names that both described our abilities and translated well. We weren't all trained the same way, or even in the same rooms. Whatever skills you were inclined toward, you'd get custom augments and training. My code name was Ghost because I was good at being silent, invisible. I could stay alone for days at a time, sneak into places without anyone noticing me. I'd achieve my objective and sneak out."

"So, Hunter is good at finding people?"

"Exactly. He's a tracker. Clairvoyance to find his prey. Telekinesis to help capture and detain, or to evade his own capture if necessary. Only he didn't finish the training. I have no idea what he's capable of now or how he's progressed. There's no telling what other abilities he's discovered."

Sarge studied Ghost's face as she lapsed into silence. "There's so much of this stuff I don't understand," he said. "So much of your past life that I never asked you about. You know I'm not one to pry. I've always respected your privacy, always avoided these questions. But I need to know some things. I need to know what's going on and what we're up against."

"Then ask," she said, her voice faltering, choked on emotions welling up inside her. For a moment, again, she was Shelly. Confidence flew away with her dignity and she turned her head away from Sarge to hide her flushed features.

"He mentioned services, and Venus Station."

"I'm a ghost, a silent killer, an assassin," Ghost said, then paused. She took a deep breath, wiped at her eyes, and turned to face Sarge before continuing. "That's what I did for them, for years. Those of us in the program used to joke about what we did. We referred to our assignments as 'services', like putting a nondescript label on the killings could help us bury the truth of what we were doing. All of our assignments, every one, was in the spirit of cleaning the government. Everyone who fought against unification was removed. An accident here, an unexplained murder there. It was all done for the good of our race.

"A few years ago, I had an assignment in Beijing. The last general, the leader of the nation formerly known as China, had been captured by United Earth soldiers who were very public about having him. They were planning a trial on some trumped-up war crime charges that never would have stuck. I was sent in to eliminate the general. Without a leader for their military, China collapsed. Now the UEF is united, finally. All nations under one flag. My job was done. Our job, as a collective unit, was done. Every other operative from the program has been sent to Venus Station. Cryogenic storage. Locked away in case the government decides they need us again some day. I didn't want to go.

"So now I'm here, with you. I always figured they'd send someone after me, to take me back to Venus Station. But now... now it's happening, and they no longer want me back. I've put you all in danger."

"Sounds like he had a contract on us anyway."

"That's what he said, on the Orion ship. He was surprised to find me there."

Sarge placed a hand on her shoulder. "All right, I think I understand now." He reached up and brushed a tear away from her cheek. "I think I've heard what I need to know about that. Now what about this guy? Hunter? What did you say his name was now?"

"Woden."

"What does that mean? What sort of man is he?"

"Brig's parents were big medieval history buffs. Hence the name Brigan-dine. It was a type of armor back in those days. The name 'Woden' is Old English, from Anglo-Saxon mythology. Woden was the leader of the Wild Hunt, a phantasmal hunting group usually seen as a precursor to war or death. Woden was the one who carried off the dead. There are other interpre-tations of the name, other links to different mythologies, but that's the one he always liked. As for what sort of man he is? Manipulative. Charming. Decep-tive."

"Is he dangerous?"

"Yes."

"Can we take him?"

"You? No."

Sarge paused and studied her face. She was regaining her composure, returning to her cold countenance. "Can you?" he asked.

Ghost paused and bit her lower lip. She turned to face the viewscreen again, seeing her hazy reflection in the tinted plastic. Finally, she said, "I don't know. I really can't know until I see what he's capable of now. We'd be in for one hell of a fight, that's for sure." Ghost turned her head and looked him in the eyes. "You up for it?"

"Always," Sarge said with a smirk. He pressed the button in his cheek. "Listen up, team. This mission is a capture and detain. We'll try to apprehend the three deserters and deliver them to Doctor Carter for analysis and treatment. Shoot to kill only if you have to." He cut off the transmission.

"You didn't tell them about Woden," Ghost said.

Sarge turned and looked out the window. "Cross that bridge when we have to."

UNSCHEDULED LEAVE

G oddard tapped his boot on the polished floor of the landing bay while the young man in front of him flipped through virtual pages on his computer. Behind him, the ship they'd arrived in made clunking noises as its engines cooled. The Private tapped the edge of the screen again and again, each tap widening his frown. "I'm sorry, sir, I don't see 'Goddard' on the expected list."

"Well what kinda place do you run here?" Goddard snapped.

"I'm only a private, sir, I don't run this place at all."

"Well can't you find someone more senior to work that thing?"

Bryant opened his mouth to add something but Jane placed a hand on his arm. She indicated an approaching figure, marching toward them, footsteps echoing in the landing bay. Jane and Bryant snapped to attention and saluted. The Private noticed this, turned to face the figure, and saluted as well. As the figure got closer, they could clearly see lieutenant's bars on his uniform. The Lieutenant stopped beside them and cleared his throat. Goddard turned to face the interruption and gave a shoddy salute.

"At ease," the Lieutenant said. "What seems to be the problem?"

"Sir," the Private said, "Corporal Goddard claims he and his companions are here on shore leave, but I can't find any record of it in our database." He handed the tablet to the Lieutenant and pointed at the screen.

"Last minute change," Goddard said. "Decided to come here and hang out with my little brother for a few days."

"I see," the Lieutenant said. He tapped the screen a few times and frowned. He didn't appear to be paying much attention to the screen, eyes roving over the three assembled before him instead. He tapped, glanced at the screen, and pressed the device to his chest. "Last minute changes are usually problematic like this. Dismissed, Private. I'll take it from here."

The Private saluted again and departed.

The Lieutenant motioned for the trio to follow him, and started walking down a side hallway. "This sort of thing happens often. People decide at the last minute to visit CrossWorlds, so they aren't in our database yet as being authorized for shore leave. I'm sure you understand that we have to verify those orders, that's all. Standard operating procedure. In the meantime, we have a special lounge set aside where you can relax and unwind a bit. It's not much in the comfort factor, but it's still better than most bunks. Where did you say you were stationed?"

"MP-2184," Bryant said. Goddard glared at him.

"Ah, Mars," the Lieutenant said. He tapped his fingers against the computer's surface while nodding slowly. "Been there before, before terraforming was completed. Absolute hell."

Goddard snorted. "Hasn't gotten much better since."

"No, I imagine not."

The Lieutenant motioned to a large window on their left, a thick pane of nanoglass that afforded a view of the main gaming floor. "Did you come to see the final rounds of the tournament? Lots of excitement down on the floor today."

Hundreds of people milled about, looking like a swarm of ants from this distance. Many eyes were focused on a raised dais in the center of the crowd, where two contestants were playing chess. Their board was mirrored on a dozen large telescreens hanging at regular intervals around the ceiling of the gaming floor. One of the central screens showed closeups of both opponents, facing each other. The one on the left looked bored. The one on the right was sweating.

The player on the right made a move, and the other countered within seconds. The latter leapt to his feet and started jumping up and down. A light whirred on its axis and a siren blared. The telescreens all displayed the word "CHECKMATE!!", then declared the tournament round completed. The winner was a man who went by the name of Tempest, a well-known competitor with a huge following on Earth.

The Lieutenant started to make a comment on the news, but noticed Goddard had already resumed walking down the hallway. He moved to catch up and led the three into a side room. "Here's the lounge," he said. "Make yourselves comfortable."

"You know my brother?" Goddard asked, then added, "sir?"

"Private Goddard, sure, works mostly in communications."

"Can you let him know we're here? Can he visit us in the waiting room?"

"Hmmm..." he said, tapping the screen on his computer. "He's assigned to hallway patrols at the moment. I can give him a short break, but any more than a few minutes and you may as well wait until your leave is approved and he's off duty. I'll see what I can do. In the meantime, let us know if you need anything."

The Lieutenant left the room and the door slid closed. From this side, the door was a solid sheet of metal. Beside it was a control panel with a ten digit keypad and a blinking red light that said "LOCKED". Jane sat on one of the chairs and watched Goddard and Bryant pace.

PROTOCOL

Weasel almost fell off his chair when Sarge made his request. It was one of those few moments when he'd heard something so insane that he'd forgotten he was tethered and tried to leap to his feet so he could confront the absurdity. Calling for docking procedures was routine, but on a military channel? To a civilian base? He patched the call through anyway, not expecting anyone to answer it. It should have been a dead channel, but it was answered promptly. Weasel sulked. He didn't like being wrong. Ghost gave her access code to the attendant on the screen and Sarge asked for the call to be patched through to General Hanson.

"General, we have a situation," Ghost said, standing slightly in front of Sarge and staring directly at the screen. "Three marines docked with your station a short while ago."

"Yes, yes, I saw them come in. Shore leave, they said. I'm well aware of who they are. I've already spoken with Doctor Carter and Colonel Robbins."

"Then you are aware they are infected with the Nano-Morphine?"

"Quite aware. I've already had them quarantined in a private lounge. I have a bright young lieutenant and a pair of guards watching them."

211

"General," Ghost said, "with all due respect, sir, these marines are very dangerous. I think this situation calls for more than-"

"I will not be told how to run my base," General Hanson barked. "They are locked in a quarantine room under constant supervision. As far as my staff is concerned, they are there waiting confirmation of their orders. Only two people on this base know any more than that."

"But-" Ghost started.

"But what?" General Hanson replied. He appeared to be getting more agitated with every word. "But I should tell my marines what they are dealing with? I should tell them all about a classified research project and risk widespread panic? I've told my men what they need to know. If that is all, I have-"

"General," Sarge said, "there is something else. Someone calling himself 'Woden' is chasing us."

"I'll handle it," General Hanson replied, curtly. The transmission cut off.

Sarge stared out the viewport.

"Well," Ghost said. "That went... well."

Sarge shrugged. "Making a general happy is not in our job description. Have you received the docking authorization yet, Weasel?"

"Yeah, Sarge," Weasel replied. "We'll dock in a few minutes."

Weasel turned the ship thirty degrees upward. CrossWorlds Station slowly slid into view, replacing the starry blackness of space with smooth titanium and nanoglass windows.

Sarge watched in silence as Weasel piloted the ship into the hidden military docking bay. Massive metal constructs watched their ship float into the bay, robotic guardians wielding more armament than most ships could carry. Zulu Prime drifted past them without incident, occasional bursts of corrective jets fighting the pull of the Station's gravity field. The ship reached the end of its trip and was intercepted with magnetic clamps that gripped it tight. The crew levitated into the air momentarily as their ship's artificial gravity field synchronized with the Station's.

"We're in," Weasel said, releasing the controls on his virtual panel.

Sarge and Ghost left the bridge and went straight for the loading bay, where Tank, Tex, and Collins were already waiting. Tank hit the button to open the cargo doors. Sarge accepted a pulse rifle from Tex and checked it. Ghost pulled her pistol from its holster and checked the charge.

"Listen up, team," Sarge said while he watched the cargo doors start their descent. "Nobody here knows what's going on, not even the marines. Nobody's heard of Nano-Morphine or re-peeps. So keep the chatter to a minimum. Get in, grab or kill the three we're after, and keep the gunfire and bleeding to an absolute minimum. There are about ten thousand civilians on this station. The last thing we want is an outbreak of this shit here. Questions?"

Sarge looked over his team. Every one of them was stone-faced, ready for combat. The cargo door touched the docking bay's deck with a metallic thud. "Alright then. Zulu, let's move out."

Sarge trailed behind Tank and Tex as they exited. Collins followed closely, with Ghost beside him.

All around them, the hangar was alive. Flight crews worked on the combat ships lined along the walls. Men and women in flight suits milled about, some entering cockpits while others exited. The stench of fuel hung heavy in the air. Sarge looked around the perimeter. He counted twelve exits from the hangar, hallways and doors leading to the interior of the station. Three were marked, but the other nine could go anywhere.

Tank shouldered his pulse cannon and said, "Well, Sarge, where to? I count ten exits."

"Twelve," Sarge corrected. "You probably missed the two by the stairs on the left."

Ghost closed her eyes and tried to concentrate, but the commotion in the massive hangar was too much of a distraction. She gave up after several attempts and considered retreating into Zulu Prime to get a better read on the area. She turned and was about to speak when she saw a young officer emerge from behind Zulu Prime's hull. She tapped Sarge's arm and indicated the officer with a quick nod.

"Sorry I'm late, I'm Lieutenant-"

"We don't have time for formalities," Sarge said, "nor do we have time for any hassles. We're here looking for someone."

"Yes, of course. So you're Fireteam Zulu. General Hanson assigned me to accompany you."

"We don't need the help or the hindrance."

"I'm not entirely interested in what you need," the Lieutenant said. "It is a matter of protocol. I'm to assist with getting you past sentries, through locked doors, and take you directly to the waiting room with the three marines you are looking for."

Sarge looked the Lieutenant from polished boots to finely shaved chin and nodded. "Understood. Let's move out."

"I'm not particularly pleased with the assignment," the Lieutenant said as he led them down a hallway. "Not exactly a glamorous job for someone of my rank, all this escorting. If these marines did something wrong, I really don't see why I didn't escort them straight to the brig in the first place. And why did General Hanson bring *you* in to escort them back out? He's usually a stickler for protocol. But then the General did give me the orders personally, so I can only assume he has his reasons. Still... something about this doesn't seem quite right. You ever get that feeling?"

"Always," Sarge said with a snort.

AN UNEXPECTED GUEST

L anding at CrossWorlds had been trivial -- a forged authorization handed down, supposedly, from Gabrielle Anderton herself. Woden parked his ship in one of the civilian docking bays, and not one of the crew members there had the stomach to question the official-looking document. Woden snatched the document back with a snarl and walked right past the guards. He walked tall, moving as if he knew the layout of the station. When he was out of sight, he ducked into an access hallway. At the first guard station he came to, a schematic mounted on the wall gave him a good idea of how to get to the administrative offices.

He moved with alacrity, skirting around marines, ducking past automatic scanners, working his way through maintenance tunnels and access pathways. He paused at every corner, peering around with his extrasensory perceptions, waiting for the right moment to move. When he reached the entrance to the central offices, he paused. Nobody was in the hallway with him, so he projected his astral body around the corner. There was one entrance. One exit. The lobby was large and well-lit. The exit was directly across from the entrance. A long desk on his left stretched the length of the room. Behind sat two secretaries. One was talking to a telescreen. The other was reclining in her chair with her eyes closed. Most likely jacked into the Solar Net and doing work there. Each woman had an armed marine standing watch behind her. Two more marines stood guard at the other entrance.

Woden returned to his physical body and considered his options. He could simply stroll up to the desk, flash the forged authorization letter, and hope they were too scared to verify it. That carried the risk of bringing more attention than he wanted. He was hoping the guards in the docking bay wouldn't call it in. There was no way to be sure, but it was a risk. Flashing the same letter here would almost certainly call attention to himself. Fighting the guards was unacceptable for the same reason. Neither was really an option, considering his current desire for a stealthy approach. It was times like this that he envied Ghost's abilities. She could have simply willed herself invisible and walked right past security.

While trying to come up with a third option, he saw a door open down the hallway, swinging into his view and exposing a room beyond. He made for it, casually strolling past the lobby entrance without even glancing in, and found the room beyond the door to be a maintenance room, currently empty. A quick search revealed an access panel for the ventilation system. He crawled into the air duct and stopped.

He closed his eyes and concentrated, using his telekinetic powers to carefully close the access panel behind him. When it had sealed, he projected his astral body in front of his physical one. In his astral body, he flew down the air ducts, twisting and turning, trying every passageway that led deeper into the administrative offices. Each time the ducts turned to carry air elsewhere, he floated back to try another path. After several minutes of searching, he found a duct that ended in a corner of General Hanson's office.

Woden returned to his physical body and concentrated again. This time, he used his telekinetic powers to lift his body, allowing him to float silently through the air duct, slowly maneuvering his way around corners, working his way to the General's office. When he reached the grate, he stopped. It was locked and trapped, linked to an alarm. From the outside, he probably could have picked it, but he wouldn't have known where to start with suppressing the alarm. He could hear General Hanson from here, talking to an adjutant about an incoming call.

Woden stared at the floor on the other side of the grate. Teleporting was something that weakened him, but then this was such a short distance. It couldn't weaken him that much, could it? He didn't have much choice. He knew he did not possess the technical knowledge to bypass the alarm. He could try, but he'd never get his hands through the grate to pick the lock. And why bother when there was a much easier solution?

He closed his eyes, concentrating on a mental image of the room beyond. It was cloaked in shadow, with a hint of light from beyond. Probably no more than a desk lamp. His eyes had adjusted to the darkness enough to per-mit him a clear space large enough to teleport into. He was sure he could do this undetected. But how much would it weaken him? He chased the thoughts from his mind and focused. His insides twisted and for a moment he felt like getting sick.

When he opened his eyes, he could see he was now laying on the floor inside the General's office. He took a deep, slow breath and exhaled. He had been right, or lucky. It was such a short distance that teleporting had had no effect on him. He twisted into a kneeling position and looked. He had arrived next to a small bookcase, providing even more cover than the darkness did. General Hanson was sitting at his desk, attention engaged by a phone call. There was a single light in the ceiling, shining on his desk. That and the glow from his computer screen were all the light in the room.

Woden hid in the shadows, watching the conversation unfold. Ghost was talking on the other end of the connection, and the General was not at all pleased with her tone. He wasn't used to people giving him orders, and he was taking it out on her. She had gotten too used to being above the normal ranks and rules of the military. Woden considered butting in, to add his taunts to the mix, but there was no sense in playing his hand now. Fireteam Zulu didn't know he was here. Surprise was an asset best kept in reserve.

"Only two people on this base know any more than that," General Han-son said.

"But-" Ghost's voice said, sounding less confident than usual.

"But what?" General Hanson replied. He leaned into the screen and shook his fist. "But I should tell my marines what they are dealing with? I should tell them all about a classified research project and risk widespread panic? I've told my men what they need to know. If that is all, I have-" he moved his hand over the button for terminating the connection.

"General," came Sarge's voice over the communication channel, "there is something else. Someone calling himself 'Woden' is chasing us."

"I'll handle it," General Hanson replied. He slapped the button to end the call and the screen went black, leaving only the single light in the ceiling to illuminate the room. He mumbled something and leaned back in his chair, obscuring his face in shadows.

Woden took a step toward the center of the room. "And how, exactly, do you plan to 'handle' me, General?"

"How did you get in here?" General Hanson asked, casual.

"Clearance code from Mrs. Anderton," Woden said. "Followed by some creative use of your corridors and, shall we say, some of my own personal skills. You don't appear startled."

"Give me some credit, Woden. You're good, but you can't evade detection completely."

"Fair enough. Stealth was never my forte. I'm here to capture Fireteam Zulu. I expect your cooper-"

"You forget yourself, Woden," General Hanson said, standing. He placed both hands on his desk, leaned forward, and stared Woden in the eyes as he spoke. Confident, clear voice resonating in the small office. "You are but one man. I command a dozen others like you. Others who, arguably, are even more powerful."

"Ah, yes, but they're all on ice in the Venus Station, aren't they? How long does it take to defrost a person, anyway? Assuming you haven't already kept them too long, that is. The military still hasn't solved the problem of freezer burn, last I heard."

General Hanson straightened and folded his arms behind his back. "Not all of them are on Venus Station."

Woden started to reply but then the hairs on the back of his neck stood at attention.

Hello, Hunter. Woden. Whatever you are calling yourself now. It's been far too long since we've had a chat.

The voice echoed in his head. Woden glanced around the room but wasn't able to find the source. There were some other places in the office with shadows, like where he had hidden by the bookcase, but he couldn't detect any movement.

Oh you needn't bother looking around the General's office, Woden.

There was a pause. Woden felt a shiver snake its way up his spine. It had been a long time since he'd felt that. There was only one person he'd ever met who could make him feel that way. It had been so many years since he'd been subjected to it. Part of him had wondered if he would still be susceptible. Another part didn't want to find out. Both felt the fear.

"I noticed," General Hanson said. "Lights on."

Something in the ceiling clicked, entire panels warming and casting rays of artificial light. The shadows slinked away as the lights grew brighter. Woden glanced around the office again, turning to see all the corners. He was alone with the General.

"I believe you've already met Major Cho," the General said. "Now, I want you to listen to me *very* carefully, Woden."

HUNGER

J ane watched Goddard, staring intently as he scratched at his collar and started to break out in a sweat. His skin looked paler than before, pupils dilated, nostrils flaring with every shallow breath. He sat up straight, took a deep breath, and exhaled hard. Bryant didn't look much better. He dragged his hand across his forehead and wiped the sweat on the cushion of a nearby seat. Something in her knew that she would start to feel the same way soon as well. They were becoming like those other soldiers. Infected.

"You okay?" she asked Goddard.

"Sure, fine. What's taking them so long?"

"Well," Bryant whispered, "prolly has somethin' to do with us not really havin' authorization to be here on leave."

"Oh, *that*," Goddard said with a grin. "Damn I'm hungry." He stood and wandered to the other side of the waiting room.

The room was small, pristine white walls, tiled floor. More like a doctor's office back on Earth than a receiving room on a space station. The chairs were uncomfortable, barely more than slabs of plastic with legs. Half of them had thin cushions, adequate for a few minutes of waiting, if that. The magazines were unreadable civilian trash with too many animated advertisements. He stared down at one he had thrown across the room minutes earlier. It had landed open and had been playing the same pharmaceutical advertisement in an endless loop. He watched as the ad reached the end part that listed all the possible side effects of using the miracle cure of the week, reset, and started asking if he felt tired or lonely again. Every one of those ads was the same and had been for decades. The only thing they changed was the drug they were trying to sell. He kicked the magazine closed and turned to look at the only exit, a single metal door set in a wall, the entrance they had come through, now sealed with no means to open it from this side. Beside the door was a mirror that he was sure hid at least one observer.

Goddard looked back at Bryant and Jane. "Are you two hungry? I'm hungry. How long have we been here?"

Jane shifted in her seat. "We haven't been here that long. Fifteen minutes. Half hour maybe. We just had a snack on the ship before we docked."

"Well I'm hungry," Goddard said. He walked to the mirror and pounded on it. "Hey you. Hello? I know you're in there. Can we get some chow in here?"

There was a scraping sound, behind the mirror. A hidden panel slid open beside the mirror with a hiss, revealing three MRE packets, neatly stacked. Goddard grabbed them and the panel slid closed. He tossed one each to Jane and Bryant, then tore into his. From it, he extracted a nutrition bar and took a big bite out of it.

Jane nibbled half-heartedly at her bar, eyes still focused on Goddard. Bryant stood while he ate his bar and started to pace. Goddard was already halfway through his bar, cradling it with two hands like a rabid hamster, biting and chewing in quick strokes, vanilla and saliva foaming around his lips. He finished his bar and looked inside his MRE packet. He pulled small packets out and dropped them on the floor. "TP, gum, toothpaste... Shit," he said, "that's it?"

"Standard meal bar," Bryant said. "Half-day of nutrition, scientifically engineered to expand-"

"I know, *I know dammit!*" Goddard watched as Bryant took another bite and chewed. "But I'm still fucking hungry." He sprinted toward Bryant, grasped the hand that held the remainder of his meal bar, and took a big bite out of it.

Bryant screamed and tried to pull away, but Goddard held fast. Blood poured from his hand, seeping around Goddard's hand and dripping onto the floor. Goddard took another bite, getting another chunk of the bar and the rest of Bryant's thumb in the process. Bryant gathered his wits and punched Goddard in the chest with his free hand. He struck again, hitting Goddard in the nose and bloodying it. Goddard twisted his hands and sent Bryant to the floor. He pounced and straddled his friend, grasping both wrists with his hands.

Jane dropped the rest of her nutrition bar as she stared in horror at the scene unfolding before her. She lifted her legs to her chest and shivered. Goddard leaned forward and bit Bryant's cheek, tearing most of the skin from his face. Bryant howled again and fought against his attacker with all the might he could summon. But might was not enough. Every time he managed to work a wrist free, Goddard's arm would dart to grab it again. Every time Bryant shifted his weight to use his strength advantage, Goddard would pull in another direction and catch him off balance. Goddard bit Bryant again, this time in the throat, sending a fountain of blood spewing against the wall, staining the pristine tiles.

"My... God..." Jane managed to finally say. "Wh- why?"

Goddard paused and turned to look at her. The glaze in his pupils was gone. His countenance lacked remorse. There was nothing left of the man she knew. Not that she liked him much in the first place. "I'm hunnnngry," he said in a raspy voice. "Sooo damn hunnnngry." He leaned forward and took another bite from Bryant's inert body.

The door opened and three soldiers rushed into the room. One of them aimed his pulse rifle at Jane. She held up her arms slowly. Goddard let go of Bryant and turned on the other two soldiers, momentarily stunning them with the vision he presented. He hissed at them, blood trickling down the front of his uniform, small chunk of Bryant's flesh still hanging from his lower lip.

One of the soldiers raised his pulse rifle but he didn't fire. The other took a step back. Goddard took the opening and leaped at the first, pushing aside his rifle and biting his hand as he brought him to the floor. The soldier yelped, but went silent when his head impacted the floor. The other soldier ran into the hallway and shouted for help.

Goddard jumped on the back of the soldier who was covering Jane and bit his neck. The soldier clenched and fired a round through Jane's shoulder. She fell to the floor and rolled under the seats. Goddard spun around and used his momentum to pull the soldier face-first into the wall. He dropped his pulse rifle and collapsed. Goddard paused, surveying the carnage. Two soldiers, dead. Bryant, on the floor, mouth still opening and closing but no sound coming out. His wounds were starting to close.

Goddard stooped to take another bite from the soldier he'd just killed but stopped short. He could hear footsteps pounding in steady thumps emanating from the hallway. Two more soldiers? No, four, at least. Maybe six. He picked up a pulse rifle and limped his way to the mirror. He raised and fired, sending rounds into the mirror and the room beyond until the pulse rifle's clip was spent. He dropped it and dove through the opening.

The control room beyond the mirror was even smaller than the room he'd just left. Monitoring equipment lined the far wall, smoke and sparks pouring from the holes he'd made in them. Two privates lay on the floor in pools of blood. Goddard knelt beside one, licking his lips, but again he paused. He could hear the footsteps enter the waiting room.

He'd have to wait. He pushed open the control room door and ran into the hallway beyond. His vision blurred and he tripped, hit the floor, and skidded several meters before stopping.

The infection, he thought. *Those other soldiers... on the base... they... weren't...*

He stumbled to his feet and staggered into an open doorway. Elevator. The doors closed and the elevator started to move down. His stomach turned and he doubled over in agony, falling to the floor with a loud thump. *They weren't...* he thought again, but his thoughts trailed off. Focusing on things became harder with every attempt he made. He tried to think of his brother, somewhere on this base. He could help, couldn't he? But what could a private do to help someone in his situation? He had to figure this one out on his own. He focused on the words, saying them out loud, hoping it would help.

"Those," he said, pausing to focus on the next word. "Ssss... ssssooold... errrrs," he added after some time.

The elevator pinged and the doors opened. Before him he saw a room full of civilians, playing a series of games for another heated round of the tournament. Someone jumped and cheered. Another winner who was instantly surrounded by other players congratulating him. Bright lights from a scoreboard flashed to announce the second round of the tournament had been completed.

Goddard knew there was something he was trying to focus on.

Something about soldiers.

But he was so damn hungry.

UNREQUITED

Sarge entered the waiting room with Ghost close behind him. He took one look at the bodies and blood, casually sizing up the room. He could see someone cowering under a row of chairs against one wall, but couldn't make out who. Footsteps from the rest of the team entering behind him. His gaze fell on the smashed mirror and the control room beyond. "Collins?" Sarge asked.

"That looks like Bryant on the floor," Collins said. "I don't see Jane or Goddard."

"Copy. Tank, Tex, go that way," Sarge said while pointing at the control room. "LT."

"Yes?" the Lieutenant asked as he stared at the carnage.

"Alert the base, seal off all corridors that control room leads to. Go. Go!"

The Lieutenant darted down the hallway as Tank and Tex moved into the control room. Ghost asked for permission to join them. Sarge agreed as he tried to move cautiously toward the person underneath the seats. The figure leaned forward and he could make out her face.

Collins followed Sarge's gaze. "Jane?" he asked.

Jane pulled herself out and stood, wavering, hands shaking. "Collins, I-" she cut herself off as she looked at Bryant's body.

Collins followed her gaze. "Shit," he said. The blood had mostly congealed, but there were large patches of tissue glistening in the artificial light on his neck and face. As he watched, a gaping wound in Bryant's neck stitched itself closed. Before he could turn back to Jane, he saw the corpse stir. Bryant's eyes fluttered open and he rolled onto his stomach. He pressed his feet against the wall and pushed, sliding across the floor on a river of blood, directly at Collins. Collins fired, but missed his target, his shot clipping Bryant's foot. Bryant hit Collins in the ankles and latched on.

Collins tried to take a step back and nearly fell. "Sarge!" he yelled. He grimaced as he felt teeth puncture his ankle. He couldn't get an angle on Bryant's head that wouldn't also hit himself. The pain was already intense, so he took the shot anyway, right through Bryant's shoulder and into his own foot. He yelped and fell backward, hitting the wall. He couldn't concentrate or aim well enough to get the angle.

Sarge had been watching Jane, covering her to make sure she wasn't going to attack. At Collins' warning, he looked down and narrowly averted the outstretched arm of one of the dead soldiers. The soldier was squirming, fighting the infection, not yet conscious of what he was becoming. Sarge aimed his gun and fired, splattering the soldier's brains against the floor. Then he took aim and fired at Bryant, hitting him in the back. He tried to line up another shot, but there was no way to shoot him in the head without hitting Collins.

"Do it!" Collins shouted as he saw Sarge's hesitation. "Shoot me, do it!"

Sarge nodded and took aim again. He squeezed the trigger and sent a single round through Bryant's left eye, shattering Collins' ankle with a loud snap. Collins screamed, tears streaming down his face. Bryant's grip relaxed as his body went limp. Collins pried the corpse from his leg and limped away. He leaned against the wall and sank to the floor. He tried to slow his breathing. The pain made his eyes tear up.

"Thanks. Shit. Guess we were too late," Collins said through clenched teeth.

"This is one we're chasing," Sarge replied, indicating Jane.

"You have to shoot me," she said, walking to the center of the room so Collins could see her better. "In the head. I don't want to be like them."

"No," Collins said, "Listen-"

"No, *you* listen, it's too late for me. You have tooo dooo it. Riiiight now."

"What?" Sarge said, turning his head to face the control room. "Repeat that. Copy. On my way." He turned to face Collins. "You got this? My team needs assistance. She doesn't look like the others did. Just take her to Doctor Carter; he can help her."

Collins stared at Jane. She looked different, definitely a little more like these reanimated people than the woman he had trained with all this time. The woman, he was beginning to admit, he loved. He started to raise his rifle but stopped. Sarge cleared his throat and asked again if things were under control. Before he could get a response, Jane reached around from behind and pulled Sarge close. He was caught off-balance with the surprise attack and alarmed at the strength with which she gripped him.

"Yoooo... haaaave to... kill meee," she slurred.

Collins took aim but hesitated. She was still... Jane. He wasn't sure what the holdup was. She was one of those things, a freak of science, an anomaly that needed to be erased. But all those times he stared in her eyes, all the times he ordered her to back him up, all the times he thought of her, and missed her. There was something there, something more than a friendship, more than the relationship between soldiers. She was plain, but somehow beautiful. He looked into her eyes.

"Kill meeee..." she repeated. "Richard, I... I'm sooo... hunnn-greee."

With that she tilted her head and bit Sarge in the neck, catching him in the jugular. Sarge ground his teeth and grunted, eyes wide with the pain, in-voluntary tears flowing down his cheeks, blood pouring down his neck. He dropped his rifle and flailed his arms about as he staggered back under the weight pulling at him. He reached one arm up and grabbed a fistful of her hair. He yanked, pulling her head away from his neck. She stared at the hole in his neck, pure lust, watching as blood spurted out, looking as if she were about to lick her lips in anticipation of the feast.

Collins gasped, hands shaking. He inhaled and held it to steady his aim. Jane heard him and glanced in his direction. He looked into her eyes again. In them he saw nothing of the woman he had grown to love. He pulled the trigger.

WHAT THEY WEREN'T

T he screaming was somehow delicious to his ears.

Goddard dropped the corpse of the young woman he had recently cradled, her warm blood dripping from his jaws. People ran
from the hall, pushing past each other, trampling those unfortunate enough to
stumble. Several of those fallen ones had been trampled so thoroughly they
no longer moved. Whether they had died or not was irrelevant to him; they
were easy pickings and that's all Goddard cared about. He took a step toward
another as a marine ran out from a hallway and knelt, aiming his weapon.

"Freeze!" the marine yelled.

Goddard turned on the intruder and hissed at him. The marine shook but
kept his weapon trained. Goddard took a step forward. The marine opened
fire, sending a burst of three pulse rifle rounds toward his chest. Goddard
dodged to the side, but one of the rounds caught him. It burned but somehow
it didn't hurt. The stench of burnt flesh reached his nostrils, bringing a fresh
wave of hunger. He inhaled deeply, savoring the aroma. Then he leaped at
the marine, taking another burst of pulse rifle fire to his abdomen in mid-air.
The marine dropped his rifle when Goddard slammed into him. He tried to

push Goddard away with his bare hands, but Goddard pushed down, forcing the marine onto the floor. The marine's clawing slowed as he stared at Goddard's face.

"J... Jimmy?" the marine said.

Goddard paused, staring at the marine beneath him. Something inside registered a familiarity. But that was soon replaced with another feeling, the burning hunger deep inside. He leaned forward and took a bite from the marine's neck, whose mouth opened to scream but was silent. Blood gurgled out of the open wound, spilling into a slowly expanding pool. Goddard grasped at the marine's uniform, trying to pull it apart to get access to more of the tasty flesh. His gaze rested on the name tag sewn into the uniform, half-crumpled between his clenched fingers.

dard.

He released his grip.

Goddard.

He felt a tear form and opened his mouth, letting a surprised gasp out. Blood dripped from his mouth and splattered on the marine's chest, covering the name tag. He felt something more than hunger, but only for a moment. The hunger returned, chasing all sense of emotion from his mind, leaving him only a shell of a man bent over his latest meal. A shot rang out from his right. Single round of focused plasma punched through his hip. Another burning sensation without any accompanying pain.

He turned on the newcomers and rolled to avoid another incoming projectile. More marines, firing wildly. One of them dropped his gun and vomited on the floor. Goddard chuckled and rolled again, this time coming to a crouch before a marine as he entered from a side hallway. He grabbed the marine's arm and snapped it with a twisting pull, then flung the marine over his shoulder. Behind him, the hallway was quickly filling with more marines. He turned and sprinted to the center of the gaming floor, and was forced to dodge to the side again to avoid another volley of pulse rifle fire. One of the rounds nicked his shoulder, another took his left ear clean off. He glanced to his left and saw another group of marines entering from another hallway. The gaming floor, already littered with corpses, was taking on a new influx of marines.

Goddard tumbled over a woman's corpse and dove toward the docking bay, the only place that looked clear. The blast doors were open, and in the distance he could see his ship, the one he'd stolen back on Mars. His vision clouded and his stomach churned. He shook his head, succeeding in adding to the disorientation. He knew he wasn't himself, but he wasn't about to let that stop him. He had to get out of here, had to get somewhere else to get a chance at sorting out what was going on in his head. It was the strangest sensation. He wondered if the other soldiers had gone through the same thing. The hunger hit him again, forcing him to his knees as another round of weapons fire tore through the air where he had been standing.

Those other soldiers, he thought, while kneeling over an older man, staring into lifeless eyes. He brushed the man's gray hair away from his forehead and considered taking a bite to sate his hunger. *They... weren't... dead...*

He leaned forward and took a bite from the man's cheek as the marines closed in.

*   *   *

Ghost was the first to dash onto the gaming floor. Tank followed closely and leveled his pulse cannon in the direction of a cluster of marines, who appeared to be closing in on a central point. Standard tactics, aiming low, covering each other and slowly advancing. Tex was last in and had both pistols drawn.

"Looks like they got it under control," Tank said, gaze still focused on the center of the action.

Ghost aimed her gun toward the mass and stood still. "We don't know that yet. Be prepared."

A figure leapt from the center, rising a full four meters into the air. The marines reacted by swinging their weapons skyward and opening up, peppering the air and the ceiling with pulse rifle rounds. The figure in the air roared as rounds tore open his legs, filling the air with a shower of blood.

"Dear God," Ghost said, "they're all gonna get infected..."

The figure hit the floor on the outskirts of the mass of soldiers, whirled, and attacked. He swung with bare hands and ripped open three of the marines before they could even aim in his direction. The rest of the marines fanned out, firing wildly in the general direction of the action. Four more soldiers went down from friendly fire before they realized the mistake they were making. By then Goddard had already sprinted away and was now running full-bore toward the docking bay. A small group of marines ran out of the docking bay, knelt, and opened fire.

"This is a fucking bloodbath," Tex said. "Think he'll get overloaded like Tank did?"

"Perhaps," Ghost said, "but how many will he infect before that happens? We have to do something."

"Yeah," Tank agreed. He tapped the communications button in his cheek. "Sarge? Sarge I think we're gonna need some backup here. Sarge? This is a big fucking mess here, sir. Please advise. Sarge?"

Ghost tilted her head toward Tank without removing her eyes from the carnage. "Tank? What's going on?"

"No reply from Sarge. What do we do?"

She watched as Goddard rolled into the mass of marines and came up in the center of them, ripping another two open with his bare hands as they tried to fire down to where he was. He grabbed another by the throat and drove his forehead into the marine's nose. The marine yelped and collapsed. A group of marines split off and ran for the far hallway, dropping their guns as they went. Goddard laughed as rounds continued to hit him, but none of the marines were aiming high enough, and he kept coming at them.

"There ain't many marines left, Ghost," Tank said. "Why don't they shoot him in the head?"

"They're aiming at center of mass, to incapacitate," Tex said.

Ghost took aim, but Goddard was dancing around another group of marines, ducking in and out of their bodies. She lowered her weapon. "They don't know what he is."

"We have to get in there," Tex said.

"I agree," she replied. "Let's go."

"Ghost," Tank said, "you're the fastest. Seal the exits. All of 'em. Probably our only chance of containment at this point."

They took off for ground zero of the worst massacre any of them had ever seen. Civilians and marines alike were thrown all around the gaming floor. Every step met with a squish. Walking was hard enough on the slick ground, and they soon found they couldn't run anymore. Some of the earliest casualties were starting to stir. Tex pointed out the movement to Tank, holstered his pistols and retrieved a pulse rifle from one of the fallen marines. He took aim but Tank pressed down on the muzzle.

"Don't," Tank said. "They're just starting to heal and awaken. It's too early. Carter can still help them."

Ghost split off toward the docking bay door controls as Tank and Tex moved closer, hoping for a clear shot. The last marine tried to punch Goddard, but he grabbed the young man and bit into his throat before he had a chance to even cry out. Goddard dropped the marine's corpse and started moving toward the docking bay.

Ghost dove past Goddard, sailing the last few meters through the air, aiming for the door controls. She caught them just in time. She hit the big red emergency button and the blast doors came crashing down with a thunderous echo of metal meeting metal.

Goddard roared and swung at her. She stepped back, dodging the attack. He was fast, the fastest opponent she'd ever come into contact with. It took all of her concentration to avoid his swings. Duck, lurch, dodge. She tried to keep low, using her smaller body to her advantage, hoping to give her companions an opening. Goddard roared at her, saliva and blood dripping from his chin. This distracted her for a moment, long enough for him to drive his fist into her ribs. She yelped and danced back, tripped on a body, and slammed into the floor.

Tex opened fire with his pulse rifle, two rounds and it was out. He dropped it and pulled his pistols out, firing in rapid succession. The plastic bullets hit Goddard in the chest and head, sending him stumbling back a few steps. Ghost pushed against a marine's corpse and slid away on the blood-coated floor. When she was far enough from Goddard, Tank pulled his trigger. His pulse cannon warmed up and peppered Goddard with rounds, making him dance and showering the blast doors with blood. Ghost swung her legs out, catching onto two corpses and ending her momentum. She drew her pistol and took careful aim, counting the tempo.

Three two one lurch.

Three two one lurch.

Three two one -- she pulled the trigger, sending a single burst of focused plasma into Goddard's skull. Tank released his trigger and Goddard fell to the floor. Ghost cautiously stepped over the corpses, making her way to where Goddard lay. When she got closer, she saw his eyes still open. He blinked and his head lolled to the side. Her shot had grazed him, taking part of his skull off but not destroying his brain. Part of the exposed tissue sizzled. The rest of his body was riddled with holes.

"I'm..." he said, voice croaking and interrupted with a cough that sent blood dribbling down his cheek.

"What?" Ghost asked.

"I'm... not..."

Ghost aimed and fired, sending a blast into the center of the exposed brain tissue. "Dead," she said.

"Guess we didn't need help after all," Tank said with a shrug. He waited a moment, then tapped the communicator in his cheek again. "Sarge? You still there?"

"You okay?" Tex asked Ghost as he looked her over, gently pulling on her arm so he could examine her back. Her entire backside was soaked in blood.

"I'll be fine," she replied.

"Maybe we should backtrack," Ghost said. "Check up on Sarge and Collins?"

"Go ahead," came the strong voice of General Hanson. "My boys will take care of the rest of this." He paused as he surveyed the carnage with sadness.

Ghost tightened the grip on her gun when her eyes rested on Woden. He stood beside the General, occasionally glancing at him with obvious distaste. Ghost narrowed her eyes and Woden rolled his in response.

"Ghost," came a woman's voice, familiar. As they watched, a woman materialized in the area behind the General and Woden. She was mid-stride, stepping over a corpse. She came to a stop beside Woden.

"Who?" Tex asked.

"Major Cho, ma'am," Ghost said, casting a warning glance at Tex. He fell silent.

"You know I've never been one to mince words," Major Cho said. "You are a fugitive. You've gone AWOL. I'm mostly retired now, or I'm sure they'd have sent *me* after you." She smirked at this, and swept her hand to indicate the room. "This is quite a mess, and Mrs. Anderton herself has asked that the bloodshed end here. This station is too precious a commodity, and we've a lot of cleaning and explaining to do. Today you've earned a reprieve. But if I ever see you near CrossWorlds again, I will kill you myself. Is that understood? Now, I'll keep Woden here with me a while," she said, resting her hand on his shoulder. He winced. "We have some catching up to do. But you and your friends should go."

Ghost thought of responding, but couldn't think of any appropriate words, so she just nodded, turned, and motioned to Tex and Tank that they should follow. They retraced their steps, hearing echoes of the General's commands floating up the hallway behind them.

ALWAYS

Sarge fell to the floor under the weight of Jane's corpse. Collins dropped his rifle and limped over to help extract Sarge, unwinding and moving Jane's arms with a care they no longer needed. Sarge grunted and pressed his hand to the gaping wound on his neck. Blood spurted above and below his hand and leaked between his fingers. Collins sat on the floor and used his good leg to prop up Sarge's back.

"I'm... sorry..."

"What for?" Sarge barked, then coughed.

"I hesitated. I shouldn't have." Collins tried to examine Sarge's wound but his hand wouldn't budge. He quickly patted his pockets to see if he had any patching gel or morphine, but came up empty.

"You loved her," Sarge said. He coughed again and his eyes closed. "That much I... can understand."

"Yeah, I think I did."

Ghost entered the control room and stopped. She willed herself to fade, at the same time motioning Tank and Tex to stay back and be quiet. She faded into the shadows of the room and watched as Sarge coughed, fresh blood squeezing between his fingers. She could see even from this distance that he was mortally wounded and wouldn't last more than a minute. Neck wounds were the worst. Even the tube of patching gel she had taken from the Martian base wasn't going to help at this point.

"Love complicates things," Sarge said. "Always does. At least you... did the right thing," he said, breathing becoming more shallow. "In the end. You did good." Sarge tensed and grunted. "Need you to... do something... for me..."

"What's that?" Collins asked.

"Watch out for... my team," Sarge said.

"I will. You hang in there. Doctors are on the way."

Sarge coughed, smile slowly creeping onto his face. "You're a... shitty... liar. But a... good... marine. You shoot me... you hear? I don't want... to turn... like them."

"You can make it. C'mon Sarge, hang on," Collins said. "Doctor Carter can-"

"No!" Sarge barked. He coughed and gagged. "You... shoot me. In the head. End it. Promise..."

Collins was starting to tear up. He'd seen more than his share of death today. "You aren't ready to die... are you?"

"Always ready," Sarge said. "Always."

Ghost turned her head, not wanting to see what she knew would come next. She inhaled deeply and held her breath.

Collins watched as Sarge breathed his last. He hung his head, partly from shame of not acting faster, and partly from the sadness of seeing a fellow soldier expire. He shifted Sarge's body and laid it on the floor. He winced as his damaged ankle throbbed from the movement.

He picked up a pulse rifle and aimed for Sarge's head. He knew it had to be done, but it still didn't feel quite right. *Always?* Always ready to die? How could anyone be like that? What would drive a man to that length? Collins sniffled as he stared at Sarge's tired face. He looked serene, at peace. It was obvious that he'd seen more than his share of combat. He hadn't known Sarge for very long, but if the stories he had read about Fireteam Zulu were true, then these people didn't take breaks. There were always more pirates to fight, always more people to save, always... always more to do. No matter how many times they deployed, there were always more distress signals to answer. Always fighting. Always helping. Always pushed to the edges of your abilities and beyond. Always moving to find new people to help. Always running from the law. Always finding more people to save. Always thrusting yourself into danger. Always ready to die, because you had to be. You had to risk your life to help the people who couldn't defend themselves.

He knew what he had to do. He hadn't actually made the promise, not in words, but he had in his heart. That was enough of a contract for any marine.

"Sorry," he said to the corpse. "I'm so sorry."

Collins pulled the trigger, looked once to confirm that his aim was true, then dropped the rifle. He fell backward and hit the floor, tears in his eyes and a feeling of something grabbing at his chest. *I'm next*, he thought. He reached for the rifle again, intending to finish himself off. But the exhaustion of his day and the throbbing pain in his ankle overtook him.

Ghost exhaled. A single tear escaped her eye and worked its way down her cheek.

*   *   *

None of the men assembled in the docking bay knew the man whose funeral they were attending. All they knew was that a fellow marine had fallen. An ex-marine, some had whispered, but they knew he had served the United Earth Federation at some point in his life.

That was enough to warrant respect.

There were many others who had fallen that day. Funeral detail was going to last for hours. This was just the first in a long line of coffins to be honored, saluted, and loaded onto a cargo ship for burial back on Earth.

Tank walked into the bay, wearing a borrowed dress uniform, gently pushing Sarge's coffin along on well-oiled wheels. Behind him, Tex and Ghost marched, heads held high. General Hanson waited until the coffin reached the proper point and then launched into a speech about soldiers and honor and duty. It was rehearsed and dry, but nobody was in any position to complain. Considering the number of funerals they had to cover today, he was only going to give this speech once. Every successive coffin would be wheeled in, the marine inside would be named, everyone would salute, and they would continue with the next. When General Hanson finished his speech, he motioned for Tank to wheel the coffin forward so it could be loaded onto the cargo ship. Tank wavered and slowly shook his head.

"You have something you want to add, son?" the General asked.

Tank stood at parade rest. "Yes, sir," he said, his voice loud and clear in the docking bay. "You spoke of honor and duty and sacrifice, and that's all fine and well sir. But there are some things you just can't teach. I believe honor is like that. It's not something you choose to do. It's who you are. It's something you're born with. Or, at the very least, it's something you strive to be. Either way, I don't believe it's a choice. I believe that when situations present themselves, you either act with honor, or you don't. And sometimes, you act with more honor than anyone ever thought possible. I'd like to tell you a story about Sarge. So all of you here today will know what kind of man he really was.

"Many years ago, I was with Sarge, fighting some separatists on Mars. Some of you remember that war. As for me, I was a green recruit, in a squad full of green recruits. This man we call 'Sarge' was our leader. He led us into a bunker filled with thirty defenders. He lost his arm in that fight, but he sealed the wound with the heated muzzle of his rifle and pressed on. We made it to the bunker. The first kid through the door was killed. Sarge used to say he blacked out and couldn't remember that battle. I think it broke his heart to think of that kid. So he didn't. He convinced himself it didn't happen.

"Anyway," Tank continued, "when we got back to the barracks, he called the kid's mother to give her the news. I was there for the conversation. He gave her the standard speech about her son serving and dying honorably. He told her the military arranged transport of her son's body, but it would take two days. She started crying. Not because her son had died. She took that news well, for some reason. She was crying because of the transport. She told Sarge that her people believed that a person's soul could be stolen if the body were left alone before it could be buried. The dead had to be guarded to prevent this.

"Sarge didn't even flinch. He didn't waver. He never questioned or mocked. He didn't even pause. He offered to guard the kid's body, all the way to Earth.

"'You will do this thing?' she asked, shocked. 'You will guard my boy all the way home, for the entire journey? You would give up your time for another like this?'

"'Always,' he said. And that's all the explanation she needed. The very same day, Sarge boarded the transport with the kid's coffin. Our lieutenant didn't seem to mind, since Sarge lost his arm and needed a medical leave anyway. Medics on Mars, medics on Earth. Didn't matter much to him.

"An old friend of mine was working on that flight. I talked to him a few days later. He said Sarge stood there, beside the coffin, dressed in his uniform and wielding his pulse rifle. He guarded that coffin for the entire trip. Two *days*. He sat twice. Once for the liftoff from Mars, and once for the landing on Earth. A damned one-armed marine vigil for two days to make sure a corpse didn't lose its soul to some ancient superstition. My buddy and his friends asked him several times if Sarge needed anything, if he was alright.

"'Always,' Sarge replied, loud and clear, every time they asked. He refused food. He refused water. He refused rest. He let nothing distract him from his task.

"When the ship arrived, the boy's mother met them. She didn't have to ask if Sarge had done what he said he would. Everyone could see it in his face. His body was exhausted. He was on the verge of collapsing. But still he stood there as workers loaded the coffin into the mother's truck. Sarge held a salute until he could no longer see the coffin. Then he collapsed and the medics took him away."

Tank choked up and turned his head to the side. "He-" he started, then forced a cough. "He didn't even know the marine who had died. Just his name. Sarge spent more time with the kid's corpse than he did with the kid. That's the kind of man Sarge was. Always prepared to do the right thing. Always ready to go far beyond the call of duty. I'll remember you, Sergeant Thomas Gedderick. You and your example. Always."

Tank saluted the coffin. Every other marine in the landing bay joined him.

* * *

Collins awoke to white ceiling with long tracks of LED lights running like pinstripes. Stench of antiseptic and pure alcohol. Machinery whirred around him. He tried to glance around but couldn't turn his head far. He could hear voices but couldn't make out what they were saying. He blinked and tried to talk, hearing only gibberish come from his mouth. The voices stopped and a face came into view. It was blurry at first, but soon it came into focus.

Ghost looked down at him and smiled. "Sergeant Collins, welcome back."

Collins felt something release and he could pivot his head. Soon his hands were free and someone was helping him sit. The whole room tumbled and blurred again. He shook his head to clear his vision. Something gnawed at him. Visions of Jane and Sarge flooded in and threatened to make the tears return. But he held them back and looked around the room.

He was in some sort of medical lab, lots of machinery lining the walls, people in white lab coats moving from console to console and talking of patients and diagnostic results. It didn't look like his base on Mars, much too small, but at the same time there was more activity here. Behind him was a giant tube, like the brain scanning machines they had back on Earth, the kind you slid into on a table so they could see what was wrong with you.

Collins took a quick inventory, mentally concentrating on various parts of his body, but was unable to find any source of pain. He felt fine, like he'd just awakened from a long sleep. Tank was the one helping him to a sitting position, meaty hands supporting his back. Strong but friendly, like the times O'Malley helped him out of bed after a long night of binge drinking. Tex was behind Tank, looking rather somber. Ghost was standing by the table, hands on her hips, looking as casual as she could in full battle gear.

"Where-" Collins started to ask.

"You're on my ship, Sergeant Collins. I'm Doctor Carter."

"You... you have to kill me," Collins said. "I'm... hungry..."

His words hung in the air several seconds before everyone broke out laughing. Even Ghost, who hadn't shown much emotion since he'd met her, had turned red in the face. Collins watched them in stunned silence, not understanding the joke, feeling once more like he was on the outside looking in. Another group of soldiers to pick on the token Norm, a relic of days long dead.

"Quite normal, I suspect," Carter said, once he'd recovered. He chuckled again, then coughed and regained his composure. "Don't worry, Sergeant, you're going to pull through quite fine."

"You're a Norm," Tank explained when he had recovered. "You were infected, but it's easily curable in your case. We got you here and the doc EMP'd the shit outta them nanos."

"Electro-magnetic pulse," Doctor Carter said. "Killed off all the nanobots in your bloodstream. Without any augmentations, they weren't able to multiply like in the other soldiers who were infected. There was no risk of any other bodily systems failing."

"All... gone?" Collins said, looking down at his bare ankle. Someone had cut his pants to expose the area. He touched the area and felt no pain.

"Correct," Doctor Carter said. "But not before they fixed the wound in your ankle. Which raises some very interesting medical uses for the Nano-Morphine project in critically injured Norm patients." His colleagues echoed his excitement.

"Yeah, you'll be fine," Tex added.

Collins sighed with relief. "But what now? I mean, what happens now?"

"I guess you go back to the base when you're up for it," Carter said. "We're still in orbit around Mars."

"I'm up for retirement next week," Collins replied. "The Colonel had said I could just take a vacation and not go back."

"Well then, I guess we'll have to find some work for you then," Ghost said with a twinkle in her eye.

"What? With you?" Collins asked.

Ghost shrugged. "If you want to."

"But," Collins said, putting his feet on the cold floor. He faltered a moment and leaned against the table for support. "What do we do? Where do we go?"

"Fly around at random," Tex said. "Listen for damsels in distress."

Carter cleared his throat. "There's also the matter of this ship's cargo. Several pieces were taken by those pirates, including at least two crates of the Nano-Morphine. We can't risk that falling into the hands of... well, any-one."

"Sounds like a fine job for Fireteam Zulu!" Tank said with a clap of his hands. "But first... we need a new leader..." he said, looking at Collins.

Collins cast his gaze to the floor. "You don't want me. I... I've done things. Sarge, he-"

"I know," Ghost said. "I saw. When the time came, you did what had to be done. What he asked you to do. I couldn't ask for anything more from a leader."

"We also know how you handled those re-peeps on the Martian base," Tex said. "The way you alerted your fellow marines to a threat and showed them how to end the threat, all without saying a single word. And accuracy from that distance is impressive, even *with* augmentations. But for a Norm? Wow."

Collins frowned. "How did you-"

"Ghost told us about it," Tex said. "Plus I have to say that I was im-pressed with your assessment of Goddard. You were pretty accurate. Takes a good leader to size up an opponent and communicate that info. Coupled with the Mars thing, I'd say you've got some good tactical skills."

Collins looked to Tank, who shrugged and said, "Ghost says Sarge called you a good marine. That was enough info for my vote."

"So," Ghost said. "You up for it... Sarge?"

Collins flinched but relaxed before anyone noticed. He wasn't entirely comfortable stepping into those shoes just yet. But what else did he have to look forward to? He didn't earn much pay as a marine, and his choices were either to reenlist or go back to civilian life. The latter meant getting a job, one of those real-world jobs that were boring as hell. That was easier said than done for a Norm. Fireteam Zulu knew who and what he was, and were asking him not only to join them but to lead them. That was already more promising than anything civilian life could ever offer.

He thought back to Sarge. Always ready to die. But also, always ready to fight for those who needed him. In a way, it was part of the reason Collins had wanted to be a marine in the first place. But sitting next to a railgun on Mars wasn't helping people. The first civilian he had seen in years was the one that his automatic sniper had shredded. And Jane, whom he had secretly loved for far too long, was gone. No, he couldn't go back to the military. A civilian's life wasn't for him either. In truth, he loved the rush of combat. He wanted to help people. Sarge was right -- he had to be ready to fight, ready to defend, ready to die. In any situation, ready to put his life on the line to help those who needed assistance.

Am I ready? he thought.

He straightened his back, grinned mischievously, and said, "Always."

About The Author

Jamie was born in Western Massachusetts in 1977. He started programming computers when he was about six years old, and went on to earn a bachelor's degree from the University of South Florida in Computer Science with a minor in mathematics. He worked as a developer for a small company in Tampa for eight years before moving to  Maine to pursue his own projects. He currently works as a programmer and product designer for a company he started with his brother Paul, Lost Luggage Studios. His interests include writing, computers, artificial intelligence theory, cooking, nature, and photography.

He's also probably the only person left in the United States without a cell phone.

Author can be contacted at:
    jamie@LostLuggageStudios.com
    http://www.LostLuggageStudios.com

About Terran Shift

Terran Shift is an open universe project created by Jamie and Paul Belanger. The main goal is to construct a science fiction universe like the creators of Star Wars and Star Trek did, but without the universe itself being owned by any corporation.

There is no fan fiction in Terran Shift. Or, rather, no need for it. You can use events and places in the Core Canon, combined with your own characters and ideas. Create new planets or races, and contribute them back to the project for others. Create any fiction, comic books, games, music, TV shows, or movies you want. Everyone can contribute to the universe and everyone's work will help to promote everyone else's work. There are no restrictions on what you can do, and no need to pay royalties or request permission to be a part of the project. Anything listed in the Core Canon is done so with a Creative Commons license. Create your media, attach the Terran Shift logo, and join the open universe revolution.

The Core Canon has been designed by Jamie and Paul Belanger for use in their novels and future Lost Luggage Studios computer games. Beyond that, the universe is open to your imagination. More details will be released on the project's website in the months ahead as we announce and release the projects and stories we've been working on.

Visit http://www.TerranShift.com for more information.

Explore The Terran Shift Universe

The Bio-Tech Era (2015 - 2096)
Pariah

The Soul Bank (*in Scribings, Vol 1*)

Aftershock Era (2096 - 2149)
Secret Under the Sand (*in Scribings, Vol 2*)

Expansion Era (2149 - 2329)
Fireteam Zulu

The Sol-Bect War Era (2329 -)
The Sol-Bect War, Part 1

The Sol-Bect War, Part 2

The Sol-Bect War, Part 3 (*coming soon*)

Works Spanning Multiple Eras
Terran Shift Anthology 1 (*tentatively titled; coming soon*)

Purgatory Beckons (by Paul J Belanger)

In a world descending into moral depravity, it seems Evil has won. After a botched arrest attempt, Detective Debbie Mason's life begins spiraling out of control, forcing her to question whether fighting crime is worth the effort. But nothing could prepare Debbie for the arrival of Garrett Carmichael, a stone-cold killer sent on a mission of mass homicide by his mysterious employer.

Pariah (by Jamie Alan Belanger)

Neil Roberts, a programmer for the largest software provider on the planet, stops in a bar and witnesses a murder. His once boring life changes drastically when, through a twist of fate and a realization that his life has no purpose beyond his job, he leaves the scene of the crime and becomes a suspect. Neil's life shifts from protecting people to becoming that which he most despised... a hacker.

Scribings, Vol 1

The first volume of short stories compiled by the Greater Portland Scribists, a group of speculative fiction writers in the Portland, Maine area. This compilation contains eleven pieces of fiction written by members Lee Patterson; Cynthia Ravinski, MA; Jamie Alan Belanger; and Richard Veysey.

The Sol-Bect War, Part 1 (by Paul J Belanger)

Humanity is near the tail end of an intergalactic war that war we are losing. After a rough skirmish, a strange object is picked up by the United Earth carrier Ticonderoga. Within, the ship's scientists find something even stranger: a man, cryogenically frozen and shot into space more than 300 years ago. The fact that he's still technically alive raises questions of Fate's hand in life and war.

The Sol-Bect War, Part 2 (by Paul J Belanger)

The war against the Bect rages on. Humanity is now on the offensive. The Bect send larger forces against us. Our weapons and tactics may have improved, but our forces are beginning to dwindle. And the strange newcomer who showed us a path to victory, Peter McCabe, is Missing-In-Action and presumed dead. Can the human war machine complete what he started?

Scribings, Vol 2: Lost Civilizations

Journey into lands long lost with the Greater Portland Scribists. Scribings Vol 2: Lost Civilizations contains eight exciting stories that will take you on a trip through Ancient Egypt, Viking lands, Atlantis, and more. Includes stories from trusted veterans Richard Veysey; Cynthia Ravinski, MA; and Jamie Alan Belanger; as well as stories from new members Christopher L. Weston and Timothy Lynch.

www.ingramcontent.com/pod-product-compliance
Lightning Source LLC
Chambersburg PA
CBHW070912180626
46817CB00003B/1019